The Sky Beneath My Feet

Also by Lisa Samson

Quaker Summer

Embrace Me

The Passion of Mary-Margaret

Resurrection in May

Acclaim for Lisa Samson

Resurrection in May

". . . thought-provoking, believable and authentic. The sweet truths of the gospel emerge not only through the pain and heartache, but through the healing that eventually comes."

—*Christianity* magazine

"Samson is bold as ever, exploring big questions through her vivid writing and memorable characters . . . high marks for imagination and ambition . . ."

—*Publishers Weekly*

"Samson (*Quaker Summer*) has written a tragic story that ends in tenderness. Recommend this to readers who like stories of second chances."

—*Library Journal*

"This novel is a true gem."

—*Romantic Times*

The Passion of Mary-Margaret

". . . a page-turner with characters so fresh, funny and indelible the reader wants another 50 pages or so, please."

—*Publishers Weekly*, starred review

"Stellar characters and profound spiritual truths resonate on every page . . . this is a book to savor."

—*Romantic Times*

"Well written and enjoyable, this title will appeal to readers who appreciate intelligent fiction with a spiritual element."

—*Library Journal*

Quaker Summer

"One of the most powerful voices in Christian fiction . . . an emotionally and spiritually luminous portrait of a soul beckoned by God."

—*Publishers Weekly*

"*Quaker Summer* speaks to the heart of women. It just might set you free in ways you've never imagined."

—Mary Graham, Women of Faith

"It's not often that I say, 'This book changed my life,' but in the case of *Quaker Summer* I shout it with a hearty amen. Samson weaves a compelling, surprising, faith-awakening story with the deft skill of a writing artisan. Her characters partially materialize in the room when you're reading, wooing you to consider their lives, struggles, and questions. Samson puts a human face on consumerism, compelling the reader to give Jesus' radical call, but she does so with candor and grace. A highly recommended book."

—Mary DeMuth, author of *Watching the Tree Limbs* and *Wishing on Dandelions*

"*Quaker Summer* is a perfect example of the life-changing power of fiction . . . [Samson] manages to call into question the state of the North American church and challenge the reader to consider what life would look like if we took Jesus' example seriously. I was entertained, but I was also given a glimpse of the church doing what it should be doing—and it's changing the way I view my own spiritual walk."

—Alison Strobel, author of *Worlds Collide* and *Violette Between*

The Sky Beneath My Feet

~

Lisa Samson

THOMAS NELSON
Since 1798

NASHVILLE DALLAS MEXICO CITY RIO DE JANEIRO

Published in Nashville, Tennessee, by Thomas Nelson. Thomas Nelson is a registered trademark of Thomas Nelson, Inc.

Thomas Nelson, Inc., titles may be purchased in bulk for educational, business, fund-raising, or sales promotional use. For information, please e-mail SpecialMarkets@ThomasNelson.com.

Publisher's Note: This novel is a work of fiction. Names, characters, places, and incidents are either products of the author's imagination or used fictiously. All characters are fictional, and any similarity to people living or dead is purely coincidental.

Library of Congress Cataloging-in-Publication Data

Samson, Lisa, 1964–
The sky beneath my feet / Lisa Samson.
pages cm
ISBN 978-1-59554-545-9 (pbk.)
1. Married people—Fiction. 2. Clergy—Fiction. 3. Domestic fiction. I. Title.
PS3569.A46673S59 2013
813'.54—dc23 2012044039

Printed in the United States of America

13 14 15 16 17 QG 6 5 4 3 2 1

For Duch

Contents

chapter 1

Jesus Fish

Every once in a while, I glance at the rearview mirror and see my own eyes staring back at me. It's disconcerting. *I'd forgotten you were in there.*

And then, blink, she's gone again.

Or I am.

Maybe it's the eighties music on the radio, or the breeze coming through the old VW van's rolled-down window, the warm sun on my bare arm. Maybe it's idling on the curb out in front of the high school, waiting as the kids tramp past in twos and threes, their backpacks slung over their shoulders. I don't know what summons her up. The old me. My former self.

The hatchback pops open behind me. Without a word, Eli shoves his bike in, cocking the front wheel over the backseat. He slams the hatch and comes around to the passenger door. Some passing girls call out to him and wave, then he slumps into the seat, pulling the door shut.

Unlike his older, bookish brother, who speaks with equal

parts fear and condescension whenever the subject of public school comes up, Eli wouldn't have it any other way. He likes it. He's even popular.

"So what's wrong with your bike?" I ask.

Eli doesn't answer, doesn't even acknowledge my presence. He just reaches for the radio and changes the channel. "How can you listen to that stuff?"

"Hey, you don't know what you're talking about. My music's cool again."

"Whatever."

He flicks his hand in the air, beckoning me to drive.

"What's that?" I ask.

"Let's go."

"What was that thing with your hand?"

"What, this?" He does it again with an impish smile. "That's called a gesture."

"I'll show you another gesture if you keep it up. I'm your mom, not your taxi driver. So what's wrong with your bike, anyway?"

"Don't let the people at church catch you making rude hand gestures," he says. "Or the people on the road, now that we have the Jesus fish on the bumper."

"I told you the fish was ironic."

"Sure it is." He glances over his shoulder. "I bent the back wheel again."

"Again? You weren't doing tricks, were you?"

"Tricks?" He smiles at the word. "Yeah, I was doing tricks."

"Is that not what they're called? I can't keep up with the lingo."

"Don't try," he says. "I don't want to have the Cool Mom."

"Too bad." Reaching in the door compartment, I pull out my white plastic shades. "You already have the Cool Mom, so deal with it."

"Right," he says, dragging the word out and smiling at his reflection in the window.

"And stop admiring your own reflection."

On the verge of his sixteenth birthday, my younger son is becoming a narcissist. Born with the kind of languid masculine grace that pairs well with the square-jawed facial symmetry and thick, black hair he inherited from his dad, Eli is growing into his looks. He's handsome, in other words. Which explains both the girls waving to him from the sidewalk and his indifference to them.

"Try to be nice," I'm always telling him. Only, to be charming, Eli doesn't have to try—and consequently, he doesn't. Even at his surliest, Eli tends to get his way. That's not how the real world works, I try to tell him. But all he has to do is look at Rick's example. Whether he tries or not, everything works out for my husband.

Not that I have a problem with that. Except when I do.

At York and Ridgely, we get stuck at the red light. Eli looks around, realizing we're not heading straight to the house. "What's the deal?"

"I have a couple of errands to run," I say. "You remember the Shaws? No, of course you don't. They moved to Virginia when you were seven or eight—"

"I remember," he says. "Mr. Shaw had a silver Porsche."

Yes, he did, but that's not how I want a child of mine recollecting people. "They're coming over tonight. Your dad sprang it on me this morning, even though he's known for days—"

"I'm not gonna be there. I already told Damon I was coming over."

"Well, you can tell Damon . . . no, never mind. You made your plans, that's fine. You shouldn't have to drop everything at the last minute."

"What are they coming for, anyway? You haven't seen them in years."

"That's a good question, Eli. That's a good question."

Eight years ago Jim and Kathie Shaw moved three hours down I-95 to Richmond, saying they would keep in touch. At the time, the Shaws were probably our closest friends, Jim being one of the few people Rick could talk to about his job without fear of being judged. Once they left, the most we ever heard from them was a card at Christmas. It was a wrenching break, especially for Rick. And now they're suddenly on our doorstep again? I don't know what to think.

"So have you thought about what you want to do for your birthday?" I ask.

"It depends," he says. "Are we going to be here or out of town?"

"Your dad has the whole month of October off, and we thought we'd take a little vacation. Maybe we could go somewhere for your birthday."

"California?"

"Somewhere closer," I say. "How about D.C.? We could see all the sights."

"That's not a vacation, it's a field trip."

When Rick came home from the staff meeting over the summer announcing his four-week vacation—a *sabbatical*, he called it—he dropped the whole thing in my lap to plan. Figuring out where to go and what to do, scheming a way to get the boys out of school for a week or two without looking like delinquent parents—it was all up to me. Never mind that I hadn't known far enough in advance to put money aside. Never mind that Eli's idea of fun was visiting his cousins in California (something he's only done once before) and my eighteen-year-old, Jed, responds to every idea I come up with by saying, "Sure, fine, but you'll have to go without me."

Nobody wants to do what I want to do. Nobody can agree on anything else. And if I don't come up with something for them all—for my husband and my two teenaged sons, the men in my life—then they'll blame me for having failed in my most basic, primal duty. I just can't win.

"You know something—" I begin.

But Eli's not paying attention. He's already fished his iPod out of his jeans pocket and plugged the earphones in. He can't sit for five minutes without playing on that thing, and I've resigned myself to it. Now he taps his thumbs on the screen, absorbed in some game. I know better than to mess with the radio dial, though. He likes to blanket himself in white noise.

We pass a Greek diner, then a cluster of fast-food outlets. We pass the bowling alley and the office my childhood doctor practiced out of, then the Timonium Race Track and State Fair Grounds. I've never been to a horse race there in my life, or to Pimlico either. We pass gas stations and car dealerships, the sticker prices rising like mercury the farther north we get.

In the parking lot at Giant, Eli announces he'll stay in the car. Big surprise—I didn't see that one coming. With the door half open, I check my shopping list one last time to make sure I haven't forgotten anything. Mussels and scallops, Rick's favorites. When you're entertaining a Porsche-driving lawyer and his Ivy

League wife, you have to keep up appearances. Not that I care about that sort of thing.

"Am I forgetting anything?" I ask aloud.

Eli looks over at me, but he isn't listening.

I'm positive I'm forgetting something. Maybe. Maybe not. I always feel like I've forgotten something.

*

On my way inside the grocery store, I say a little prayer. Not a pious prayer by any stretch.

Please, Lord, don't let there be anybody from church here.

Confession: There are things you want to do in private, anonymously, and grocery shopping is one of them. When your husband works at a church of thousands, you're likely to be recognized in the most inconvenient places.

As I'm peering through the frosted glass at the seafood counter, I hear the screech of grocery cart wheels over my shoulder, followed by the high-pitched voice signifying the fact that, no, I have not found favor with my Father in heaven.

"Hey, *girrrrrl.*"

I put my smile on before turning. "Hi, Stacy."

"Hi yourself, Beth. I was just thinking about you." Stacy Manderville pulls to a halt next to my cart, her elbows propped on her own cart's handle, giving my shopping a once-over before continuing. "Got some big plans or something? I thought you'd be getting ready for the road trip."

"Not until next week," I say.

"The whole month of October, huh? What are you going to do with yourselves?"

"I have a few ideas."

"I bet you do." She looks me over now, blinking a few times, probably trying to imagine the kind of ideas a pastor's wife can come up with. But then Stacy knew me long before I was a pastor's wife. We were in high school together. That was before Stacy married into the opulently wealthy Manderville clan. "That's what I wanted to talk to you about."

"You wanted to talk?"

"About this vacation of yours. A month is a long time."

"The timing couldn't be worse," I say. "Autumn is my favorite season. With the leaves changing and the weather turning cool, our little neighborhood—"

"There's always Florida."

"Well, yes."

I wish we didn't work for such an affluent church, full of people who go wherever they want on vacation and stay for however long they want. Stacy married a doctor, so I'm sure it makes perfect sense to her that we'd pick up sticks and spend a month on Miami Beach. Sometimes ministering to the wealthy is counterproductive to attaining the peace of Christ that passes all understanding. Even if they do cut your husband loose for a month of paid vacation.

I mean, why are we having trouble raising twenty grand for the Habitat house we're cosponsoring with our sister church downtown when the parking lot on Sunday mornings is clogged with Mercedes and BMWs and Volvo SUVs, not to mention several Jaguars? (Okay, I can't help loving the Jaguars. But still.)

"Why do you have that funny look?" Stacy asks. "Did I say something?"

"What? No. Sorry, my mind was wandering. We have people

coming over tonight and it was short notice. You remember the Shaws? They used to go to the church . . ."

Her eyes study the ceiling for a memory. "Doesn't ring a bell, but the place has gotten so *huge.* I remember when it was just starting out. I think there are more people on staff now than were even attending back in the good old days! Anyway, here's what I wanted to show you." She digs in her capacious purse for half a minute only to produce a set of keys attached to a bright yellow floaty. "Here they are. And here you go." She hands them to me.

"What are these?" I ask, turning the floaty over in my hand.

"You know we have a house in Florida," she says. "It's not a mansion or anything, but it's right on the water. Beautiful stretch of beach. I already e-mailed you all the details. Do you ever check your e-mail, girl? I was starting to wonder."

"I don't understand."

"What's to understand? You have a month of vacation coming, and I have an empty vacation house on the beach. I don't care if you do like it when the leaves turn and it gets cold. When was the last time you had tan lines, Beth? And I'm not talking about on your arms either. You can go down there and soak up the sun and forget all about Lutherville and the church and the fact that we're not in high school anymore. Let your hair down and have some fun. Surprise that husband of yours."

"Are you serious?" I ask. "Stacy, this is too kind."

"It's not. You're my best friend, Beth. Of course I want you to have fun."

I wince a little at hearing her describe me this way. We're not that close, not really, but her voice sounds sincere. And it's such a sweet gesture, even if I'm ninety-nine percent sure Rick won't go for it. If nothing else, he'll object to taking the VW all the way to

Florida with its broken air-conditioning and its crank windows and no power steering.

"I can't accept this," I say. "It's very sweet, but—"

"I'm not taking no for an answer." She tucks her hands into her armpits so that I can't hand the keys back. The yawning opening of her purse lies between us. I could toss them right in.

But I don't.

I mean, why shouldn't we?

*

The Jesus fish is my own fault. I'm a Christian, but not *that* kind of Christian. Not the in-your-face culture warrior. Not the sort to plaster bumper stickers all over my car. I don't drive like a Christian, after all, and when I'm speeding or cutting somebody off, the last image I want to leave them with is that shiny faux-metal fish. But I shot my mouth off about the stupid fish and hurt the feelings of one of my study group ladies. You know the kind: she forwards e-mails to everyone in the group about liberal conspiracies and tries to sign us all up to march in front of clinics and boycott Hollywood and invest in gold.

But she's a sweet person who just never got the memo that God wants to save all types of people and not just her type. She can't imagine a decent, churchgoing person having any view other than her own. So she heard my offhand joke about the sort of people who slap Jesus fish on their minivans and she stored it away. By the time it got back to me that she was offended, I'd forgotten I ever said anything.

I went to her, because that's what you're supposed to do. I apologized. I managed to get through it without an implied reprimand too. Nothing about how she should have come to me directly and not told everybody else how upset she was. The next Sunday she presented me with the fish.

"What does she expect?" Rick asked. "You're not putting that thing on the car."

"I think she misunderstood the reason I was apologizing." I started to laugh, but Rick was still angry about the fish. Finally he gave in. "She's crazy, I know. But if I don't put it on . . ."

"I don't care what these people think about us," he said, though we both knew he did.

"When Pete Waterhouse had to shave his head, you and some of the other guys shaved yours too," I reminded him. "In solidarity. This is the same kind of thing."

"That was cancer. This is narrow-mindedness. I don't want to reinforce this kind of thing."

"What about your T-shirts?"

Rick had a closetful of kitsch T-shirts emblazoned with breathless religious slogans, most of them freebies from church-sponsored activities. "That's different. I wear those ironically."

"Right," I said. "And the fish will be ironic too."

Only nobody told the fish. Now, as I push my basket across the Giant parking lot, watching the Jesus fish glint in the afternoon sun, the fish looks awfully sincere. Earnest. He shines evenly in the sun, without so much as the hint of a wink.

Eli doesn't get out of the car to help with the groceries, naturally. Until I pop the hatch, he's not even aware of my presence. Eventually he does glance back, but just to make sure I'm not interfering with his bike. The rear wheel is distorted by an aggressive, curb-shaped bend. I fit the shopping bags in where I can, then slam the hatch.

Ordinarily I'd leave the basket in the empty spot next to the VW. But the Jesus fish is watching, so I walk it all the way over to the carousel.

When I get behind the wheel, I set my wallet on the bamboo shelf underneath the dash. (I refuse to drag around a purse because I like them too much. Get on the popular purse train and you never get off.) Eli takes no notice until the big yellow floater on Stacy's keys catches his eye.

"What're those?"

"Those are the keys to a beach house in Florida. How would you like to go to Florida for your birthday? The house is right on the beach."

He pulls the earphones out of his ears and sits up straight. "For real?"

"For real," I say.

He slumps back down thoughtfully. "Florida, huh. Cool."

I'm not immune to the boy's charm, oh no. I put the plastic shades back on.

"Who's the Cool Mom now?"

*

The traffic on the way home is heavy and my luck is such that I seem to catch every red light. Eli's headphones are still dangling, still hissing his unattended music, while he contemplates the beach house keys in his hand. He sniffs the plastic floaty, trying to catch a whiff of salt water. I can tell the idea intrigues him, which is good. If the birthday boy's onboard, Rick will have to go along.

Stuck at the light, I start thinking of ways to say thanks to Stacy. I never would have expected something like this from her.

And now that I know she thinks of me as her best friend, maybe when I get back I'll need to pay more attention to her. Maybe a girls' night out.

The light changes and we get a few cars ahead. It turns red before I can clear the intersection. On the grass verge next to us, there's a group of people gathered. On top of the noise of the radio and the traffic around us, they add another layer: chanting voices. Even with the window down, I have to pay attention to make out what they're saying: *"End the war, end the war, we can't take it anymore!"*

Some are standing and waving hand-lettered signs that say HONK FOR PEACE. Others sit in folding lawn chairs, shading themselves under wide-brimmed straw hats. They're an unlikely group of demonstrators, mostly plump, gray-haired white people with sun-pinked skin. Despite the signs, nobody is honking. The drivers all around seem, at best, indifferent.

One of them, an elderly woman with short white hair and a diaphanous sundress, reminds me of a woman I knew long ago, growing up with my Quaker family, before I met Rick and the whole course of my life changed. Miss Hannah, her name was, and she'd been a nurse in World War II and traveled the world afterward, one of those women who did amazing things back when women were expected to stay home with the kids, and subsequently didn't understand why women who didn't face similar barriers would do anything less.

Miss Hannah. I haven't thought of her in years. She'd taken my hands in hers once and fixed her hard, gray eyes on me and said, "*Do* something with your life."

And at the time, I thought I would. I couldn't even fathom why she'd think I needed the encouragement.

I look a little closer, and of course, it's not Miss Hannah, who passed away years ago. As I watch, a younger man walks among the group. He wears cargo shorts and a shirt with epaulets that makes him look like a Peace Corps volunteer, and he has a scraggly beard that can't hide the fact that he's not much older than twenty-five. He has a drum tucked under his arm and starts beating it in tempo with the demonstrators' shouting.

This catches Eli's attention. I turn to find him shaking his head.

"Hippie losers," he says.

The light changes and we drive through the intersection.

"What did you say?"

The anger comes up on me suddenly, unexpectedly. I stomp the brake, then let up. I stomp it again and twist the wheel. As the car heads back toward the intersection, Eli stares at me, baffled.

"Mom, what's wrong?"

"That's what I want to know."

"I don't understand."

And to be honest, neither do I. The VW careens back through the intersection and pulls along the curb across the street from where the demonstrators have gathered. I turn the engine off.

"Come on," I say.

"I'm not getting out."

"I'm serious, Eli. We're going over there."

"What for?"

Good question. I can't think of an answer at first.

"Mom, what for?"

"To introduce ourselves."

He pauses, then smiles. "I get it."

"What do you get?"

"This is supposed to be a life lesson, right? Because of what I said? I'm supposed to see that they're not hippie losers, just normal people, and then I'll apologize?"

"Do you *want* to apologize?"

He thinks about it. "Are we going to do this or not?"

As we cross the street, I know I've lost already. Why did it make me angry? I know he was only joking. I *hope* he was, anyway. From his older brother, Jed, that line wouldn't have surprised me, but Eli takes life as he finds it. He doesn't judge. And besides, you can't teach life lessons to a kid who's two steps ahead of you. You can't teach a boy who's always willing to call your bluff.

*

"What am I doing here?"

"What *are* you doing here?"

Up close, I can see I was wrong about twenty-five. He's older, probably in his thirties. When we approached, he greeted Eli with some complicated fist-bumping handshake, and the two of them seemed to have an understanding right from the start. But not me. This is the story of my good intentions. I sometimes act on them but always regret it. Standing on the grass among all these strangers, all I want to do is get back in the van and speed away.

"I guess . . . well, we saw you guys out here, and . . . we just wanted to say hello."

"That's great," he says. "I'm surprised you noticed us."

"It's kind of hard not to."

"I don't know about that." He smiles sheepishly under his beard. "We're shouting at the top of our lungs, but nobody in this country is listening."

The line sounds practiced, something he's said a hundred times. It elicits a practiced nod from several of the demonstrators.

Eli grins at my discomfort.

"I know this probably seems a little bit out there to people in this neighborhood," the man is saying, "but you know what I think? Most people go through life disagreeing with the politicians, yelling back at the television set, but they never say anything, not out in the open. The way we're enculturated, we look down on people who care too much and aren't afraid to say so."

"We know this isn't going to change anything," one of the others says. "That's not the point. We're here so that they know—the people in charge—that we see what they're doing and we're against it. Even if we can't stop it or change it, we're not going to ignore it either." As he speaks, his voice grows louder, but not loud enough to drown out the roar of traffic. Behind him, several demonstrators start to fold up their chairs and put away their signs.

The scraggly-bearded man checks his watch and gives the others a nodded signal.

"My name's Chas, by the way. Like I said, this may not be your scene, but—"

"Oh no," I say. "I used to be a Quaker."

He pauses, cocks his head. "Okay."

That was a stupid thing to say, a stupid way of putting it. What I mean is, I know what it's like to be unwilling to ignore things just because you can't stop or change them, and while I might not forward mass e-mails or shout at intersections, I'm not . . . I don't know what I'm not, but I'm not.

"You know," Chas says, glancing at Eli, then back at me.

"Here's what you ought to do. Come hang out with the Rent-a-Mob this weekend."

"The what?"

He smiles. "It's my little name for us. Not just these folks, but a whole bunch of us. We're not going to a demo this weekend, just working on signs, but it would be a great chance to meet everybody and see if—" He breaks off, gazing over my shoulder. "It would be a great chance—" Again, over the shoulder.

I turn around and see what he's looking at. On my bumper, the Jesus fish glows like molten silver, sparkling in the sun. A car rushes past, obscuring the fish for an instant, but then it reappears with an insistent flash. Refusing to be hidden under a bushel, or behind a passing vehicle. As I glance back at Chas, I feel my cheeks begin to flush.

"Anyway," he says, digging under the flap of his chest pocket to produce a card. "Take this."

I hold the thick card in my hand. CHAS WORTHING, it says. And underneath in red letters: ACTIVIST + POET.

Is that a thing? You can get business cards for it?

"Seriously, you should come this weekend," he says. "Every Sunday afternoon we get together. It's at my place this time."

"I wish we could. We're leaving town, going on vacation." I see Eli's smile widening. "In Florida."

"Well," Chas says, "if you change your mind, you know where to reach me."

*

"You lied to Chas," Eli says.

"Don't start in on me."

"You told him we'd be gone, but we're not supposed to leave until next week, right? Did you not want to hang out with the Rent-a-Mob?"

"Honey, sometimes—"

"You just have to lie to people, I know."

"That's not what I mean."

"You were right," he says. "That was a life lesson."

He starts to laugh. I start laughing too. I can't help it. The whole thing is ridiculous.

"I'm worried about you, Mom," he says. "I think you might have some hippie loser in you."

"You bet I do."

We turn down our street and pull into our driveway. When I pop the hatch, Eli doesn't go for his fractured bike. Instead, he grabs some groceries and helps me bring them inside. Maybe he learned something back there after all.

chapter 2

Now I Lay Me Down

One of the joys of living in a charming old house: having to use a screwdriver to shut the hot water off. Rick is many things, but handy isn't one of them.

I step out of the tub carefully. As always, I imagine my foot slipping on the tile, my hand clutching the shower curtain that circles the old cast-iron tub, pulling it loose ring by ring on my way to a hip-shattering fall. Instead—again, as always—I stick the landing. I am not as old as I feel.

Before I can get ready, I have to wipe the condensation from the bathroom mirror. Then I wipe the fog from my five-year-old cell phone to check the time. The Shaws will be here in an hour.

Yes, I'm taking a shower, my first of the day. And yes, my phone is so old that all it does is make and receive calls. No games, no music, no e-mail alert chiming every thirty seconds. Nothing but a handy clock. Which is a good thing since the battery in my Seiko died some time ago without my noticing.

Rick taps on the door. "Honey, are you done?"

"I just got out of the shower," I say, trying to keep the exasperation out of my voice.

"Well . . . there's a lot of stuff to do before they get here."

He pads down the hallway toward the bedroom. True, there is a lot of stuff, and Rick won't be doing any of it. His contribution amounted to remembering the Shaws were coming, and even that he almost botched.

I didn't wash my hair. No time for that. In front of the misty mirror, I rifle through my makeup organizer in search of my favorite blush. My makeup collection is a testament to my support of the many stay-at-home mothers at church who are trying to get a career going on the side. Avon. Mary Kay. Shaklee. Amway. Arbonne. There's more in here than I'll ever use, and I don't wait to run out before reordering.

I feel for these ladies. So many of them are ultratalented. They have the degrees I wanted but never got. Some of them do it for the extra income, but at our church there aren't many people hurting economically. It's more about putting themselves out there, finding an identity besides wife and mother. If they can't be in the boardroom, they can be Pampered Chefs.

Confession: I've never used a 1-2-3 skin-care system for longer than a week. When I admit this to the ladies, the response is always the same: "You haven't tried *this* one yet!" So I write the check and, of course, nothing changes. The bottles end up in the drawer until Rick discovers them. He never met a grooming product he didn't want to try. And anyway, everyone compliments me on my skin. "I wish I had skin like yours! What do you *use*?"

Confession (don't hate me): I don't even wash my face.

*

I dress in jeans and a gray knit top, stacking bracelets on my wrists, some silver, some tribal beads, none of which go together but somehow, when it's all together, it goes. Making a pastor's salary stretch for a family of four means not many of the clothes in my closet are original to me. I swoop down on the secondhand shops, making up for my reluctance to spend with a little good taste. I know what looks good on me, if only because I'm blessed with a husband who has no qualms about telling me what doesn't. Not to mention two sons who've learned from their dad's example.

The key to being frugal without having to host jewelry parties in my living room? It's simple enough. I don't waste time thinking about things I can't have and don't need. Things that aren't broken aren't replaced. Collections all seem designed to collect dust, and who needs more housework? I realize most of the planet has less than I do. That alone curbs my acquisitive instinct.

It also doesn't hurt if, like us, you live in a neighborhood where you could never hope to afford any of the things your neighbors take for granted. When I see Roy Meakin driving by in his vintage Rolls, all I feel is aesthetic joy. I can wave at the old guy without a trace of envy. If I'm stopped at the intersection behind someone's ten-year-old VW van, one that's old but not ancient like ours, that's when my thoughts go black. You're only tempted when the prize isn't too far out of reach.

"You look nice," Rick says, poking his head through the bedroom door. He's wearing his off-duty uniform: one of his ironic T-shirts, a pair of shorts, and his "dress" flip-flops, the ones with the leather trim.

"Thanks. I'm just gonna finish in the kitchen." I slip past him, catching a whiff of floral scent. I wonder which of my cast-off skincare products he tried today. "Eli's going over to his friend Damon's house—"

"Damon who got the new Nintendo? We won't be seeing him for a while. Does that mean Jed is joining us?"

I lower my voice. "Would that be a problem?"

"No," he says, but then he purses his lips so I'll know that it is.

"What's wrong? You aren't mad at Jed again."

He shakes his head. "It's the other way around. He's been on my case the past couple of days. I don't know what I did, but it's getting old."

"I'm sure it's a firstborn thing. He's eighteen, after all. He's trying to spread his wings a little."

Rick laughs at this. "Who, Jed? I think you're confusing him with someone else."

"Lay off," I say, emphasizing the point with a jab of the elbow.

He follows me into the kitchen, still chuckling at the thought of our tall, gangly eldest son—who's a spitting image of Gregory, my own older brother, in body and personality, but seems to have inherited nothing from Rick's genetic line—leaving the family nest. The problem is, in Rick's mind, Jed is a lump of stone waiting to be shaped into a man, and Rick is the sculptor. Everything that doesn't fit his idea of what a man should be, he tries to chisel away. The traits he wants to get rid of, though, are the ones Jed values the most. And frankly, he's right.

But then, Rick has never much cared for Gregory either.

"Where is Jed, anyway?" I ask.

Rick shrugs. "Probably on his computer. Want me to call him downstairs?"

"I'll do it."

It takes a few tries, but Jed finally appears at the top of the stairs, holding his hand-me-down laptop in the crook of his arm, the screen casting a blue haze over his features. When he hears we have company coming over, he says he'll eat upstairs in his room.

"But it's the Shaws. You remember them. Kathie will want to see you, hon. When they left, you barely came up to here. Now you're all grown up."

"I've got some stuff to do."

"Like what?"

"Just stuff," he says. "Anyway, if Eli doesn't have to . . ."

"Fine, it's your loss."

I turn to go back to the kitchen. His footsteps thunder down the stairs behind me.

"You're not mad, are you?"

He's stopped just inside the kitchen, the laptop still balanced on his forearm. The fact is, I am mad, but I don't know why. There's still so much to do, and it's not like Jed knows any better than Rick or Eli how to cook. He'll only be in the way.

"I'm just . . ." I pause to brush a lock of damp hair out of my eyes. Then I notice the back door is ajar. Through the window above the sink, I can see the light on inside Rick's shed. "Never mind. You can stay upstairs if you want."

"I'll do whatever you want."

"Don't worry about it. I'm just a little stressed out, that's all."

He takes this onboard with a nod. We understand each other, me and Jed. Not always, and not always well, but if you were going to draw a line through the family, we both know we'd be on one side with Rick and Eli on the other. "All right, then," he says, and disappears up the stairs.

I run the water and watch Rick's shadow moving across the window of his shed. It's more than a shed, really. It's a freestanding man cave, a permanent retreat from the white noise of domestic life. Originally our home was just a kind of carriage house on the grounds of the mansion next door, and the shed was an outbuilding. By late-nineteenth-century standards, I'm sure it was quite meager, but the leaded glass windows and broad-planked wooden floors make the shed rather cozy—certainly too nice for anything like a tool to be stored within. According to the neighbors, some kind of handyman used to live there, back in the days when every well-to-do household employed a couple of servants.

There's even a tiny wood-burning fireplace.

When I first saw the property, I imagined that little shed with flower boxes under the windows, a fire in the grate.

But Rick peered through the window and said, "I've got dibs on this."

I was disappointed, but still, I love my little home. Storybook style, with an arched front door complete with quaint round windows. We have three small bedrooms, a living room with a fireplace, an eat-in kitchen, and a quarter-acre lot.

The shed sits near the edge of the yard, on the paved path leading through the English garden to the big house next door. (Confession: I'm not sure what an English garden is meant to look like, but in this case it means unruly hedges and scrappy clumps of wildflowers and weeds.) Margaret and Deedee Smythe live there, a mother-and-daughter pair, the last of the family line since Margaret has been a widow for ages and Deedee never married.

Walking the block now, you wouldn't think that all the property at our end of the street had once been part of the same compound. The houses and outbuildings, erected by the Smythe family over a period of more than fifty years, reflect a variety of styles. There's a giveaway, though: our house, the big mansion, and the bungalow next door are all perched on the same swell of high ground. Standing on the sidewalk, my eyes are about level with the front walkway, which connects to street level via brick steps cut into the slope.

In back, the so-called English garden runs wild right up to an old stone wall that divides the Smythes' yard from ours. On our side, Rick keeps the sliver between the wall and the shed well trimmed. Whenever I'm in back, I feel the urge to wander along the path past the wall and into the garden, much preferring thick, unruly nature to rigid cultivation.

They're both eccentrics, Margaret and Deedee. According to Rick, I'm a magnet for "outliers," by which he means crazies. They aren't crazy, though, just a bit out of step with the modern world. Their original plan was simply to rent out the place. My husband charmed them into selling, and at a scandalously low price.

"We can't get all this for so little," I protested.

"Beth," Rick had said. "God worked out the numbers. Besides, the little old lady really took a shine to you. And it's not like they need the money."

I was doubtful. I felt as if we were taking advantage. Still, I tried to convince myself that he was right. After all, I'd never have gotten my beloved little house otherwise. I made up my mind then and there to be the best neighbor in the world.

*

I know something's wrong the moment I open the door and see Kathie Shaw's dress. It's a dark-red sheath, simple and elegant, accented by black spike heels and a patent leather clutch. She's wearing a twist of pearls that gleam like teeth in the porch light.

"Kathie," I say, holding the screen open with my hip. After a slightly awkward pause, I give her the most tentative and delicate of hugs.

"I won't break," she says, squeezing me tight.

Behind her, Jim stops halfway up the walk to push the lock button on his car key. The exotic coupe in the driveway beeps and flashes. He notices me for the first time and breaks into a smile, then envelops me in the arms of his exquisitely tailored jacket.

"Beth, Beth, Beth," he says, "it's been too long. We should have done this ages ago. Where's the big man? Is he still putting his face on?"

"You know Rick."

In the living room, the four of us give each other the once-over. Rick wears a dazed smile while Kathie gives an imperceptible wince, like she's in pain and trying to hide it.

"Let me guess," Jim says, turning my way. "We got our wires crossed somehow. I told Rick we were taking you guys out and he told you we were coming over for dinner. Am I right?" Rick starts to reply, but Jim keeps going. "You know what? This is better. This is cozier, right, Kath? Absolutely. Let's do it. I'm pumped about this. And hey, where are those rug rats? Trying to hide from Uncle Jim?"

It all comes back to me now, how much I loved this couple. Jim's way of spotting a crack in the social fabric and plastering it over with words before anyone else noticed it was there. His melodious voice accustomed to summing up for the jury, laying out a thought process, then walking us right through it. There was a time, before Rick and I were married, before Jed was born, that I had plans to become a lawyer myself. More than plans: I'd taken the LSATs, done well, and been accepted into a school.

Then life intervened. Literally. In the form of Jed.

I'd forgotten, too, the way Jim Shaw sees the distribution of domestic labor. In the space of five minutes, the re-introductions are over and Jim has peeled off his jacket and rolled up his sleeves to help in the kitchen. Rick, who acts like he doesn't know where to find anything in the kitchen, who still asks where the bowls are even though I know he knows, is squiring Kathie around the house, giving her the obligatory tour.

"He didn't tell you why we're here, did he?" Jim says.

He's found the good china without having to be told where it is. When did they stop making men like this?

"I'm totally in the dark. I thought maybe it was just for old times' sake."

"You know something?" He puts the plates down on the little island. "That's what it should be about. We had these plans when we left. We were going to stay in touch. And look at us now—it's been, what, eight years?" He shakes his head. "It's my bad. It was the job. I got sucked in and I never came up for breath. I'll tell you what—" He breaks off. "Well, who do we have here?"

Much to my surprise, Jed is standing in the doorway. He takes a step forward. Jim flings his arms wide to embrace my son, then backs up for a good look at him. "You must be, what? Seven feet tall?"

"Six three."

I haven't seen Jed like this, so boyish and bashful, in a long time. I feel something in my chest, fluttery and warm. A mommy thing. Hard to put into words.

"Just *look* at you," Jim says. "And I bet you're still the brain, aren't you? I remember how sharp you always were. Sharper than me, and that's saying something!"

Down the hallway, I hear Rick saying something about the history of the house. Whenever he walks people through, I have to stop myself from interrupting, from correcting the little details he inevitably gets wrong. The death of a thousand cuts, that's what he calls it, the way I harp on every little thing he says. It's not that he hates to be corrected. He just hates to be corrected by me.

"I saw that car outside," Jed is saying, wonder in his voice. "What is that?"

"*That* is a Maserati. You wanna take a spin? We could go out later, if your mom says it's all right."

I nod absently, still listening for Rick's voice. I can't make out the words, but the pride comes through loud and clear. You'd think he'd inherited the place and not swindled it out of a little old lady. No, that's not fair. That's my own guilt talking. I've been in a funk all day, and even this strange reunion can't seem to cut through it.

Kathie's heels tap their way into the kitchen, leaving Rick behind in midsentence.

"Is that Jed?" she says. "I can't believe it."

While the Shaws fawn over our son, I catch Rick in the corner of my eye. He leans against the door frame, arms crossed, a strange expression on his face. My irritation melts away. After nearly twenty years of marriage, I can read that man's face. Only I can't, not now. The downward curl of the lip isn't a frown exactly. It's more of a flat line of anxiety, like he's holding his breath, waiting for something terrible to happen. For a moment, I feel as if I'm seeing something I'm not meant to, something he's hidden for as long as I've known him.

I walk over and graze his hand with mine. "Are you okay? Is something wrong?"

"What?" He looks down at me blankly, then pulls away. "No, nothing."

When I look up, Kathie is glancing my way. She tries to smile, but there it is again: that microscopic wince of suppressed pain.

*

After dinner, Rick takes Jim out to the shed for a man-to-man.

"That's what he calls it," I explain to Kathie. "That's his job these days, having man-to-mans."

"That's his job?"

"Yeah," Jed says. "Dad's the Men's Pastor at church now."

"The what?"

"The Men's Pastor."

She shakes her head. "And what's that, exactly?"

"Don't get him started," I say.

"What they should call him is the Sports Pastor," Jed says, "because that's all it is. He goes to a Ravens game with some men from the church, plays some tennis, some handball, whatever. Golf every weekend, pretty much. But if they came out and called him the Sports Pastor, that would be too much. It's like the dude selling indulgences in the Reformation. People would flip out if they knew what was going on, so they call it being a Men's Pastor."

To her credit, Kathie takes all this in with a placid smile, choosing to interpret Jed's speech as an attempt at humor from an affectionate son. The reality is more complicated, as she probably realizes. The change in Rick's job description happened three years ago. The senior pastor, a Promise Keeper from way back, returned from a conference convinced that the church wasn't doing enough to meet the needs of men. We were in danger of losing them, he said, because the church had become too feminized, too therapeutic, too soft and mushy. Rick went along with the diagnosis just to humor his boss. From time to time, the senior pastor would drop hints about the succession, implying that he was grooming Rick to take over, so whenever he latched onto a new trend, Rick did whatever he could to appear supportive. Only this time, he miscalculated.

"I want you to run with this," the senior pastor had said.

"Absolutely," Rick replied, not realizing until much later what he'd signed on to do. By then, his new business cards proclaimed him the church's first-ever Men's Pastor. He only started using them once all the old Associate Pastor cards had been handed out, hoping for a reprieve. Since then, he's made the best of it.

To Kathie, who's wincing again, I say, "Rick's worked harder at being a Men's Pastor than he's ever worked at anything before."

Jed gets up from the table. "That's the *only* thing he works at."

After he's gone, I give Kathie a wan smile. "Sorry about that. At least you know we're not putting on airs."

"I feel like I'm still part of the family." She rises and helps me clear the dishes. "I guess the job has been hard on the boys? I can relate to that, you know. At the firm here, Jim set a pretty easy pace, but the new one has pretty much run him ragged. As long as we're not wearing our church masks, I might as well admit, there were times I was just about out the door."

"Not you and Jim," I say.

"Oh yes. That's all over now. He apologized." She smiles and pulls at the strand of pearls around her neck. "In fact, I'm wearing the apology right now."

"Good for you."

I leave the dishes in the drying rack and top off our glasses. Kathie leans against the counter, her back to the sink, and I prop myself against the island. Over her shoulder I can see Jim peering through the shed window. It looks like he's doing a lot of talking.

An evil thought flashes into my mind, remembering Kathie walking away from Rick in midsentence and that strange expression on his face. There are five other pastors on staff at the church, and their wives all claim to envy me. When your husband's the Men's Pastor, they say, you don't have to worry about women throwing themselves at him. "And a good-looking man like him too," the older ones add, like they've been tempted by the idea themselves.

Did something happen while Rick was giving his tour?

"What about you, Beth? Are things all right?"

"Things are fine," I say. Too quickly.

She pauses. "Really?"

I'm thinking crazy thoughts now. Of course nothing happened. This isn't me. I'm not the jealous type. Besides, Rick has never given me any reason. He's not interested in other women. Fidelity seems second nature to him. He's not a wolf, no matter what the official line might be about Mars and Venus, and the sinful nature of man.

No, we have other issues. Deeper ones.

"Okay, you caught me," I say, trying to keep my tone light. "Things are . . . I don't know. Tricky. But I have hope. I'm not sure how it happened, but the latest idea to take hold at the church is this sabbatical thing. The pastors need a break to recharge. Rick's getting the whole month of October off. He doesn't know it yet, but we're going to Florida. You remember Stacy? She's got a beach house down there and today she handed me the keys. Can you believe it?"

She sees through me. She knows I'm hiding something. But she's too gracious to push. "That's great. So, a romantic getaway, huh? Or are the boys going too?"

"I haven't thought that far ahead. They can't be out of school for a whole month, so . . . yeah, I think we need some time on our own, just the two of us. Maybe that's the answer."

"It *is* the answer," Kathie says. She reaches for my hand, squeezing it tight. "Now, listen. I know you love this house and this neighborhood. I know Jed's almost out of high school and I'm sure Eli's happy where he is. But I want you to promise me you'll keep an open mind."

"An open mind about what?"

"Jim's explaining everything to Rick now. I'll let him tell you what's going on. It's something good, though. Something wonderful. It could be like old times. So don't dismiss it out of hand, all right? Promise me you'll think about it, pray about it."

"Pray about what?"

"Jim made me swear I wouldn't—" She stops abruptly, doubling over. Her hand reaches back, trying to set her glass on the counter. I have to take it from her or she'd shatter it.

"Kathie, what's wrong?"

She straightens herself, pressing her fingertips against her jaw just in front of her ears. She opens her mouth wide, shuts it, closes her eyes in intense pain. I take her by the shoulders, not knowing what else to do.

She lets out a long breath, then lowers her hands. "It's okay."

"Are you all right?"

"It's stupid," she says. "Have you ever heard of tinnitus?"

"Of course. It's, like, ringing in your ears?"

"No, it's more like hearing feedback from a speaker. It's this high-pitched electronic whine. It started a couple of months ago. At first I thought my hearing was going bad, but according to the tests, it's all in my head. Stress-induced. I told my doctor, I've never been less stressed out than I am now, but . . . I don't know. I guess this is what it's like to get old."

"We're not old."

"Speak for yourself. I looked in the mirror this morning and, Beth, I have jowls. Look at this . . ." She runs her hand up and down the line of her chin. "These are my mother's, not mine."

I remember my own glimpse in the mirror this afternoon, my truer, younger self staring back at me.

"Do you take medicine for tinnitus?"

"Usually it's a symptom of some kind of hearing loss. I thought maybe I'd gone to too many concerts as a wild child. But no, what the doctor prescribed was behavioral cognitive therapy, which is a fancy way of saying I go to a shrink. Does it help? Not so far."

"Do you always hear it?"

"The funny thing is, you learn to tune it out. It's there but somehow you push it into the background. Then your brain starts messing with the volume knob. All night long, it's been going crazy."

"Maybe it's the stress of coming here."

She smiles. "You want to hear something funny? As much as it hurts, I don't feel like something's wrong with me. What it feels like is a part of my brain switched on and now I can hear things that people aren't supposed to hear. You know how dogs can hear frequencies that humans can't? In this analogy, I'm the dog. I never catch myself thinking, 'Why is this happening to me?' The question I ask is, 'How can they not hear it?' Isn't that strange?"

"Well," I say, "believe it or not, it isn't the strangest thing I've heard today."

Kathie smiles again and reaches for my hand. She tells me she's missed me and that we're going to stay in touch from now on, and how happy she is to have gotten to talk. But as she's saying this, I can see her eyelid fluttering slightly and her lip pulling taut. She can hear it now, I realize, that secret frequency all her own. I can't imagine what that must be like.

*

Rick and I stand on the front porch waving until the Maserati is out of sight. Once the men came in from the shed, Jim took Jed for the promised spin, then it was time to call it a night. As he turns to go inside, I loop my arm inside Rick's.

"What's going on?" I ask. "What was Jim talking to you about?"

"Haven't you guessed?"

He goes around the house turning off the lights. I turn a few back on for when Eli comes home. Rick heads upstairs, beckoning me to follow, and behind the closed bedroom door, he peels his shirt off and pulls me against him. I can't remember the last time we held each other, the last time we kissed. His lips are cold.

"It was a job, wasn't it?" I ask.

He backs us toward the bed, plopping down and pulling me after him. He pulls on my top, but I close my hand over his.

"Tell me."

He sighs contentedly. "Their church in Virginia. The lead pastor retired and now Jim's on the search committee. He's the chairman, in fact. He says they trust him to find the right guy."

"And you're Jim's guy?"

"I am Jim's guy." He kicks his shoes off, then his socks. "My talents are wasted here, he says. You know what I think about that. I feel like I don't even have a voice here anymore, and Jim says I should. I should have a big voice in the Church—the capital C church, not just ours. The church in Virginia isn't as big as ours, but I'd be the lead pastor."

"Okay . . ."

"'You'd be trading a megachurch for a megaphone,' that's how he put it. I've been 'hiding my light under a bushel,' a lot of stuff like that. He really wants me to do it, Beth."

I slide myself next to him, resting my head on his chest. "And what do you want?"

"What do I want?" He slips his hand under my top, resting his cool fingers against the warmth of my back. "I'm gonna have to think about that. I can see the pros and the cons. I've invested a lot in my current position—"

"Would we have to move? Of course we would. I don't know how I'd feel about that."

"We could make a nice little profit selling this place."

That's not what I want to hear.

"Rick, I'm not sure about the timing."

"You mean the boys? I don't know." He falls silent, his eyes studying the cracks in the ceiling. He runs his hand absently up and down my spine. I can hear his heartbeat like it's inside my own head. His slow, steady breath.

"We have a month to think it over," I say. "And guess what?"

I get off the bed and start digging through the pile of junk on the dresser.

He props himself up on his elbows. "Another surprise?"

When I turn, the keys are dangling from my hand. "These

go to a beach house in Florida. It's ours for the month of October. We can drive down on Monday. If you want, we can leave right after church on Sunday."

"The boys have school."

"They're responsible," I say. "Plus, Deedee's next door and she won't mind checking up on them, I'm sure. What do you say?"

He reaches for me. "Let's do it."

I toss the keys on the bed and follow them there.

Is this happening? It is.

And afterward, I pad to the bathroom and back, feeling better about Rick and worse about the job offer. Accepting would mean leaving everything we know. On some level, I'd be willing to do that, but there would have to be some concrete purpose, a real hope of change, and not just the prospect of living in the same rut with better pay and another rung up the ladder.

None of which I can confide to Rick, not yet. Sprawled on his side of the bed, eyelids heavy, he couldn't process any of it. Since I'm in the mood to ramble, I curl up beside him and launch into an inventory of the day's events, all the details of frenzied preparation he set in motion with his announcement this morning. When I get to the part about Chas Worthing and the Rent-a-Mob, my embarrassment at the sparkling Jesus fish, he chuckles and coils an arm around me.

"I don't know if you draw the crazies to you," he says, "or if you actively seek them out."

"Don't complain. If I didn't seek them out, we never would have met."

"Meaning what?"

I prop myself up on my elbow. "You haven't forgotten how we met, have you?"

"Of course not," he says, without elaborating.

"The Baptist Student Union, remember? One of those Monday night jam sessions they used to have on campus—"

"There was nothing crazy about that."

"There was to me. All those people holding their hands in the air, the choruses repeating over and over, the earnest, handsome man up front giving a talk from his falling-apart Bible."

He smiles. "It was in pretty bad shape, wasn't it?"

"I would never have gone in there, only . . . I don't know. Like you said, I actively seek them out."

"You can't honestly compare the BSU to a bunch of lefty antiwar nuts, Beth."

"No, of course not," I say.

"Be-e-e-eth."

"Is that the time? I feel so sleepy all the sudden."

*

My eyes open and the room is dark. If I could see myself in the mirror, I know I'd be smiling. I'd see a stupid, teenage grin, the kind of smile I haven't believed in since forever. Is it really that easy to make my problems go away? Maybe it is. My body is warm under the covers, but the air on my exposed shoulders is pleasantly cool. I roll over toward Rick, expecting his tousled hair and sleep-puckered lips. Instead, the sheets are pushed back and he's gone.

The nightstand clock says it's three in the morning. I get out of bed, fumbling in the dark for my robe. On the landing I pause at Eli's door, listening for the music he always plays to go to sleep. He's in there, dead to the world. I pad down the stairs, expecting to find lights on in the kitchen. The house is dark. Through the back window, I see the lights on in the shed.

After watching for a minute, waiting for some sign of movement, I decide to go out and check. Rick's never disappeared in the middle of the night. Then again, this has been an exceptional day. There's no way of predicting how it might end up. I left my slippers upstairs, but a pair of Rick's boots stands in the mudroom beside the back door. I step into them and let myself out.

Walking outside under the moonlight in nothing but a terrycloth robe and a pair of oversized boots is a magically illicit experience. Half fairyland elf, half little girl playing dress-up. The shed gives off a faint orange glow, last traces of a dwindling fire. Instead of the door, I go to the window, pressing myself close to the windowpane.

For such a small space, Rick has managed to pack it full of creature comforts. A little couch and chair, a bookshelf, a cast-off rug, a locking rolltop desk where he keeps his computer. All of this is lit by the flickering fire, which casts as much shadow as it does light. At first, there's no sign of my husband.

Then I see him. In only his boxers, lying facedown on the floor, his arms thrown wide. My heart jumps and I recoil from the window. He's dead, his body cooling on the floor, victim of a tragic post-coital heart attack. But no. I look again. I smile at my fright. He's not dead, he's . . .

Praying.

That thing happens in my chest again, the fluttering, heaving thing where the space that seemed so compact, so full, suddenly expands on you. This whole new capacity in your heart to love. And you feel warm and vulnerable and alive.

I pick my way around the side of the shed, the door latch cold in my hand. The door opens without a creak. I step inside, feeling the heat, the sniff of woodsmoke. I pause at his uncovered feet, then lower myself down, getting almost to my knees, touching the couch to steady myself, unaccustomed to the motion.

I want to touch him, but I don't. I want to say something, but I keep silent.

I wait.

This is a vigil he's keeping. He read it somewhere or saw it in a movie—a young knight on the evening before he was to be dubbed kept vigil all night in the church, his face to the floor, his arms spread like Christ on the cross.

"Rick," I say, exhaling his name, the slightest of whispers. I wait, listening for an answer.

My husband takes a breath, a deep breath, then lets it out in a long and tremulous snore. He is not praying. He is asleep.

So what, right? Even Peter couldn't keep watch for an hour without nodding off. This is natural, I tell myself. Absolutely normal. Whatever it is, Beth, it's not a metaphor summing up the nature of the man. Don't let yourself start thinking that way.

You're not thinking at all. You're feeling. And what you're feeling is the ground dropping from beneath your feet, leaving you to kick through thin air, falling. It makes no sense, but it doesn't have to. When did the heart start having to make sense?

I get up quietly, straighten the front of my robe, and trudge back across the yard to the house. Up above, the moonlight shines down on me like a dull throb, like a painful keening only my ears can detect.

chapter 3

Full Retreat

"I want to share something with you," Rick says over breakfast.

It's a funny word, *share*. It doesn't mean what you think it means. Ordinarily if somebody tells you they want to share with you, it means they have something nice and want you to have some too. In the Christian vernacular, it's almost the opposite. To share means I'm going to impose on you, but it's not me doing the imposing, really, it's God. Therefore you have to sit there and take it. You have to go along with whatever I share.

The boys have gone to school and it's just the two of us. Eli hitched a ride to school with Damon after extracting a promise from Rick to drop off his twisted tire at the bike shop. Now it sits in the mudroom, waiting.

During the night, Rick slipped back into bed, never mentioning that he'd been gone. But there is clearly a difference from the night before. The fraught sense of intimacy is gone. And he hasn't said a word about Jim's proposal. We're at the table, bathed in morning light, staring into the dregs of our coffee. And now Rick wants to share.

I have to force myself to answer. "What is it, honey?"

On the table, the keys to Stacy's beach house sit beside my half-eaten grapefruit. I close my fist around the floaty, dragging it down to my lap. As he talks, I find myself squeezing tightly.

"I stayed up late last night," he says, "and did some serious soul-searching. This is such a big step, the job in Virginia. I have to be honest. I don't know what to do. It would be such a change . . . but maybe a change is exactly what I need. I'm feeling stifled."

"In ministry, you mean?"

"I don't know," he says. "In life."

"I see."

"Now, don't get angry."

"Why would I be angry? You haven't said anything we didn't talk about last night."

"You sound angry."

"Do I?" I pause, trying to listen to the sound of my words, their echo in the room. "Well, I'm not trying to. Listen, we don't have to get into this right now. Let's take our time, okay? When we're in Florida, away from Lutherville and the church and everything else, you can clear your mind and we can really figure this out. You don't have to say yes or no right this second."

"I know that," he says, a defensive note in his voice.

"It's just . . . I don't think you need to do anything rash."

"Beth, I've made a decision."

"Oh."

"*Oh*? That's it?"

"It sounded like a statement, not a question."

He pushes away from the table, splashes the last of his

coffee into the sink. Lingering there, gazing through the window toward the shed, he lets out a sigh. I almost tell him about last night, how I interrupted his prayer vigil and caught him napping. Instead, I unclench my fist and put the beach house keys back on the table.

"Listen, Rick."

"I'm not going," he says.

I hear the words and weight lifts. As much as our life here can sometimes grate on me, I'm not ready to leave it, not yet. Maybe not ever. My house. My neighbors. My little niche in the world. I didn't know how much I loved it until the prospect of leaving arose. Breaking the news to Kathie will be hard. The pressure of her hand on mine, telling me to keep an open mind, saying it would be like old times. But it wouldn't. You can't go back.

At the same time, there's a flutter of doubt. Is this really me? Afraid to leave my familiar surroundings. Willing to live with a situation I can't stand out of fear. He's making the decision without me, though, so I don't need to interrogate my feelings too deeply. It's on Rick's shoulders. Let it stay there.

"All right, then," I say. "For what it's worth, I think you're making the right choice."

He turns and gives me the same inscrutable frown from last night. "No, Beth. I don't know about the job yet. That's up in the air. What I mean is, I'm not going to Florida."

"What?"

"Take the boys if you want. Or go yourself if you want. Maybe you should. You could ask Stacy to go with you."

"I don't understand. You don't want to go to Florida? Fine. We'll go somewhere else. I don't care. But we need to go, Rick. We need this time."

"Not me," he says.

"It's *your* vacation!"

"Last night something happened. God laid something on my heart. I don't know exactly what he was telling me, or what to do about it. But I know where I need to be if I want to hear him."

"Where is that?"

"Out there," he says, jabbing his thumb over his shoulder.

"In the backyard?"

"In the shed."

"You're going to the shed so God can talk to you? Will you be back in time for lunch?"

He shakes his head slowly, smiling at my mockery. "Don't, Beth. What I'm saying is, instead of some vacation, I'm going to spend that time with him."

"The whole month of October."

"If that's how long it takes, then yes."

"You're going to live in the shed?" Acid floods into my veins. "Are you even listening to yourself? What are you going to do for food, huh? What if you need to go to the bathroom?"

"I didn't say I couldn't leave the shed ever. It's not about legalism."

Legalism, in this context, means having to follow rules invented by someone other than yourself. There's no doubt in my mind this isn't about that kind of legalism. Rick is definitely going to make up his own rules and not be bothered by anyone else's.

"This is so *selfish*," I say.

"That's where you're wrong. This is the most selfless thing I have ever done in my life."

I'm not a throw-the-dishes kind of woman, but hearing those words, I can understand why they do it. He marches out, slamming the back door behind him, and part of me wishes I'd sent a bowl or coffee mug—one of the cheap ones—flying after him.

A few moments later I hear the shed door snap shut.

*

He's gone temporarily crazy, that's all. In an hour, he'll emerge from the shed and make a joke of the whole thing. And I'll make myself laugh. *You had me going there for a while.* Only an hour passes and he doesn't come out. I make more coffee and take a mug outside.

At the door, I remember last night. I pour the coffee onto the grass and turn back.

Across the English garden, from the corner of my eye, I see a familiar figure emerge from the back of the big house. Deedee Smythe steps outside in a flowing white cover-up that opens to reveal an ecru one-piece bathing suit that must have been very chic when she bought it in the 1970s. Under one arm she carries a folding lawn chair, just like the Rent-a-Mob folks I met yesterday, and under the other she has a canvas and easel. When I first met Deedee, I thought she was a recreational watercolorist, one of those people who takes it up as a hobby. In fact, she's a rather accomplished painter. Roy Meakin, one of the neighbors, filled me in on her illustrious career, and afterward I looked her up online. She's the only person I know who has a Wikipedia entry.

Seeing me, Deedee raises her hand to wave. The cover-up slips down to reveal a long, bronzed arm. She is not the sort of lady whose age you ask, but as best I can work out, she's in her mid- to late fifties. To hear Roy tell it, when she was younger all the men hovered around like bees at the honeycomb. She still carries herself that way. What I like about her, though, is how little care she seems to take. She dresses eccentrically, even badly, and never seems concerned about the impression she's making. All she cares about is painting. And keeping her mother, Margaret, appeased.

"You're out early this morning," I call.

She beckons me over. "I had to get away from her. I was supposed to get her a Zagnut after mass yesterday, and it utterly slipped my mind. To add insult to injury, I made the mistake of letting her know that, at her age, maybe it was time to cut back on the sweets. You know what she said? 'Don't make me choose between you and a Chunky with raisins.' I'm her daughter, but that only counts for so much."

Another thing about Deedee: her voice. She has the deep, throaty timbre of a blues singer, like she gargled with Scotch as a girl, like her vocal cords were aged in oak casks. Not a pretty voice, but an interesting one, the way some faces can be interesting. I could listen to her for hours. And she must be accustomed to people listening, because she tends to talk in monologues.

"So you're going to do some painting?"

"And some sunbathing," she says. "Though it's still a little brisk. I'm taking a break from the church mural. Maybe I shouldn't have agreed to the thing at all. It's not what I was hoping. I'm not happy with it at all."

"I was going to stop by and take a look."

"Well, don't. You'll only vex me, Elizabeth, and I don't need vexing at this point."

I love that she uses words like *vex*, and that she insists on using my full name. I remember her chagrin when I first insisted that Jed and Eli were my sons' names, and they weren't shortened versions of Jedediah or Elihu.

"All right," I say. "No vexing."

For as long as I've known her, Deedee has been complaining about the mural in the nave of her parish church. The artwork, she says, could have come straight from some pious child's illustrated Bible. "It's a particular sort of commercial kitsch. An affront to beauty, and probably to God too." Then a few months ago the priest called on the Smythes with a proposition. As part of the ongoing renovation of the historic building, why not commission the famous artist in their midst to paint a new mural? "'Absolutely not,' I told him. 'No way, not ever.' But, Elizabeth, the man is a Jesuit. They practically invented logic. Whatever objection I raised, he had an answer. 'You can have a free hand,' he said. 'Paint whatever you're inspired to paint.' And there was Mother the whole time, just *loving* the idea. She's never much cared for my work, but there she was just swelling with pride. What could I do? What could I do?"

Every couple of weeks I venture up to the church for a look at her progress. It's uphill all the way, so I approach the miniature spires with their recessed grottoes for statued saints with a burn in my calves. Inside, there's a musty smell that goes well with the gloom. I always look around furtively, afraid I might be interrupting some arcane ritual. But usually the place is empty. Like a small-scale Michelangelo, Deedee has erected a scaffold and screened off the wall with a swath of plastic sheeting. When she's at work, the shop lights inside the enclosure make the plastic glow white, and you can see her silhouette pacing back and forth.

The last time I checked, however, Deedee wasn't working. She'd painted over most of what she'd already done.

"I should never have agreed," she says. "I'm not a religious artist. I don't understand religious art."

"Maybe you shouldn't think of it as religious. Just do what you do."

This stops her for a moment. She studies me closely. "You know who you sound like? The priest."

At the edge of the garden, beside a low stone wall half sunk in the earth, she erects her easel, unfolds her chair, and unslings the shoulder bag full of paints and caked brushes and other paraphernalia.

"You wouldn't be more comfortable in your studio?" I ask.

She shakes her head. "That's where I work. This is where I think."

Her studio is another one of the former outbuildings, perhaps twice the size of Rick's shed and equally stuffed, with beautiful skylight windows in the roof. The only examples of Deedee's work I have seen in person are the canvases stacked on one side of the studio under a drape cloth. She paints very detailed, almost photographic pictures, but with a surreal flatness to them, so that they appear both real and imaginary at the same time. I'm no art critic. To the extent that I have any taste at all, I'm drawn more to folk art. Deedee's work is nothing like that. I love it, though, mainly because I love her.

"What are you doing out here, anyway?" she asks. "Not that I mind. It's just, you're usually running around like a decapitated chicken. I'm not used to you standing still for this long."

"Hmm," I say.

Rick doesn't like me sharing family business with the neighbors. It's not about keeping up appearances. What's private is private, that's all. Not to mention, he tells me, we don't want to reinforce people's stereotypical view of Christians. By the stone wall, we're within earshot of his shed. He's probably eavesdropping right now.

"The thing is," I say, glancing toward the shed's window, "my husband had a psychotic break this morning. He's holed up in the shed right now, saying he won't come out for a month, not until God talks to him or something . . ."

Her eyes widen. "Oh, it's like that book. The one where the man goes to the shack and it turns out Oprah is really God."

"Not exactly."

"No, really," she insists. "There was a thing about it in the *Times*."

"Oh, I'm familiar with the book." Boy, am I! Both of the ladies' book clubs I belong to read it in turns. The first one wanted to shellac the book in gold dust and the second one wanted to burn it. "I'm just saying, I don't think that's where Rick got the idea. But who knows?" I raise my voice a little. "I wouldn't put it past him to rip off somebody else's idea."

One, two . . . and there it is. The shed door swings open and Rick appears. He doesn't glance our way. He pretends he doesn't know we're watching. Closing the door with exaggerated care, he beats a path back to the house, eyes down.

"Well," Deedee says, "I don't know if it was God he heard or you, sweetheart. But he doesn't look too keen. Maybe you're being a little hard on him."

This coming from a woman who never married. A woman who, according to Roy Meakin, was nothing if not hard on the men who entered her life. Those who don't know are always quickest with their advice.

"Maybe. Then again, he's being pretty hard on me."

*

The silent treatment. Rick's at the kitchen table, not even acknowledging the fact that I've entered the room. He sits crouched over a spiral notepad, scratching out some kind of note. I put the empty coffee cup I've been carrying around on the drying rack. No, wait. I pick it up, fill it three quarters of the way full, and stir in some half-and-half before setting the cup at his elbow. He glances at the coffee, not at me. On the pad in front of him, he's written down a supply list.

Utz crab chips (3)
Bottled water (3 cases)
Snickers minis (4 bags)
Juice boxes, apple (3)
Bread (2)
Peanut butter
Nutella
Tuna (10)
mayo (1)

"What is this?" I ask. "Are you going to the grocery store?"

"I'm trying to make a list of everything I'm going to need."

"Maybe you should fast instead. That's how it's supposed to work."

He puts the pen down heavily. "Listen, Beth. I don't expect you to understand. I'm not even asking you to. This . . . It could be the most important decision I make."

Resting my hand on his shoulder, I slide into the chair beside him, trying hard to bottle up what I'm feeling and appear sympathetic. He tenses, lowering deeper into his crouch, his head halfway to the tabletop like he's bracing for whatever's about to fall on him.

"Don't you think this is an important decision for both of us?" I ask. "Instead of cutting yourself off from the rest of the world, from your family, from me, maybe we need to work through this together."

"If I could explain what I'm thinking, I would, but clearly I can't."

"We need this time together, Rick. We *need* it. You and me. I can't put it any plainer than that."

"I heard what you said out there. My psychotic break."

"You're not listening," I say. "We need time together, away from everything. We need to work on us before we make any other decisions."

He scoots his chair away from me, pulling his shoulder free. "You can't make this about the relationship, okay? This is more than that. Deeper. It's not about us."

"It's about you."

"No, Beth, it's not about me. It's about him. Don't you get that? What I need from you is support and you're just cutting away at me, all these little slices until I'm bleeding to death. What's wrong with you? You know I'm committed to my ministry. You know what my life has to be. You've always known, right from the start. And I thought you *believed* in it."

"So if I don't go along with this craziness, it's because I don't believe? That's my problem—really? You really think that because I don't want you to spend your vacation living off crab chips and Snickers and bottled water that I must not have faith? Maybe I don't, not in this. I mean, if you put some locusts and honey on your list, I could at least take you a little more seriously."

He gets up again and walks out. He has this way of doing it too, like he's wasted all the time he can spare on my issues and needs to get back to what really matters. Used to be, we'd have a spat like this and I'd break down, waiting tearfully for him to come back and apologize. Then I learned that Rick never comes back. Not because he's still angry. He's simply put the whole business out of his mind, filed it away with all the other minutia.

Fine. I rip the page off the top of his spiral pad, delighting for a moment in the jagged spine of paper left behind in the rings. I grab the car keys and my wallet. If my husband wants to live off crab chips and candy bars, fine. Either he'll choke on his Nutella or he'll come crawling back in from the shed, hungry for real food, and admit he was wrong the whole time. With any luck, he will break on Day One and we can leave for Florida as planned.

"Honey," I call with caustic sweetness, "I'm running to the Giant. Don't forget about your son's bicycle tire. And he's got a birthday next week too, in case it slipped your mind."

*

The Rent-a-Mob is back at the corner. Trapped by the red light at the opposite intersection, I gaze at them with something akin to longing. Chas Worthing straddles a fat drum, beating a tempo while a half dozen others chant slogans at the top of their lungs. Even with my window cranked down, the noise of the traffic drowns out everything but the beat. *Ramming speed!*

How nice it must be, how wonderful, to set up in the middle of the bustling world and give yourself permission to scream. Even if your voice is overwhelmed, even if no one can make out a word you're saying, to fill your lungs and let go, emptying yourself into the sound . . . It must be liberating. I can see why they'd do it, no matter what the cause. The rest of us, we keep our opinions to ourselves, and we certainly don't yell about them. Or if we do, we only yell at the ones who love us and know us best, the ones least able to hear a word we say.

The light changes and the east-west traffic yields to us north-southers. As the VW chugs up to speed and I coast past them, I extend my hand out the window. I wave. Not good enough. I lean closer to the window, letting the wind buffet my face, and yell—"Whooooooo!"—as loud as I can. Chas Worthing doesn't look up. The Rent-a-Mobbers can't hear me any more than I can hear them.

But the driver behind me beeps his horn.

"Sorry!"

I say it out loud, then mouth the words into the rearview mirror, then give an exaggerated shrug. Sorry, you big SUV. Sorry for costing you a second of time. Sorry for swerving a little in my lane. Sorry for opening my big mouth and trying to speak.

chapter 4

Blue Throbbing Fullness

If it was Jed's birthday looming, everything would be different. Weeks in advance, his brow creased with anxiety, he'd want to talk through all the details with me, explaining what he wanted and what he didn't want, which of his tiny circle of friends should be invited and which shouldn't. He'd have a list of presents for my consideration, mostly arcane widgets for his computer that can only be ordered online. There is never any chance of Jed's birthday slipping past us. He wouldn't let that happen.

By contrast Eli seems so laid back that, on the way to church, I feel the need to remind him.

"Don't forget what's happening next week."

In the backseat of the van, he looks up from his iPod screen. An absent smile forms on his lips. "Ha, ha."

I'm driving the boys—or rather, Jed drives while I ride shotgun. Rick always leaves first thing in the morning, meeting with the staff for prayer and then helping with the 8:00 a.m. service. This morning he asked me not to say anything about his plans for October, worrying that if the men of the church knew he was still in town, they would expect him to show up for handball and midweek Bible studies and hot wings at the sports bar. "Are you at least going to tell the boys?" I had asked. He said it would probably be better coming from me.

"Before we go in," I say, "there's something you need to know . . ."

As I explain, I try to gauge their separate reactions. Jed flares up immediately, while Eli seems to shrug off the unpleasant news. I know better, though. Like whisky in a sauce, Jed's wrath will burn away quick enough. In the long run, Eli will take it harder.

"So no beach," he says. "No Florida."

"It doesn't have to mean that. The three of us, we can still go."

He glances at the screen again, then tucks it away. "Yeah, I guess."

"And anyway, I won't be surprised if he changes his mind."

In the church parking lot, I give them final instructions. Don't say anything to anyone. Act normal. If Stacy says something about the beach house, just thank her profusely. As soon as I'm done, Eli trots off to his youth group class. Jed hangs back, walking beside me in solidarity.

"We should go," he says. "We should go without him."

"We'll see."

Crossing the lot is a challenge all its own. The various quadrants are labeled and color-coded, and you file through hundreds of cars to approach the building, a bit like a crowd of ancient Romans on their way to the Coliseum. Once the international headquarters and East Coast manufacturing hub of a now-defunct plastics company, the building had to be gutted and rebuilt from the ground up when the church signed the lease. Despite the vast size, I never feel as dwarfed as I do when I sneak into Deedee's parish church (which isn't even a cathedral). The big box is slung low to the ground, like a shopping mall or community college. What it lacks in height, though, it makes up for in sprawl.

I kind of hate it.

The past few years, as the church got bigger, its name was sliced smaller and smaller. For the past eighteen months, we've been The Community. My best friend on staff is Holly, the director of aesthetics. (I kid you not, that is her title.) "What's next?" I asked her. "Are we gonna cut it down to just Unity?" She gave me a serious look. "Don't laugh. And whatever you do, don't spread that idea around."

In the old days, I had a lot of friends in church. There didn't seem to be so many barriers. Now my status is, at best, ambiguous. Being the wife of a pastor is one thing. You're on a kind of pedestal, always scrutinized, which can be unnerving. There are advantages, though. You occupy a natural role in people's lives. To borrow a metaphor, they have a pastor's-wife-shaped hole inside.

All you have to do is fit in.

This changes when you're the wife of the Men's Pastor. No one is quite sure what to do with you. My husband is the one who keeps their husbands out at night, the one their men confide in, the one they share their problems with instead of sharing them with their wives (who are, after all, sometimes the problem). Even people who knew me before Rick's title changed aren't as open as they used to be. I'm still a part of their lives. I still go to their book clubs and buy their makeup and vitamin supplements. But I could never talk to most of them, not honestly. I'd be too afraid of what they thought.

Holly has a little cubby of an office in the admin wing. When Jed and I split up in the cavernous atrium, instead of heading for the adult Sunday school classes, I grab two coffees at the Sacred Grounds Café ("Sandal Removal Optional") and walk them through the security door into the office corridor, where I find Holly's door ajar. It's only polite to knock, but have you ever tried knocking with a steaming cup of coffee in your hand?

"Knock, knock," I say.

"Sister, get in here. I need that coffee *stat*."

I slip inside, nudging the door shut behind me.

There's no desk in Holly's office, only a round table laden with architect's sketches for the next build-out, swatches, paint chips, and cardboard file boxes bulging at the sides. She sits on an orphaned conference room chair wheeled down from the other end of the hallway, beckoning me to take the other. As always, she looks impressive in her uniform: a crisp white blouse, a wasp-waisted jacket, and sculpted jeans, her straight blond hair cut in a severe bob. She's one of those people who decide young what they look best in and stick with it no matter what the occasion. The only real variety in Holly's wardrobe is whether her sunglasses are on or off.

When she calls me *sister*, I melt. I never had a sister growing up, and until now never had a stand-in. There have been women I could confide in to one degree or another, but not like this. With Holly I am unguarded, never afraid of being judged, always confident that what I say will be understood. That's the important thing, understanding. You need someone in your life who *gets* you. Holly gets me.

Behind her on the computer screen in the corner, the video feed from the auditorium shows the last lingerers filing out of the early service as the worship team wraps up for the thirty-minute break. The volume is muted.

"It was good this morning," Holly says, popping the lid off her coffee to help it cool. "The sermon wasn't bad—or the 'talk,' whatever we're calling it now."

"Don't spoil the ending for me."

"I wasn't sure if you'd make an appearance this morning. I saw Stacy just now and she told me the whole family was packing up for the month and moving to Florida. What's up with that? You say we're friends, and I have to hear it from her?"

"Maybe if you had a beach house in Florida, I'd keep you better informed."

"I can get one, if that's what it takes."

She's joking, but the fact is, she could. Holly's an architect by trade, in her midthirties, now semiretired thanks to her husband, Eric's, fortune. He may be fifteen years older—old enough that Holly's stepdaughter is about to graduate college—but in finding each other, the two of them discovered their soul mates. If you believe in such things. All I know is, they're good for each other.

And yet.

There are two things you need to know about Eric. First, he is a professional fund-raiser. His job is squeezing money out of the rich, and he's very good at his job. Before they met, he made his millions (literally) in the finance sector, then walked away to spend the rest of his life finding money for worthy causes. I'm not sure if it's guilt that motivates him or altruism or just the thrill of the challenge. Whatever it is, the work keeps him on the road a lot. Wherever there's a tsunami or an earthquake or a disaster of any kind, Eric Ringwald is on the first plane down, working the phone the whole way.

Yes, that's the second thing you need to know. His last name is Ringwald.

Which makes her name Holly Ringwald—just one letter of separation between eighties *Breakfast Club* sweetheart Molly Ringwald—and she married him anyway. She didn't even put her maiden name up front and go hyphenated. That is love, if you ask me. They are in love, Eric and Holly, and yet . . . I can tell that my friend is lonely. Lonely in her marriage. Maybe that's what brought us together in the first place, our unacknowledged common ground.

"Oh, Beth, you're in a funk, aren't you? I can always tell. Is it the vacation planning? Everything's up to you again, isn't it?"

A funk? That hardly describes it. I'm bitter as cursed well water. You take a drink and you can't get the taste out of your mouth ever again.

"It's not just that. There's Eli's birthday next week."

"That's *right*." She reaches for a ballpoint pen and writes something down on one of her canary-yellow legal pads. That scribble will translate into something nice and shiny for Eli, I'm sure. "Eric's down on the Gulf Coast again, so if you need any party planning assistance, you know who to call. Assuming you're not going to leave for Florida until after the party."

"I don't even know if there's going to be a party."

"Why? What's wrong?"

"Don't make me spill it. Not now."

"Beth, really, what's going on?"

And so it all comes tumbling out, and so do the tears. Crying really does make you feel better, the same way shock makes hiccups disappear. The more immediate trauma erases the longer-term one. For a time. By the end of my story, we're both dabbing our eyes and then she's hugging me and patting my back.

I pull away. I try to laugh. "Just look at me. I can't go out there like this."

"You don't have to go anywhere," she says with conviction.

If I was an eccentric old spinster in a Merchant Ivory movie, I'd want to share my lovely cottage with Holly and that's the truth. I'd do the cooking and leave the decorating to her, and we'd be inseparable.

"Thanks."

"It can't last, Beth. It'll never last. He'll be begging to get back in the house this time tomorrow. If he doesn't give up the idea before then. Rick's not stupid. The real question is, are you going to leave me high and dry? Richmond is the dumps, believe me. You couldn't drag me any farther into Virginia than Arlington, and even then I get nervous when I'm out of sight of the Washington Monument. Eric thinks touring Civil War battlefields is romantic, but, sister, it's not."

"You don't have to convince me. I couldn't imagine leaving my friends, our little house, Lutherville—no way." As I say the words, they ring false in my ears. The fear goes deeper than this. I can't bear trading this life for a new one with the same problems and none of the outlets. "But Jim knows how to bait a hook. You know what he said? 'You'd be trading a megachurch for a megaphone. You'll be a big voice in the church.'"

"A big voice in the church."

"With a capital C."

"Wow. All that versus being a Men's Pastor. I see what you mean."

"And you don't know any of this. He'd flip out if he knew I'd said anything."

"It sounds like he's flipped out already."

On the screen, the crowds are flowing back into the auditorium. The Community logo flashes onto the projection screens and the lights on stage start to flare. In the old Quaker meetinghouse I remember from my youth, everyone sat in the round with no front or back. You stared into the faces of other people, or at the ground. Deedee's parish faces forward, including the priest at times. He does some of whatever he does with his back to the audience, as if there were someone behind him looking down on them all. Not us. We march in and the band plays and the screen fills with soulful faces and lifted hands and swaying bodies, our own images reflected back to us, all but unconscious of the symbolism.

"Beth," she says, seeing my eyes fixed on the screen. "Feeling sorry for yourself?"

"It's what I do, Holly." The on-screen service starts to come alive. "You know what? I'm going to go. I think I need it."

"I'll go with you, then." She smiles. "It was a good sermon. I don't mind hearing it again."

*

We sit side by side on the extreme right edge of the auditorium, right under a suspended speaker pumping out the bass notes. A high-pitched vibration rides along with the sound. I can feel it between my teeth. Like the middle-aged woman I am, I cast my eyes back over a sea of worshippers toward the centrally located sound booth, willing them to turn the noise down. Next to me, Holly seems oblivious to it. Buttoned up as she is, Holly's a kinetic worshipper, a side-shuffling, clap-your-hands Jesus freak the moment the music starts. She sings and closes her eyes and, if everyone else does, raises open palms to heaven. All the while I watch her from the corner of my eye, acting like she's a bride dancing at her wedding. We are not sisters in this regard, not at all. More evidence that opposites attract.

The poison rages in me. I glance around and it all seems so fake, so false.

You're projecting, Beth. You're assuming the condition of your own heart is the condition of everyone else's. I know, I know. I'm sitting in the seat of the scornful, and I've brought my cushion.

Up on stage, the vocalists trill into their microphones and the lights up above throb in prearranged patterns. I try to tune everything out, to make it all go away. I clear enough space in my mind so I can offer up a prayer.

Confession: I don't pray much, not these days. Not for a long time, actually. I might offer up the random request, like my supermarket wish not to run into church people, but as far as deep, heartfelt communication, not so much. Sometimes I tell myself God and me, we're like an old married couple, so much in sync that they don't really have to say anything. Only I don't know any old married couples like that. Other times I worry what this two-way silence signifies.

Nothing happened that I can remember, no telling trauma. I simply fell out of the habit. Now, when I try to pick it back up again, it's hard to shake the feeling that I'm just talking to myself.

I have shared this with no one, not even Holly. Certainly not Rick.

Sometimes Rick will switch on a television preacher and watch a few minutes of snake oil. As the toll-free prayer line crawls across the screen, he chuckles at the craziness of it all, the blue-haired old ladies who sign away their life savings to men in shiny suits wearing gold nugget rings and improbable comb-overs. One of these charlatans, banging his Plexiglas pulpit on the subject of prayer, berated his audience for not letting God get a word in. "You pray and you pray and tell 'im this what you want and that what you want—but do you listen, praise Jesus? Not at all! You do all the talking, then you say God don't listen! Brothers and sisters, are *you* lis'nin? That there's the problem!"

So I heard this, and I stopped doing all the talking. I left pauses for God to fill. The pauses remained empty. I told myself I was foolish to listen to a TV preacher—but doesn't God use the foolish things of the world to confound the wise? I mean, if he can use a Chick tract to speak to somebody, he can use anything, right? But he wasn't speaking to me, not anymore.

I started to wonder if he ever had.

Yes, he did. It happened once, if only that. He spoke without using his voice. He spoke with his presence.

It was the summer after I graduated from high school, when Miss Hannah, the Korean War doctor, took me to a place she said I needed to experience. I don't remember how she knew our family. She seemed always to be there when I was growing up. The frail shrivel of old age had gotten hold of her. Even so, she did the driving that day, making me nervous with her weaving and her not wearing a seat belt. ("I'm too old to learn now.") We arrived in the late afternoon and entered a one-story brick building that looked from the outside like a dentist's office. Indoors, though, we found a large room with a vaulted ceiling and the familiar wooden pews arranged to face each other.

At the center of the meetinghouse ceiling was a glowing square of light. There were a few people already inside. They tilted their heads back so they could look at the roof—or rather, *through* the roof, because the square of light was simply a hole in the ceiling, opening up the room to the sky.

"You've never been here?" Miss Hannah asked.

I shook my head. She led me to one of the front benches. To my surprise, instead of sitting, she stretched herself out on the wood full-length.

"It's okay," she said. "My neck stopped bending that far a long time ago."

Tentatively, I sat next to her. I looked at the other people, uncertain what was going on. Miss Hannah told me to watch the sky.

At first it still looked like the sky. The edge of a graying cloud was visible. The occasional bird shot across the opening. As the sun lowered itself, the nature of the light began to change. Minutes passed. After some fidgeting, I found a comfortable way to arrange myself and let my body go numb.

"Keep watching," she said.

The light was blue now and pure. Bright and glowing. The longer I stared, the closer it seemed to get. Could I touch it? I almost thought so. Once my sense of distance was gone, I lost all concept of time as well. This experience required waiting.

So blue. I'd never seen anything like it before. Not in a museum, not at the movies, not in the carnival tents at the fairgrounds. Yet there was no trickery, no sleight of hand. There was no variation in the hue, no sense of depth. We were gazing into infinite color. The wonder of it was, there was no wonder at all. This was a spectacle available to anyone with eyes to see, always at the same time or thereabouts. Still, I had *never* seen it, I realized. I had never seen the sunset.

And I wasn't seeing it now. All this was, when I stopped to consider, the change that happens to a little patch of abstracted sky when the sunlight dies. I sat there unmoving as the time ebbed away, an ocean tide washing away the deep indigo to leave purple midnight in its wake.

"That was amazing," I said on the way out.

Miss Hannah looked at me sideways. "You think so? I come here whenever I need to remember what the world really is. Sometimes I forget how to look. If that happens to you, you'll know where to go."

When my brother called long distance to tell me she'd had a car accident and it didn't look promising, it was finals week of my first semester. Coiled up with academic anxiety, the news hit me hard. I promised myself that during the Christmas break I would go back to the meetinghouse with the open roof and watch the sunset again. I'd felt a presence there—not just Miss Hannah's, but the blue throbbing fullness up above and all around me. I wanted to feel that again.

Back home, finals behind me, I tried to find the place where she'd taken me. Though I reconstructed the journey as best I could, I was never able to discover that meetinghouse again. I described it to my parents and to Gregory, but none of them had ever heard of such a thing. And then Miss Hannah got better, but my world became crowded and, well, isn't that just the way of things?

Up on stage, the worship team transitions from one of their slow numbers, then lowers the volume to a quiet hum. One of the leaders intones a transitional prayer. A haloed floodlight comes on in the rafters, projecting a gold circle at center stage. Rick appears from the darkness, taking the mike stand in one hand, tilting it toward his mouth.

"The Fall Men's Retreat is coming up in November. We've already had a record number of men sign up. If you haven't made a decision yet, let me share three reasons why you should today . . ."

This is how I first laid eyes on my husband, standing on stage in front of a crowd. He'd seemed so handsome to me, so beautiful, a perfect, symmetrical man gone from marble to flesh. And he had a voice that sounded like the one in my head, a deep and friendly voice, always reassuring. It was Rick's voice that had drawn me into the BSU meeting, hearing him speak between the songs as I passed the open door. With the lights dimmed, it felt like he was speaking directly to me. I loved the idea of him right away, and came to love the reality soon after.

Now, under the harsh light, his untucked, slim T-shirt clings to his shoulders, proving he still works out. He looks his age under the lights too, making the shirt and the whiskered blue jeans and the white-walled Keds a study in trying too hard. I feel for him, on display, the oldest man on stage apart from the senior pastor, delivering a sales pitch for a church retreat when he's been told he ought to have a big voice in the church. It also pains me because his anxiety is apparent, the fear of aging and death, the fear of losing something he didn't make better use of when it belonged to him.

The moment he's finished, the floodlight switches off. The other side of the stage springs into action, one more upbeat praise song before we settle in. I watch the darkness where Rick's shape disappeared, looking for the edges of the man I'm trying to love. Too far to make him out, I give up trying. Next to me, Holly starts clapping her hands. I slip into the aisle and make my way to the exit.

*

"You bailed on me," Holly says. She sounds understanding over the cell phone.

"I had to. The noise was killing me. I have a headache coming on."

"Where are you?"

I laugh. "Sitting in the parking lot."

"I'll come out."

"Don't bother. I think I'm going to head home. The boys can catch a ride with Rick."

"I'll tell them if I see them."

"That would be great."

The van shudders awake and rolls unhappily through the parking lot, out through the exit where an orange-vested traffic cop is sipping coffee straight from the thermos. At least, I assume that's what he's drinking.

A few years ago I never could have made it out of the church without running into a dozen or more friends and acquaintances wanting to talk. Now I can simply vanish and no one knows I'm gone. It's not such a bad feeling, to be honest.

*

ACTIVIST + POET.

See, if the last part was meant to be taken seriously, it would have come first. I turn the card over in my hand. Nice and thick. The letters are indented into the paper the way old typewriters used to do it, only the font seems a bit fancy for a Remington or an IBM Selectric. Interesting. I punch the phone number in, resting my thumb on top of the Send button.

This is a bad idea.

Chas doesn't even remember me. "Beth? Ahhh . . ."

"The lady who stopped the other day, when you were on the median. The one with the teenage son? That's me."

"Oh, right. Yeah, I remember. Did you have a change of plans?"

"Yes," I say. "I mean, I got my dates mixed up. You know what? Forget about this—"

"No, wait. It's perfect. There're a bunch of us here at my place. Biggest turnout in a long time. There's a big demo coming up in, like, two weeks. Everybody's amped. If you want to meet the Rent-a-Mob, this is your chance. Worst thing that could happen is you get some paint on your clothes and get your horizons expanded."

That chafes a bit, his assumption that my horizons need unnarrowing. Thank you, Jesus fish.

"I don't know what I'm doing here."

"None of us do, Beth. You'll feel right at home."

"That's truer than you realize," I say. "Fine. How do I find you?"

I write the directions down, then double-check them at the computer in the kitchen. It's past two and the house is empty. Rick and the boys haven't come home or called. He probably sensed the need for damage control and took them to the Outback at Hunt Valley or the California Pizza Kitchen. Where would Rick want to go for his last cooked meal before October 1? Probably Andy Nelson's to suck down some barbecue.

On my way out the door, I rip a page from Rick's pad, write a note, and peg it with a fridge magnet: GONE TO MEET THE RENT-A-MOB.

Let him chew on that.

chapter 5

Rent-a-Mob

Given the job description on his business card, I was expecting Chas Worthing's address a few blocks from the Towson University campus to be some kind of multi-unit slum dwelling. How much money can an activist-poet be pulling down, after all? To my surprise, the hilly, tree-lined lane is home to a series of largish bungalows with peaceful, shrub-cloistered yards. I drive past a line of Subarus, Priuses, and old Volvo 240s, park at the tail end, and walk up the slope toward Chas's house.

The hedge hides my approach. On the other side, I hear Johnny Cash playing on the radio and smell meat on the grill. There are people talking, laughing. I catch a whiff of aromatic smoke too—charred vanilla? I stop in my tracks.

Confession: I'm a chicken in social situations. My palms sweat and I get self-conscious about my body, my clothes, my hair. I can't think of what to say, afraid that anything I do say will make me seem idiotic and uninteresting. I want desperately to be interesting. Don't we all?

"Are you looking for Chas's?"

I turn to find a young woman at my elbow, a fine-boned, pale-skinned girl with light freckles and a prominent nose ring, her hair a tuft of dirty-blond dreads and complicated braids. She can't be much older than Jed. My first thought, quickly suppressed, is what a shame it is to hide such a pretty face under all those piercings and dreadlocks. How suburban of me. How soccer mom.

"Oh," I say, struggling for words.

"I'm Marlene. You're . . . new?"

"Yes," I say. "Beth. I'm Beth."

"Good to meet you." She ushers me toward the gap in the hedge, her touch light on my elbow. "Chas told me you might be coming."

"Oh," I say again. "Are you his . . . are you dating?"

She gives a crooked, charming smile. "Um, no. Chas must be, like, thirty." She says *thirty* like it's the same as a hundred, and I laugh nervously at my own stupidity. "No, he told me because I'm kind of the organizer. I help with the planning."

Through the hedge and into the front yard. Chas stands at the grill on the front porch, dressed in a striped apron. He waves at us with a shiny spatula. On the lawn, there's a ring of folding chairs, half of them empty. The other half are occupied by some of the older ladies I saw on the median. A pile of cardboard sheets, paint buckets, and brushes anchors one side of the ring, but no one has gotten started on the signs. Instead, they're chatting in groups of twos and threes.

"This is Barber," Marlene says, leading me up to the nearest man.

Barber takes a briar pipe from his lips to say hello. The charred vanilla I smelled through the hedge is from his smoldering tobacco.

Though he's not much older than Marlene, in addition to the grandfatherly pipe, Barber sports a waxed Victorian mustache that curves up at the corners. All he needs now is the monocle.

"You're the lady with the Jesus fish," he says. "Chas told us all about you."

I wilt a little. "Yeah, that's me."

"The Quaker thing, I'm down with that. If I had a religion, pacifism would be it. But I like the pipe weed and the microbrews too much to give them up."

"Quakers can drink," I say. "And smoke."

"That's cool."

"Come on," Marlene says. "Let me introduce you around."

Too many names in too short a time. I can't keep track of them all. There are several younger people like Barber and Marlene, most of them in the tribal dress of whichever social faction they hail from. There's a guy in bike shorts and a green-and-white jersey. A girl in tight black jeans and a black tank top, her arms a pair of tattooed totem poles. A pudgy woman with a crew cut, the sleeves of her white T-shirt rolled all the way up. Then there's a missing demographic—people my age. The parents of the younger set, the children of the older. Where are they? The fiftysomethings make a strong showing, though, with a few wizened retirees.

There's a lanky, gray-haired man named Vernon who wears pleated khakis and a plaid sport shirt. He comes over and shakes my hand, letting me get a good look at the lapel pin dangling from his chest. Around a green marijuana leaf, the words read LEGALIZE MY MEDICATION. He seems sharp-witted and vivacious. If he's suffering from a debilitating illness, Vernon gives no sign. After chatting with him for a moment, Marlene leads me up the steps to where Chas is grilling burgers.

"Is Vernon sick?" I ask her under my breath.

"He's not sick," she says. "He's a doctor."

"Oh."

Chas flips a patty before turning. "Well, what do you think?"

"I was expecting more vegans, to be honest."

"There's some salad if you prefer," he says, cracking a smile. "We're a motley bunch, I admit. We're for a thousand different things and against a thousand others, but the thing we have in common is that we insist on being heard. How about you?"

It feels like a sales pitch. "I'm not ready to sign on the dotted line or anything. But I appreciate the invitation."

Again he smiles. "No pressure. Why don't you show her around inside, Marlene?"

She opens the screen door and motions me inside. The interior comes as a bit of a shock. The bungalow has been stripped to its bones, the wood floors polished to mirror finish, the trim and the walls painted sterile white. The furniture looks like it's straight out of the Design Within Reach catalog (a more accurate title would be Design Out of Reach), steel-and-leather chairs and sofas known best by the name of the designer. They're arranged more like museum displays than objects meant for sitting on. I can understand why Chas entertains in the yard.

"What does Chas *do*?" I ask.

"His family is loaded. They'd have to be—to name their son Chas, right?"

"I guess so."

The dining room has been converted into a library, the books perfectly aligned at the lip of the shelves. I'd be afraid to take one down for fear of ruining the line.

"How did you meet him?"

Marlene shakes her head. "This takes some explaining. He was protesting at a pro-choice rally. Protesting *against* the rally, I mean."

"Chas is pro-life?"

"He's not pro-anything. Or anti-anything. He's just . . . Chas. He was holding this sign he'd made. A WOMAN'S RIGHT TO KILL, it said. Screaming at the top of his lungs, but clearly he wasn't with the other pro-life people. They seemed kind of scared of him, to be honest. And somehow I got into a shouting match with him, and he started cracking up. We talked for a couple of hours, and I only realized toward the end that he didn't care at all about the cause. It's the experience, that's his thing."

"The experience of being pro-life."

"The experience of being anything. I'm not like that, don't get me wrong. Most of us aren't. But for him, that's all it is, a release. He says he doesn't understand how people can get so worked up about things, so passionate. He wants to, though, which is why he does this."

Glancing around the room, what she's saying makes sense. This is the lair of someone who doesn't get passion. So squared away, so cold. But still . . .

"You don't feel like he's mocking you?" I ask. "I mean, he's basically faking it."

"To him, it's like creative nonfiction. He's after an artistic truth rather than a literal one. And to be honest, seeing it through his eyes, I kind of understand. Everybody in the world is pro-choice, basically, but not everybody is out there marching. The experience adds something. Even if you don't believe in the cause."

"That's a little hard to get my head around."

"Yeah," she says. "Some of us go with Chas and try it. We made a bunch of NRA signs and went to a big Second Amendment demo. I thought I'd throw up at first, but if I tuned out the words and just felt the emotion . . . I don't know, I kind of fit in."

"I can't imagine protesting something I wasn't against."

"Neither could I. It's weird, I know. But if you stick around Chas, that's the kind of thing that happens. He opens your mind to things in a strange kind of way."

*

Once the burgers are gone, along with most of the beers in the Igloo cooler, I install myself in one of the folding chairs to see what will happen next. I'm determined to see the afternoon through, even if coming here was a mistake. What was I thinking? My life needs less crazy at the moment, not more.

Chas stations himself on the edge of the ring of chairs, motioning the stragglers forward, making sure everyone has a seat. Marlene sits on the ground next to my knee. Sucking contemplatively on his pipe, Barber sinks into the chair beside me.

"The question is," Chas begins, "who's actually going with us to the Big Demo? I was hoping we'd have more people here, and it makes me worry that if we go through with the plan of renting the bus, it'll be half empty."

Marlene turns to me, whispering, "There's a peace demonstration in D.C. the weekend after next. With all the troops pulling out, this could be our last chance."

"They're not going to stop having wars," Barber says.

After some hemming and hawing, Chas asks for a show of hands. The results disappoint him.

"Vernon, you're not going? Come on, man, you're the backbone of this thing."

The elderly doctor waves away the suggestion. "What's the point? I only have so much effort to give, and I want to invest it where it'll make a difference. You're not going to stop them going to war, like Barber just said. We should be focusing on something achievable, something that'll make the world a better place to live. Without legalization—"

"Not again." The girl with the tattooed arms rolls her black-rimmed eyes. "Legalization is fine and everything, but it's only going to drive the prices up. As it is, nobody's having trouble getting what they need, right? Anybody hard up for weed?"

One of the grandmotherly types raises her hand, and the others giggle.

"Medical marijuana isn't enough," Vernon continues, ignoring the others. "As long as they're still arresting people for possession—a disproportionate number of those people being African American—I don't see why we should focus on *anything* else."

"Okay, so Vernon's not going." Chas turns to the tattooed girl. "But what's your excuse?"

"I have to work that weekend. We don't all have trust funds."

"Ha, ha. Marlene, you're going, right?"

"I'm in."

"What about you, Beth? I know you're new to this, but if you've never been to the Mall for one of these things, it's a mind-blowing experience, I can tell you that."

I shrug.

"Seriously," he says. "You really ought to do this. Bring that son of yours too. It's the ultimate civics lesson. You'll open his eyes to a whole new reality."

"With any luck," I say, "we'll be in Florida."

"In two weeks? That's a pretty long vacation."

"My husband has the month off."

"Sweet," Barber says, exhaling a puff of smoke. "What's he do for a living? That's the kind of job I need."

Deep breath. Come right out with it. "He's the Men's Pastor at The Community."

Blank stares.

"It's a church down the road in Lutherville."

Vernon's face distorts into a frown of consternation. "The *big* one? The one that bought the old plastics factory?"

"That's the one."

And just like that, I've killed the conversation.

They're all looking at me like I'm a plant from the Establishment. If they're looking at all. Marlene, I notice, is staring at the clasped hands resting in her lap, probably replaying every moment since my arrival.

"The Life Chain," one of the grandmothers says. "They're the ones that sponsor the Life Chain every year. That . . . abomination."

I'd forgotten about the Life Chain, thousands of suburbanites standing hand-in-hand along the highway out in front of the shopping mall on behalf of the unborn.

"That's the one," I repeat. Own it. There's no other choice.

Chas tries to save the situation. "Still, you should come. Like I said, it'll be eye-opening. And if you're already out there protesting, then . . ."

The women across from me are muttering to each other while Vernon drills me with laser beams from his eyes.

"So that's a *Quaker* church?" Barber says. "I had no idea."

Before I can untangle his assumptions—something I should have done from the start—Vernon gets out of his chair and wanders off, prompting an exodus. My cheeks are burning, and though I hate to confess it, my feelings are hurt. A few moments ago I was thinking of them as crazies, the way Rick would, but now I'm hungry for their acceptance.

Shouldn't they be more tolerant and accepting?

Marlene gets to her feet, brushing imaginary grass from her jeans. No, I can't expect them to be any more tolerant than my own tribe would be if one of them turned up. Imagine bringing Marlene to the ladies' book club, watching the girls swallow the ice in their tea when she drops the bomb about everybody in the world being pro-choice. She'd be lucky to get out of there alive.

"I'm sorry to break up the party," I say, putting a brave face on the situation. I make my way toward the gap in the hedge, Chas trailing in my wake with a confused expression.

"You don't have to go," he says.

"I think I probably should. But thanks for inviting me. I enjoyed it. Really."

On the sidewalk, hidden once more from their scrutiny, I feel myself shaking with anger, maybe self-pity. I should have fudged when the question came up. At the very least, I shouldn't have mentioned where Rick works. The Community is too high profile not to have rubbed some of these people the wrong way. But no, I am who I am. There's no point denying it. There's a Jesus fish on my bumper, and that's all you need to know.

I pause at that bumper, staring down at that fish. He's looking a little dim and dirt-speckled. Part of me wants to kneel down and wipe him clean. The other part wants to pry him off.

"Beth, wait."

Marlene comes up behind me, tentatively, her earlier confidence gone.

"It was nice meeting you," I say.

"You're not mad, are you? Don't go away mad."

"No, I'm fine. I knew there was some potential for culture clash. It's not a big deal."

"Good," she says. "Anyway . . ."

"I'd better get going."

I open the door and pause. She's standing on the curb, hesitating, wanting to say something.

"What is it?" I ask.

"I used to go there," she says. "To your church. My parents made me when I was in high school."

"Oh."

"I remember your husband, I think."

"You do?"

"I always thought he was nice. The youth pastor, some of the others, I always thought they were full of themselves. But he was different."

"Thanks for saying that." She's probably confusing Rick with someone else. But no, that's unfair. He is different, only I lose sight of it sometimes. I mean, there's nobody else on the pastoral staff planning to spend his vacation in a shed waiting to hear from God.

*

I drive home in a cloud of pipe smoke and guilt. As judgmental as it sounds, implying her life is off the rails, the words keep repeating in my head: *We failed that girl.* I failed her. And I didn't even know who she was. She's a college student now—at Towson, she told me—but a couple of years ago she was in the same youth group as my son Jed. They might have known each other, or at least recognized each other by sight. And now, going soccer mom again, I'm reinterpreting everything about her—the hair, the piercings, the pro-choice advocacy—as a reaction *against* her experience with us. The Community.

I want to talk to Jed, see if he recognizes her. I want to talk to Rick too. It can't be a coincidence, me running away from church and straight into Marlene. I want to tell him what she said, in case it might encourage him. Remembering him on that stage this morning, so different from the man he used to be, I *want* to encourage him.

Eli is in the driveway with his bike standing upside down on its handlebars. He looks up from tinkering with the new wheel, waiting for me to park.

"Where's your brother?" I ask.

"He went to the movies with some kids from church."

"Okay. What about your dad? His car's gone."

"He said he was going to Sports Authority. He needs a new sleeping bag."

"I see."

He spins the bicycle wheel, watching the chain dance around the hub. "So, Mom . . . how was your afternoon with Chas? I bet he was surprised to see you."

"Chas thinks I should bring you to the big peace demo in Washington DC two weeks from now. It'll open your eyes, he says."

"It sounds lame. Maybe Jed should go instead."

"Maybe so. All fixed?"

He rights the bicycle and throws a leg over the top tube, rolling back and forth to test the weight. Satisfied, he kicks forward, rolling down the driveway and into the street, where he circles once or twice before waving good-bye. I stand there and watch him disappear.

Then I turn toward my empty house. I walk in.

chapter 6

Desert Father

There's an elephant in the room, a big, gray elephant swaying his snout back and forth over the breakfast table, probably astonished at how completely we're managing to ignore him. The boys do most of the work. Eli can talk for hours about dialing in his bicycle, about the shortcomings of his aluminum frame compared to carbon fiber, about track-standing (whatever that is). And Jed fills the gaps with questions about Marlene. He remembers her well, it seems. Maybe he even had a crush on her once upon a time, the way freshmen can fixate on unattainable seniors. "She was planning to go to law school," he says, which makes me wince a little. There was a time when I was planning to go to law school too.

Rick sits listening, stirring his Grape-Nuts with a contemplative spoon. Not his usual choice. He brought them back from his provisioning trip, along with the new sleeping bag, some gallon jugs of water, and a big box of generic-brand cheese crackers.

When the boys get up to leave, so does Rick. They go out the front as he slips out the back, saying good-bye over his shoulder like he'll be back in an hour or two. No sense of occasion, my husband. Or maybe he just wants to escape.

As he lopes across the yard toward his shed, I watch him from the kitchen window. There's a magnetic timer on the refrigerator. I set it for an hour, ruminate a little, then knock it back to forty-five minutes. He'll be back by the time the clock runs down. He'll hear the ping and know why. And I won't have to say a word.

*

But the clock runs down and Rick doesn't return. An hour passes, two, and I start to realize this could go on longer than a morning, or even a day. I have laundry to do, but between each step—clothes to the washer, clothes to the dryer, shrinkables to the drying rack (assuming I haven't already shrunk them)—I pass by the window for a glance at the shed. No movement.

Selfish, that's what it is.

Leaving me like this. All the work on my shoulders.

And it's pretty dangerous too.

Try it out, he's saying. *This is what life without me would be like. This is a trial run.*

*

Holly, who isn't the sort to drop by unannounced, drops by unannounced the first afternoon. She joins me at the window for a few minutes.

"He's not coming out, is he?"

I shake my head. "I guess not."

"Well, you can't wait around for it to happen. You've got better things to do. Come on, there's a birthday to plan, right? The boys are going to need some normalcy if this"—she nods toward the shed—"is gonna keep up. Let's go shopping."

"Retail therapy? I'll pass."

"It's not for you, silly. It's for Eli."

"Do they have a store that sells new dads?"

She loops her arm through mine and starts edging me out the door. "What he needs isn't a new dad, Beth. He needs the old one to get fixed. Let's leave him in his cocoon, and when we come back, maybe Rick'll come out a butterfly."

"I'd like to see that."

On the sidewalk outside, we intercept Deedee with Roy Meakin in tow. Roy of the vintage Rolls, who's carried a torch for Deedee Smythe for going on thirty years. When he's around, it usually means Deedee is going to the market and needs a bearer. Or that she's listed another huge, ornately carved piece of mahogany furniture on Craigslist and wants a man around when the buyer turns up.

I make the introductions. Roy seems delighted by my tall, blond friend. "You're Eric Ringwald's wife, aren't you? I know Eric quite well."

Roy and Holly talk finance for a minute while I smile at Deedee, waiting for it to stop. She's not so patient. Pulling me to one side, she says, "You look distracted. What's wrong?"

"He started up this morning in earnest."

"Who, Rick? He's out in the shed?"

I nod. "Since eight o'clock this morning, with no sign of movement."

"Well, well." Her eyes sparkle with mischief. "Maybe I'll drop in on him and wish him luck."

"Wish who luck?" Roy asks.

"Elizabeth's husband is channeling the desert fathers. He's holed up in one of the old outbuildings to wait for a sign from God."

"The desert fathers," Roy says. "Are they the ones who climbed up on poles and wouldn't come down for years? I hope *you* don't have to wait that long."

"I think it's rather exciting. Who's even heard of such a thing in this day and age? I can't imagine you sequestering yourself for a whole month, Roy."

"Not even for a day," he replies.

"I'm telling you, Elizabeth, they simply don't *make* men like that anymore."

"But did these desert fathers have wives and kids?" I ask. "Did they climb up their poles with pork rinds and a jar of Nutella?"

Holly butts in. "Well, it was nice meeting you both."

They continue down the sidewalk, discussing the merits of various ancient hermits, while Holly packs me into the passenger seat of her car.

"I thought you were gonna explode back there."

"Don't worry about Deedee. She's impossible to offend."

"If you say so, sister. She really seems to like her monks, though."

She heads down York to Towson Town Center, deciding our first stop should be the Apple Store. Holly quickly marshals the youngest of the hipper-than-thou employees, guiding him around the shop asking one question after another about what an about-to-turn-sixteen-year-old would want most. I watch for a while, then wander off, browsing the sterile white shelves disinterestedly. What would they do if I suddenly whipped out my antique mobile phone? Would they even recognize what it is?

I find myself standing at a table full of iPods. They stand on plastic pillars, tethered in place to foil thieves, with various types of headphones plugged into their jacks. Across from me, a middle-aged Indian man in a rumpled gray suit slips on a pair of over-the-ear cans. Back in the pre-Walkman era, when I was a girl, these were the only kind of headphone around. He adjusts them carefully, then snaps his fingers. The sound is loud enough, even in the bustling store, that several people turn to find its source. Cocking his head slightly, he snaps again. Then he notices me and smiles.

"Just a little test," he says, slipping the headphones off. "Noise-canceling, they say, but I snap my fingers and I can hear it perfectly well."

"Are you hitting play? I think you have to turn the music on."

"To cancel noise, you need more noise? No, thank you."

He walks out, not angrily, but with the light step of a man who's once again seen through the world's lies. A contented gait, unless I'm imagining it. If Deedee were here, I'd tell her, no, it's *this* sort of man they don't make anymore, the one who walks into the Apple Store to remind himself of what he doesn't need.

"You think Eli would want headphones?" Holly asks, still towing her teenaged assistant along.

"I'm not looking, I'm just standing here."

In the end, she decides on an indestructible-looking messenger bag with a shoulder strap and a brushed metal buckle straight off an airline seat belt. Eli will love it, and while I make a point of not asking about the price tag, it can't be as expensive as half the stuff in here. I'm relieved. Sometimes Holly doesn't understand why I wouldn't want her giving my son a thousand-dollar laptop or a handmade bike that will only get stolen at school.

We tour around the shopping center until Holly starts complaining about having to walk in high heels. "You don't have to walk in them," I remind her. "You choose to." Then we stop for a half hour of iced coffee and people watching. I tell her about my afternoon with the Rent-a-Mob and how it ended, which makes her cringe in sympathy.

"So what were you talking to the Indian guy about? In the Apple Store?"

"That was nothing," I say. "He didn't care if the earphones played music, he just wanted them to make all the noise go away."

"Like a cone of silence."

"Pretty much. You remember Kathie Shaw?"

"Wife of Jim, who's trying to get you to move to Richmond."

I nod. "She was telling me she has tinnitus. She hears this ringing sound in her ears. It looked really painful too. What she wouldn't do for some peace and quiet."

"I bet."

She swirls her straw around in the ice, hunting for the last ounce of coffee.

"Is this what I do?" I ask. "Complain all the time? You must get sick of having to listen to it."

"You weren't complaining, Beth."

"I should be in Florida right now. That's not too much to ask, is it?"

"Now you're complaining. But yes, you should be in Florida. And listen, if Rick doesn't come out of his cave, why don't the two of us go? After the birthday party, we could hop on a plane—"

"A plane? I was going to drive."

"That van of yours would never make it. Besides, you'd spend half your vacation on the road."

"Florida's only a day away. I like having time to transition. Leaving Baltimore and stepping onto the beach an hour later doesn't seem right. There should be some kind of journey in between."

"You really are old-fashioned," she says. "One day that car is going to break down for the last time and your phone is going to die, and you'll be forced into the twenty-first century."

"Kicking and screaming. Anyway, it's not the twenty-first century I have a problem with. It's all the stuff that goes with it."

"Same difference. You can't have Now without all the stuff."

*

At dusk, the lights inside the shed switch on. It would be easy to walk across the yard. Rick didn't lay down any rules. He didn't forbid us to interrupt his isolation. But no, I can't bring myself to do it. He has to come in before I can go out.

I let the boys talk me into pizza. Jed takes the keys and they return in a half hour with a large pepperoni, devouring most of it between them. I have no appetite. They don't ask whether we should save any for Rick, and I don't suggest it. On his way upstairs, Eli tells me he's going to his room until God decides to talk to him. I smile. It's the first reference to Rick's self-imposed exile all day.

"Mom," Jed says. "Are you going back to that group?"

"You mean the Rent-a-Mob? I don't think so."

"Well, if you do . . . I might want to check it out."

"Really?"

He shrinks under my scrutiny. "Or maybe not. I'm just saying."

"I'll keep it in mind."

Now, this is a surprise. Maybe I'm right about that freshman crush. While Eli is the son who'd tease me about Chas, Jed would be more likely to scold. In his early teens, chafing at Rick's expectations, he took a sudden interest in Christian doctrine so he could argue with his dad. For a while, they went at it about everything, constantly butting heads to my exasperation and Eli's detached amusement. Whatever Rick would say, Jed would take the more conservative, in his mind more biblical, position. At the private Christian school we sent him to, his teachers started sending home notes about how much Jed was applying himself, never imagining the reason why. Then he got into computers and started spending hours on discussion forums. He progressed in leaps and bounds. Instead of arguing with him, Rick now didn't have a clue what he was talking about.

"It's the Christian *tradition*," Jed would shout. "Deal with it!"

To be honest, this phase impressed me and scared me all at once. This was just how Gregory had acted at the same age—though his rebellion went in the opposite direction, which is how he ended up as a self-professed Marxist literature professor (albeit at a community college in northern Virginia, thanks to the glut of PhDs in the world). Jed's mental acuity amazes me sometimes. The fear comes from realizing how easily a rift could open between father and son. I know firsthand.

All this to say, if Jed is suddenly interested in hanging out with a bunch of lefty war protestors, he must have really had a thing for Marlene. Of course, I suspect she didn't have a nose ring or dreadlocks when she was in the youth group at The Community.

With the downstairs all to myself, I brew some decaf tea, put some music on, and stretch out in front of the television. By the time I find out there's a series worth watching, it's usually off the air. Fortunately the library has most of the good stuff. I pick through the pile of movies on the shelf—a three-to-one split between science fiction thrillers (Rick, Jed, Eli) and quiet dramas set in stately English manors (yours truly), but nothing looks interesting. I flip channels, watching five minutes of a singing competition, five minutes of reality housewives (most of whom aren't even technically wives), five minutes of cooking, five *more* minutes of cooking.

Through the side window in the living room, I have a view of the Smythes' house. The fairy lights are on around back. Roy and Deedee are sitting at the wrought-iron table, a silver cocktail shaker between them along with a pair of glasses. He's a sharp dresser, Roy, in gray flannel pants and a thick navy shawl-collared cardigan, a gentleman at leisure. It's hard to figure those two out. He's in his sixties, a widower, and I get the impression he'd propose to Deedee at the drop of a hat if he thought she was even a little bit interested. They spend enough time together it seems like a no-brainer. Clearly there is history I know nothing about. When I broach the subject—always with Roy, never with her—he smiles enigmatically and sighs, "If only!"

The home telephone rings. I don't recognize the number, but I answer anyway. A telemarketer is company, if nothing else.

"Hey, Beth, it's Jim. Is the Big Man around?"

"Not at the moment," I say.

"Too bad. I tried to call him a couple of times today, but he must have his other phone switched off. I just wanted to check in and see where he's at. No pressure or anything."

Do I tell him the man he wants to hire as the leader of his church is closeted out in the shed waiting for a sign? Would that work in Rick's favor, or just the opposite? I'm not sure, so I'd better say nothing at all.

"You want me to have him call you?"

"That would be great. And what about you? Where are you at on this thing?"

"Me? I'm just waiting to see where Rick comes down. It's his decision, and I'll support him no matter what." The words come out automatically. Because they're expected, not because I believe them. Maybe I do, though, on some level. You play a role long enough and you do believe in it. You can't tell anymore which face is the mask and which is real.

"Well, I'm sure he's already told you, but between you and me, Beth, lemme make one thing crystal clear. You guys will be taken care of. I know you've both made a lot of sacrifices in ministry, but this won't be one of them. The workman's worthy of his hire, right?"

"Don't muzzle the ox, I know."

"That's the spirit."

"Jim," I say.

"Yeah, Beth?"

"Do you remember, years ago, I told you I'd been accepted to law school?"

"Sure I remember. This was before you had Jed, right?"

"Right. I asked you if you thought it was a mistake, not going."

"And I'll tell you now what I told you then. You don't have to go to law school to make a difference. Most people don't."

"Sometimes I do regret it. I mean, that was my *plan*, you know?"

"Listen, Beth, if you feel that way, it's not too late. We have some great law schools down here. And with the nest emptying out—"

"I'm just thinking out loud. Never mind me. By the way, I was sorry to hear about Kathie, the thing with her hearing."

He goes quiet. "Yeah, it's pretty bad. But, hey, I appreciate that. I'll tell her you were thinking about her, all right?"

After the call, I replay the words. *That was my plan*. Strange to think, I did have a plan. I grew up with a purpose in life, a sense of calling, and now . . .

Best not to think about it. They're still cooking on TV.

During one of the commercials I glance outside and notice Roy standing at the edge of the patio, looking off into the yard. Deedee is nowhere to be seen. Curious, I creep over and cup my hand to the glass. There she is, walking gingerly through the English garden, martini in hand, turning theatrically to put a finger to her lips, shushing Roy.

I go to the kitchen for a better look, careful not to switch on the lights. Deedee crouches stealthily toward the shed.

"What are you doing?" I ask aloud, remembering the mischief in her smile this afternoon.

She goes on tiptoes at the window, steadying herself with her free hand. The light inside illuminates the impish expression on her face. She sets her drink on the windowsill.

I dislike her spying on Rick this way. It may be funny to her, but to me it's halfway to tragic. Plus, he's my husband. Just because I'm mad at him doesn't mean it's open season. But does this bother me enough to intervene? Do I really want to make an issue of it?

Deedee freezes, her expression hardening, the muscles going

slack. Now I can't read her at all. She draws back into the shadows a step, denying me the chance. But she's still watching.

What is Rick doing in there? Is he sprawled on the floor the way I found him two nights ago, twisting his body into the shape of a cross? Is he watching movies on his laptop, or eating miniature Snickers bars, or sitting on the couch in his unzipped sleeping bag, clipping his toenails? Whatever he's up to, Deedee seems fascinated. She watches for more than a minute. Impatient, Roy calls out—I can just hear him—but she doesn't respond at first. After a pause, she takes her drink off the sill and makes her way back.

I return to the living room window in time to see her speaking to Roy. She takes the cocktail shaker and goes inside. He stays, gazing in the direction of the shed. Then he turns and looks right at me, raising his hand in a cautious wave.

I wave back and Roy goes inside.

*

I put clean sheets on the bed before crawling in. Despite the fresh scent, I can't get comfortable, can't go to sleep. So I switch the lamp on and pad downstairs to the bookshelf for something to read. When I turn on the lights, I see a gap in the uppermost row of spines. Rick has taken an armful of books into the shed with him.

My husband is not much of a reader. Most of his books are purchased on the recommendation of men at the church, so they split pretty evenly between American history—the lives of famous presidents, the Civil War, World War II—and business leadership—build your team, make your money, move the other guy's cheese before he moves yours. His taste in fiction: Tom

Clancy–style thrillers, thick sci-fi paperbacks, though I notice he tends to start novels without ever finishing them. When he brings a new book home, he sits on the couch for an hour or two, browsing over the pages. Speed-reading, he calls it. Jed dubs it "skimming." The whole point of the exercise is to be able to get through a conversation about the book with whoever recommended it.

But the missing books don't fall into this category. They're the smaller group Rick has accumulated over the years, the ones he thinks he should read based on what he's heard people saying. G. K. Chesterton, Flannery O'Connor, Walker Percy—"All Catholics!" Deedee would crow. The collected works of Francis Schaeffer is gone too, and he's taken the matched set of Spiritual Classics passed down to him from his grandparents. The last time I flipped through one, the pages were still stuck together by the fancy gilt edging.

Also missing: an enormous King James Bible full of woodcut illustrations, a gift from a couple at church who must have imagined we had a carved wood lectern in our living room just waiting for such a behemoth to land.

What is going on out there?

Is he following after the Irish monks who supposedly saved civilization, hand-copying books by firelight as some kind of spiritual discipline? *Is he actually reading them?*

I laugh out loud, and not out of spite. No, I'm certain of that. Holding the laughter up to my ear, listening again, what I hear sounds almost joyful. If he is reading them, then good.

I could always go and see for myself.

Then again, I did that once before and didn't like what I found. If there's any joy in this situation, I'd better grasp it like a fragile ember. Better that than to barge into the shed and find him drooling onto the raised initials in that fancy King James Bible.

*

The next morning I'm up before the alarm. I throw on some sweats and go downstairs, wondering if Rick will join us for breakfast or not. He won't. He can't. He may be out in the yard, but already it feels like he is a thousand miles away.

I put coffee on, drop some bread into the toaster, and glance through the kitchen window into the gray-lit morning. Against the door of the shed, their petals wet with dew, a heap of freshly picked wildflowers lays scattered on the threshold.

What in the world . . . ?

As I watch, the door opens. Rick doesn't appear, but I can sense him looming just out of sight. The door half closes. Low to the ground, his hand reaches out. He gathers the flowers by their stems, taking them inside. The door shuts. At the window, his silhouette appears. The same hand that gathered the flowers presses itself against the glass. And then it's gone.

I didn't leave them there. I want to run out and tell him. It must have been Deedee returning in the night, laying tribute at her desert father's door.

My, oh my. What will Rick make of that?

I would stick around and watch for more of a reaction, but I have my study group this morning.

Confession: There's not much study in the study group these days.

Originally, when the group was much smaller (small enough

to meet around Kathie Shaw's dining table), we kept up a pretty lively and stimulating conversation, usually guided by some assigned reading in the Bible or a popular theological tome. After the Shaws left for Virginia, the location moved to Stacy Manderville's cavernous, ever-expanding mansion, the group growing considerably in size but stretching much thinner when it comes to content.

Most of the ladies prefer it that way. The study group consists mostly of stay-at-home (or these days, work-at-home) moms, the only people free during the workday. By definition, we are over-committed. Several of the study group ladies are also members of one of my book clubs, so it's not like they're lacking for intellectual stimulation. What they lack is time.

I drive over to Stacy's, bracing myself for questions. Why aren't we in Florida? When are we leaving? How long will we stay? Part of me wants to skip out, pretend I'm already gone. But as long as I have that key, I'll feel a sense of obligation.

The Manderville house, over toward Loch Raven, is a faux castle, turrets and all, perched on a hilltop approached via a long, winding drive. The family goes as far back as the 1700s, and I imagine there are a few ghostly patriarchs turning in their fancy crypts at the thought of the former Stacy Root having married into the line. She's a loud, plump woman with wild hair and expensively bad clothes, who loves weaves, fake nails, rhinestones, and country western music. When she redecorated the stately home, she dedicated a whole bedroom to her favorite movie character, Scarlett O'Hara. Her husband, Lynn, raised no objection. In her presence, he goes kind of limp, contentedly overwhelmed.

I let myself in—the door's always open on study group mornings—and Stacy greets me with unfeigned enthusiasm. "Hey, girrrrrrl! I thought you'd be down at the beach by now. Great to see you."

"Stacy, about that . . ." I produce the beach house key and make to hand it over.

"What's this?"

"I don't think the vacation is going to work out."

"Why? What's wrong?"

"Nothing," I say. "It's just, getting the boys out of school, you know, and Rick was thinking we might stay closer to home, and . . ."

"I thought you *wanted* to go."

"I do, but . . . you know."

"Let me talk to him, girl. I'll set the man straight. The problem with men is, they can't take a hint. You have to draw a great big picture for them, then you have to stick their faces in it. I'll bet you're dropping hints, right? Hoping he'll pick up on your little signals. But, Beth, they never do. Trust me, I haven't dropped a hint in fifteen years. When I want something, I let Lynn know. It's not that they don't *want* to give us what we're after, they just have no idea what that is. You have to give them a clue!"

"Oh, I gave him a clue. It's just not going to work out, I'm afraid. Here, you take the key. I really appreciate the offer, and I wish I could take you up on it."

"Beth, you do me a favor. Hold on to that key. If you go down there, great. If you don't, so be it. Just know that you have the option."

"Are you sure?"

"How long have we known each other? I'll tell you this: I think you *need* some time away."

"You're probably right."

As we're talking, other ladies file through, saying their hellos, stepping down into the huge sunken living room. Although the house is old, back in the seventies, Lynn's parents spent a fortune gutting the place and remodeling along contemporary lines. Then Stacy added her own touch, filling the wide-open rooms with dainty-looking but massively scaled furniture, big tufted sofas with floral print covers, glass-topped tables, and enough accent pillows to open an accent pillow boutique. She likes dolls too. Two-foot porcelain farm girls in ruffled calico stand in every corner, and if you bump into one, her jewel-tone eyes blink. It's so bad that the overall impression is pretty wonderful. As long as you don't have to live there.

I sit on a couch beside Nat Waterhouse, whose husband, Pete, has been battling cancer for the last two years. She's a serene, calming woman in her late fifties who's always pulling her sleeves down because she's self-conscious about the age spots on her hands.

"How's Pete doing?" I ask. "And the girls?"

"Oh, fine," she says, "just fine. Our youngest is getting married, did you hear? It's a relief, I'm telling you, such a burden lifted. Once the kids are settled in life, I'll feel like I can finally relax."

"I've got a few years ahead of me, in that case."

"Your Eli is turning into quite a handsome young man. I saw him Sunday and, from a distance, I mistook him for his father at first. You'll have to shake the girls away with a stick."

"Hmm. He does a pretty good job of that himself. Anything that comes too easy, he's not very interested in. And Jed . . . well, I can't remember the last time he had a girlfriend."

"You'd better find some wood and knock on it, Beth. If you're right, then all I can tell you is, luck like that won't last forever. It wouldn't surprise me, though, if you're wrong. There might be more to those boys' love lives than they share with their mama."

She laughs, and I join in. I'm used to these talks. Until I had children of my own, I never understood how much parents live vicariously through our kids, how we project ourselves into their lives. When they grow old enough not to want to share the tedious details of their daily experience, the effect on us is similar to being suddenly weaned off a strong narcotic. You start pumping them for information, for concrete detail, anything that will help you visualize their existence apart from you. And you end up in silly conversations about your teenagers' love lives.

By a quarter past ten, there are twenty-two ladies gathered round, some on couches, some on chairs, a couple sitting casually on the armrests. Stacy takes a break from doling out refreshments to offer up an opening prayer, then Peggy Ensign raises her hand.

I sigh inwardly, cutting a glance at Nat, who gives a microscopic shake of the head.

It was Peggy Ensign who gifted me the Jesus fish.

"Before we get going," she says in her singsong, schoolmistress voice, like she's speaking to a roomful of children whom she suspects of being a little slow, "I'd like to make an announcement for those of you who didn't make it to my Sunday school class this week. There have been some ominous developments in the courts recently that it behooves us as Bible-believing Christians to take a stand on." She pauses to dig through an oversized tote, producing a stack of stapled handouts. "I printed some things off so everybody could follow along."

Stacy plops down on a side chair, conceding the floor.

I haven't read an etiquette manual in years. (Actually, I don't think I've ever read one.) Maybe the rule about not discussing religion or politics at the dinner table no longer applies. Over the years, though, our study group has evolved an etiquette of its own, classifying certain topics as off-limits for the good of the group. No arguments about homeschool vs. private school vs. public school. No speculation about the End Times or the best Bible translation. Generally speaking, if it's a topic the evangelical world at large is divided over, we tend to steer clear—not just for the sake of harmony, but out of respect for those with differing views.

Unfortunately, this etiquette was never written down, or even voiced aloud. It had more to do with good manners (and a few awful experiences early on) than premeditation. And Peggy Ensign, like the men Stacy was just describing, doesn't know how to take a hint.

She's only been a member of The Community for a couple of years, but she volunteers tirelessly for every church program, teaches a Sunday school class, and generally makes her presence felt. She wields an awful lot of influence. If Peggy's not happy, the staff hears about it from above. As a result, she pretty much runs roughshod over anyone less vocal or more well mannered.

At Rick's behest, I once tried to have a heart-to-heart talk with her, hoping to help her fit in a little better. Big mistake. What I discovered surprised me, and left me feeling conflicted.

"I'm not like most of you," Peggy confided. "I didn't grow up a Christian. Most of my life, I didn't even believe in the existence of God, let alone love the Lord. When I got saved, I made a promise to not have anything to do with the secular world anymore. I won't expose myself to any of those influences any longer, and I can't understand why any of you would want to."

Where I might look at The Community and think our problem is that we're too evangelical, too conformed to a comfortable subculture that scratches our religious itch without requiring more of us than that we be entertained by Christians instead of unbelievers, Peggy thought the church was far too secular. The music was too loud, too fast. There were too many references to movies in the sermons, and not Christian movies, but films from Hollywood.

"I don't think Jesus went around quoting from Shakespeare!" she said.

I wanted to explain about anachronism, and how in AD 33 it would have been tricky to start quoting lines that wouldn't be written for another fifteen hundred years, but I knew Peggy would not only be suspicious of the word *anachronism*, she'd be suspicious of me as well. Plus, if anybody *could* have quoted the Bard in the age of the Caesars, Jesus would have been the guy.

Clearly, my attempt to rein in Peggy ended in failure. I felt conflicted because, as irritating as I found her inflexibility and her uninformed confidence, the fact was, I saw something beautiful in her simple faith. It's not so easy to dismiss people you disagree with when you sense God working in their lives too.

Later, when I shared the remark about Shakespeare with Rick, expecting him to get a kick out of it, he grew quite angry and resentful.

"Did you tell her about Paul and Mars Hill?" he snapped.

"No, why should I?"

"How he quoted the pagan poets? I mean, come on! Beth, you can't let these people get away with their ignorance. What Paul does . . . I mean, it's worse than Shakespeare—"

"What's wrong with Shakespeare?"

"Nothing, Beth, no, that's not what I mean. From Peggy Ensign's point of view. Paul's quoting poems written to praise

Zeus as if they were true, only they applied to the true God rather than Zeus."

In hindsight, it occurs to me that the apostle Paul might have understood Chas Worthing's take on creative nonfiction a little better than I do.

But I digress.

Most of my friends at The Community, though we're part of the evangelical world, view the whole thing with a certain level of self-criticism. We're conscious of the excesses, the embarrassments. We would rather not speak out than risk speaking out and being misconstrued. But Peggy has never been separated from her opinions. She loves everything that bears the Christian label and hates everything that doesn't. Which is why, even if Jesus didn't have a Jesus fish on his chariot (or for that matter, didn't have a chariot to begin with), she thinks every Christian ought to have a Jesus fish on her minivan bumper.

Now, however, the issue isn't Jesus fish. It's the Ten Commandments. In particular, a statue from the 1950s at a public high school out in the county, a patriotic bronze that symbolized our great anti-Communist, Judeo-Christian heritage with two symbols: a scroll bearing the words "We, the people . . ." followed by a row of lines meant to represent the text, and a camel-humped stone tablet that says DECALOGUE across the front.

Yes, that's right. There's a photo on Peggy's handout.

None of the actual Ten Commandments are written on this tablet. Nothing about stealing or killing or committing adultery. Just that single word DECALOGUE in raised letters running underneath both humps.

For years this thing was in storage at the school, until a board member found out and insisted that the "censored" artwork be put on display again. Which led to a lawsuit, then an appeal, and now to an impassioned twenty-minute harangue from Peggy Ensign about how, if we don't do something, we're going to lose this nation's Christian heritage for good.

I flip through the handout, waiting patiently for this to end. Next to me, Nat starts inspecting her manicure, then tugging at her sleeves.

"It breaks my heart to see what's happening in America," Peggy says, dabbing at her eyes.

Funny thing is, she'd be a great fit for the Rent-a-Mob. Better than me. If she could ignore the particular issues, I suspect the experience would be quite cathartic, like it is for Chas. Peggy wants to scream at people. She wants to force them to hear. Even now, as she wipes tears from her cheeks, I know she resents the fact she's the only one in the room who's crying. She's not satisfied with the ladies. None of us measure up to her standard. We're not outraged enough, not vocal enough, insufficiently bent out of shape. She'd probably yell at us if she thought she could get away with it.

Instead, she has to cry at us.

Over a vaguely religious piece of civic art that's been in storage since before I was born.

When she's finally done, Stacy rises to her feet.

"All right," she says. "I think we need a bathroom break."

All but one of the ladies in the room break out in nervous laughter.

chapter 7

Man Gave Names to All the Animals

Adjusting to an absent husband? Not so hard, it turns out. After the second day, I stop keeping watch at the kitchen window. After the second night, I start sleeping in the middle of the bed, forcing myself to spread out even though come morning I'll be curled in my usual tight ball on the edge of the mattress. Hermits don't need their laundry done either, and their meals don't have to be cooked. Their opinions don't need polling whenever there's a decision to make.

I could get used to this.

With Rick gone, the nature of time itself starts changing. I used to be so busy, running from one errand to another, anticipating his wants and requirements, trying to allow for last-minute surprises. And all the relationships I had to maintain! The chats over coffee, the ladies' lunches, finding myself thrust into the role of counselor by virtue of being a pastor's wife. The beginning of Rick's vacation brings an end to all that.

He's gone, so people assume we all are. My phone stops ringing. Pure bliss.

Problem is, with the boys at school and no one's needs to fulfill, I sit all alone in the house, listening to the radio, reorganizing shelves that are already tidied up (though nowhere near as razor-sharp as Chas Worthing's bookcases), taking apart the hot water knob in the shower to see if I can fix it once and for all. I've never been a clean freak—when a house reaches a certain age, it's earned the right to be a little dusty—but now I find myself digging under the sink for cleaning products, spraying and squirting and shining every surface I can get my hands on.

From the upstairs bathroom, working on the grout with Rick's toothbrush, I notice movement down in the backyard. When I push the sheer to one side, I have a clear view of the hermit. Hunched over, looking around every other step, he makes an approach on the back door. I tap the window and the noise startles him. He scoots his way back, disappearing into the shed.

I know from the empty toilet paper rolls and the damp towels that he sneaks into the house at odd intervals. He waits until we're all gone.

At first this discovery irritated me. He's already living in the shed, so why does he have to avoid us entirely? That's taking things too far.

No, they were already too far. What do you call it when you go too far, then go even further?

I'm not irritated anymore. Now it cracks me up.

"You'll just have to hold it," I say, and resume my scrubbing.

Confession: I've also been talking to myself out loud a lot the past couple of days. Out loud, having whole conversations. A house full of cats can't be far behind.

*

I decide to surprise Eli after school. He rides past me on his bike, oblivious. So I blow the horn. He circles, dismounts, and starts the walk of shame. All of his classmates are watching. He makes a point of approaching the driver's window, keeping the bike between us.

"What's up? Is something wrong?"

I slide the sunglasses off my nose. "Hop in, sport."

"I don't need a ride."

"Just throw your bike in back. The longer you wait, the more people are gonna see."

With a defeated slump of the shoulders, Eli complies. All I have to do to embarrass the kid is show up. Why is that? I'm not even blaring eighties music today.

"It's your birthday tomorrow and you still haven't told me what you want to do."

"I don't want to do anything."

"Are you too old for a party now? We could invite some of your friends over—"

He gives a violent shake of the head. "No, that's okay."

"You don't want them coming over? Because of Dad?"

"It's not that. Not *just* that. I don't want a party, that's all. I'm turning sixteen, not six. I don't need the cake and candles."

"What about a present? You want a present, don't you?"

He shrugs.

"Well, you're getting one," I say. "You're getting a cake too."

"Whatever."

"I love you, you know that?"

He nods.

"Your dad loves you too."

"I know."

"Your brother practically plans his birthday for me," I say.

"He cares about that stuff. I don't."

"Well, what do *you* care about these days?"

Again, he shrugs.

Until you've had a teenage son, you can't understand. Every conversation is like a jailhouse interrogation. An invisible lawyer leans toward him, saying, *"Plead the fifth."* Pulling teeth doesn't begin to describe it. Something could be terribly wrong in there, or he could be as placid as a summer lake, and you'd never know from anything he says.

"Peanut butter cup."

"What?"

"If I have to have a cake, I want an ice-cream one with peanut butter cups. And here—" He brings his foot up, scraping his shoe against the dashboard. "If you want to get me something, how about new shoes?" He pulls a flap of delaminated sole away from the toe of his sneaker, then lets it slap back into place. "Or I could just glue these."

"Shoes. Good. You might have to be more specific, though. Are Reeboks still cool? And I'm not getting you anything the kids at school will shoot you for and steal."

"For Reeboks, they just shoot you and leave your shoes on."

"That's more like it."

When we get to our neighborhood, he asks me to let him off on the curb. "We're gonna ride the trails, a whole group of us." He pulls his bike out and comes alongside the van.

"Be home by dark."

He nods. "Hey, Mom . . ."

"Yes?"

"You didn't *make* him move out, did you?"

"What? Of course not. Eli, where did you get that idea? I already told you what happened. It was the Shaws. They want us to move to Virginia so Daddy can work at a different church. It's a big decision, and he's trying to think it through."

"All right," he says. "I was just wondering."

"I don't *want* him out there, Eli. I'm as shocked as everyone else. And anyway, he's not on the other side of the world. He's just in the shed. You can go talk to him anytime you want. Maybe we should all go, the three of us."

He shakes his head. "It's not a big deal."

Eli rides away, leaving me to wonder if we're not as big a mystery to our children as they are to us.

Instead of going home, I wheel the car around so I can order the cake. The bakery refers me to an ice-cream place, where they seem incredulous that I need a cake for tomorrow. In the end, though, the manager promises it by two in the afternoon. Then I stop at the Foot Locker and puzzle over a dozen pairs of indistinguishable, neon-colored sneakers. Some of them seem to glow in the dark. Some would double the size of your feet. It wouldn't surprise me if they did double duty as flotation devices either. And at these prices it's hard to imagine any of them being made for a penny apiece in sweatshops. They'd be much cheaper in that case, right?

Right?

I should have taken advantage of Holly's expertise when I had her. On the verge of giving up, I call Jed on his mobile number. "You've gotta help me out. Your brother wants new shoes for his birthday."

"Cool. Get him some Rockports."

"Is that what he likes?" I ask, glancing around at the names on the boxes.

"No, get him some Crocs. He *loves* those."

"You're not helping. I'm serious, Jed. I finally know what he wants and I'm getting it. I just don't know which ones to choose."

"How should I know? Who bought him the last ones?"

Duh, me. But I'm not thrifting sneakers for my son's sixteenth birthday. "Jed, help me out."

"Ask the dude who works there."

Lowering my voice: "I already tried that. I think they work on commission."

"If you can't make up your mind, do a gift certificate. Or give him cash. That's what I'd want."

"I never have any trouble knowing what *you* want," I say. "I'm not giving him cash. That's cheesy."

"Fine, then get him some black Nike Airs."

"Black?"

"Yeah, black. He'll like those."

He'd better. As I check out, I can't help reflecting that at this price, the Nike Airs better be made by seasoned Italian craftsmen who get long lunch breaks in a workshop somewhere in Tuscany.

"Would you like to look at some socks?" the salesman asks.

"What, the socks are extra?"

A long pause. He clearly doesn't get the joke.

*

I make it home with plenty of sunlight left. No need to worry about sneaking the shoes past Eli. There's a strange car on the curb, maybe one of Jed's friends. Then again, he only has three or four and they hardly ever come over. What's the point? They do all their fraternizing via Skype. "They don't need bodies at all," Rick says. "They just need broadband." One of his hobbyhorses, though it didn't keep him from tinkering with the wireless network until he could get a strong signal out in the shed.

As I park and get out of the van, someone emerges from the strange car.

"Gregory," I say.

My older brother stops at the curb, giving me a scarecrow shrug. "Did I get mixed up? Where's the birthday boy?"

"Come here." I put the Foot Locker bag on the ground and give him a hug. As always, he squeezes tight and lifts me off my toes.

"Hey, sis. How you keeping?"

"Don't tell me you drove down for Eli's party. We weren't even planning to be in town."

"Let me look at you," he says, holding me at arm's length. He wears an old corduroy blazer he's had for years, a lumpy sweater, baggy pants, orthopedic-looking leather shoes, all of it far too big and an inch or two too short for his frame. In school they nicknamed him Lurch. He started using the name himself, though I never did.

"Where are you staying?"

"Over at Dad's." He jerks a thumb over his shoulder, as if our father's house were across the street and not out in the sticks. "I've been down here a couple of days."

"Is everything all right? If he had another doctor's appointment and didn't call me—"

"Eliza, chill. Nothing's wrong with Dad."

"And the two of you are getting along now?"

He seesaws his hand. "To be honest, I don't think he's got a firm grip on recent history. Have you noticed he's kind of in a muddle? He seems fine if he's talking about boats, the sea, that kind of thing, or grousing about politics. When you get him on the subject of people, though . . ."

"I know," I say. "He's getting old, that's all."

"That's not *all*. But anyway, I didn't drop by to talk about Dad. I have a favor to ask."

"So Eli's birthday has nothing to do with it."

He smiles. "I brought him a card."

"His birthday's not until tomorrow."

"Tomorrow? Perfect."

I bring him inside, depositing him in the kitchen while I take the Foot Locker bag upstairs. Then I brew coffee while he peruses the bookshelf in the living room, sighing at what he finds, thinking I can't hear him. One of the first things I did was rearrange the books, minimizing the gaps Rick left behind.

Jed comes down the stairs, curious about the voices.

"Your Uncle Greg dropped by. Go entertain him."

Ordinarily he would retreat back to his room, but at the mention of Greg's name, he lights up. The two of them start talking computers, picking up where they left off—what was it?—two years ago at Christmas.

We both managed to disappoint our father, Gregory through alcoholism and a lackluster academic career, me by eloping with a "fundamentalist nut job" (Dad's words), settling for the barefoot-and-pregnant life when I was intended for better things. In my dad's eyes, you could deny the Virgin Birth and the Incarnation, pretty much anything in the Bible, and you'd still be a fundamentalist nut job just for going to church. He was down on Quakers too, though—an equal opportunity skeptic. What really set him off, of course, was the hypocrisy of it all: the fundamentalist nut job knocking up his daughter.

"What, he doesn't believe in rubbers?"

My dad has a way with words.

Rick's family, for the record, was much more supportive. They sensed I wasn't quite one of them and were just relieved I was going to have the baby. Like they assumed you *had* to be one of them not to solve the problem by having an abortion.

My elopement and Greg's drinking both came out around the same time, within a year of our parents finally splitting. Mom went back to Pennsylvania, remarried, and owns a real estate agency in Altoona. Dad bought a crappy little shack overlooking Tar Cove and became a weekend sailor until his heart problems were diagnosed. I visit him out of a sense of duty, doing what I can to make him comfortable. He whiles away his retirement drinking black coffee in greasy-spoon diners, wearing a stethoscope around his neck.

The first time I saw it dangling there, I was perplexed. "What's that for?"

"So I can hear I'm still breathing," he snapped, clamping the chest piece against his skin to demonstrate. "See? Still going strong."

Maybe this was his way of reassuring me. It didn't work.

Despite our issues, I don't want to lose my father any more than I want my marriage to fail. I have a funny way of showing it, I guess.

For half an hour, Gregory and Jed keep talking while I look on, contributing occasionally. It amazes me how easy Gregory is with young people—I always remember him as being socially awkward. Of course, he's used to classroom interaction. That must explain it. On Jed's side the fascination makes sense: an intellectually stimulating grown-up who doesn't talk down to him, and his mirror image to boot. Here's an alternative vision for him to latch onto of what it means to be a man.

"Anyway," Gregory says. "Your mom and I need to have a talk. Don't you have some homework to do? Or better yet, isn't there some young lady out there sitting at home, pining away for a phone call from you?"

Once Jed disappears upstairs, Eli turns up and hits the reset button. The whole process repeats, but this time it's my youngest who pleads a prior engagement and slips away to his room.

"They're growing up," Gregory says.

"Yes, they are. So what's this favor?"

"When does Rick get off work? Maybe I should get that over with before we dive into things."

"Don't worry about him," I say. "Just spill it."

"Hmm. Maybe we should go for a walk."

*

It's dark outside, a pleasant autumn night. The smell of woodsmoke on the air. Gregory turns up the collar of his jacket, though it's crisp at best, not cold.

Most likely scenario: Gregory is back on the bottle, ran someone over under the influence, and is here looking for an alibi.

Second most likely: Gregory has met the woman of his dreams, and she happens to be an underage college student, and now needs me to cosign on a loan so he can buy the girl her dream house. I'm hoping it's the alibi. He's not getting me to sign anything.

"There's this girl," he begins. "One of my students."

Oh no.

"Are you sure you want to tell me about this?"

He laughs. "It's not what you're thinking. This is a bright girl, a really promising girl. Her mom teaches at the college with me. We're good friends."

"Good friends?"

"The mother and me. More than good friends. I like her, Eliza. They're from back home. Here. Baltimore. Moved down to take the job at the school. We haven't gone out or anything—I haven't known her *that* long—but I really like her. The thing is, her daughter's done a runner. She's got a problem."

"What kind of problem?"

"No, a Problem." He presses his finger down on one nostril, sniffing loudly through the other. "Not just blow. She's done it all—and the girl still hasn't hit her bottom."

"And what does this have to do with me?"

"I know where she is. She called home, and she's at this halfway house in West Baltimore. Called Mission Up. You ever heard of it? No, I guess it's not your beat. Anyway, something happened, a scared-sober moment, and she called her mom. She revealed where she was, but she wouldn't come home. I figure I've got some experience in this line and the girl trusts me, so I offered to come down and reason with her. I want to talk to her, and I want you to come with me."

"Why me? Can't you talk to her yourself?"

Sheepish grin: "I already tried, Eliza. It didn't go very well. So I thought, maybe *you* can get through to her."

I turn to look in his face. The moon is up, sitting like a halo behind his head. "You thought *I* could get through to her? Why?"

My record on getting through to people isn't great. Just look at Peggy Ensign. Or for that matter, my husband.

"I don't know—you're a woman. You're a mom. Look, I'm kind of desperate here. Help me, Obi-Wan."

"I am *not* your only hope. What you need is some kind of professional. A drug counselor or maybe a social worker. There are people who do this, Gregory. It's their job."

"Leave it to the professionals? I know you don't believe that. Listen, I'm sorry if this is outside your comfort zone, and ordinarily I wouldn't even be asking. But there's a life at stake. Don't shake your head, Liz, I'm not being melodramatic. You should see this place, the halfway house. It's one rung higher than hell. If we don't get her out of there, I can tell you exactly what's going to happen."

"And all you want me to do is talk to her? Convince her to go home?"

"That's it. One conversation. We could go first thing in the morning."

"Not tomorrow," I say. "Eli's birthday is tomorrow."

"It won't take long."

"It will if it works."

"Come on, Eliza. You know you're going to say yes."

He puts one of his large hands on my shoulder, pulling me awkwardly against him in a semi-hug. For a second, I'm fifteen again, looking up to my big brother, called by the nickname my family gave me, Eliza. It was Rick who started calling me Beth.

No, I'm not blaming him.

I liked it.

Eliza was a calico-and-lace kind of name out of *My Fair Lady*, Audrey Hepburn singing in cockney, her high cheekbones rouged in faux filth. Becoming Beth freed me from that.

And just imagine: it takes *audacity* to rename someone, to play Adam to the animals. Rick did it almost without thinking, like it was his right. Staking his claim the very first time we met. Before he had any designs on me at all.

Months would pass before he changed my last name along with the first.

"I don't think it will make a difference," I say, "but if you want me to, I'll go."

"Thank you, sis. Seriously."

He leans down and kisses my forehead, the most affection he's shown in as long as I can remember. His lips leave a damp impression, cooling in the night air. I lean my head against his chest, content.

"I hope the neighbors don't see me, cuddling with a strange man."

"I'm sure they're a broad-minded lot," he says. "People with money usually are," then laughs at the hilariousness of his own joke.

"Spoken like somebody without any."

We walk back, the heels of his leather shoes clicking on the sidewalk. A breeze stirs through the trees. It's really beautiful here, especially now. A garden of tranquility on the edge of the big city, and here I am smack-dab in the middle, as riddled with useless anxiety as the corseted ladies who used to recline on Dr. Freud's couch. Oh, the ingratitude.

"I'm glad you came," I say.

"Really?"

"I've been thinking about old times. You remember Miss Hannah?"

"How could I forget? She had a glare that would take the paint off a barn."

"Well, she never used it on me. I was remembering the other day about that place she took me, the meetinghouse with the opening in the roof."

"Ah, right. Did you ever figure out where it was?"

I shake my head. "If it weren't for that vivid memory of her stretching out on the bench, I'd tell myself it was all in my imagination."

"Have you been reliving more episodes from your past?"

"What do you mean?"

"It's about that time. Your midlife crisis. I'd say you're pretty much overdue."

"Ha." A midlife crisis. If only he knew. There's a crisis in the family, no question about that, but it isn't mine. "Gregory, you're going to find out soon enough, so I might as well tell you. You asked when Rick was coming home and I told you not to worry about it. That's because Rick is home. He's living in the shed in the backyard."

"He's what?"

"I didn't put him there, if that's what you're thinking. He made the choice himself. He's unfulfilled at work and conflicted about a new job offer he just received, so naturally he decided to wait for an answer from God. Meanwhile, he's sequestered himself in the shed. As people do."

"Right. Of course. This is the same Rick we're talking about—my brother-in-law, the ultimate sportsman, deep as a ditch?"

"Not anymore. My neighbor thinks he's becoming a mystic. I think she left an offering of flowers at his door."

"Wow." He stops in his tracks, takes his arm from my shoulder. "I mean, *wow.* Eliza, that's weird. It's, like . . . messed up. I've never even *heard* of something like that before. He's really gone off the deep end?"

"I'd say that's a fair assessment."

"You seem pretty calm about it. I'd be freaking out."

"Trust me, I've been freaking out. My son's birthday is tomorrow, and as far as I know his father isn't planning to be there. I have the keys to a beach house in Florida on my nightstand, I have permission slips to get the boys out of school, and I don't have a husband anymore to go with me. I'm like a single mother all the sudden, except there's a crazy man living in the backyard, sneaking into the house when I'm not around so he can go to the bathroom."

"Liz," he says. "Oh, Liz."

"I know. And the really insane part is, I'm used to it now. It's only been a couple of days and I really don't miss him. The boys don't either. They barely talk about him. But they're afraid to bring anyone home, afraid their friends will find out."

"Oh, Liz." He puts his long arms around me and pulls my face into his chest. My shoulders heave, my cheeks burn wetly. I'm pumping tears into the fabric of his jacket. Letting go, drifting free. "Oh, Liz," he's saying, "oh, Liz, Liz, Liz," over and over, a voice across the water calling me toward the distant shore. He holds me tight but I'm floating, my eyes prismed, floating off to the dissolving dark.

"Maybe," he says, much later. "Maybe," as we walk very slowly, side by side, pacing ourselves so we never make it home. "Maybe this isn't about him."

I wipe my hand over my face. I sniff. "What does that mean?"

"Maybe this isn't his time, Liz. Maybe it's yours."

"My time to hear from God, you mean?" I give him a lopsided smile. "My time to find myself?"

"Is that so hard to believe?"

"I'm not into all that psychobabble. 'Finding yourself.' I never lost myself."

"You didn't? You could've fooled me."

"Don't talk," I say. "You're ruining the moment."

"Sorry." He gazes up at the whirling, faceted anarchy of the Smythes' Victorian mansion, the moonlight shining dimly in the grimy leaded-glass windows. "Since I've already ruined it, I might as well say something else."

"If you must."

"You know that Eli's smoking weed, right?"

"What?"

"I could smell it on him when he came in the house."

chapter 8

Good Christian Lady

Definition of hypocrisy: this daydream I'm having, in which I slap a fat joint from Eli's lips, snatch it in the air between my finger and thumb, and grind out the smoldering cherry in the middle of his peanut butter ice-cream cake.

Gregory drives, trying to munch down his McDonald's hash browns before the grease melts through the bag. He doesn't look over at me, knowing no good will come of it.

Shocking news plus a sleepless night plus an unwanted errand equals recipe for volcanic eruption.

If Gregory hadn't arrived first thing, ringing the doorbell with his fast-food offering in hand, there would have been an eruption all right.

And where is his father? Cloistered away while his son puffs himself into a stupor. Is that where Eli goes every day after school? Is he being metaphorical when he calls it riding the trails? Is he laughing at me behind my back?

"You shouldn't have told me," I say.

"I gave you the red pill when you wanted the blue one. Or is it the other way around?"

"I'm serious."

"What? It's *The Matrix.* You don't really think that ignorance is bliss. Anyway, you weren't such a little teetotaler back in the day."

"Neither were you." Low blow. "Sorry, I shouldn't have said that."

"No big deal. I can take it. Twelve years sober as of last month."

"That's great."

"So you can understand why this means something to me, helping this girl."

"I thought you liked the mom."

"I do," he says. "But it's not just about the mom. Kind of hard to explain."

"You don't have to. I understand."

"I'm not telling you to go easy on the kid. I wouldn't. Nail him to the wall if that's what it takes. Just wait until tomorrow. It's his birthday, after all."

"Do you think Jed knows?"

"I wouldn't be surprised. You knew when it was me."

"What if he wasn't the one smoking it? Maybe he was just around people who were smoking."

"Could be," he says, doubt in his voice. We're taking the Jones Falls Expressway into town. Speeding one minute, sitting still the next. He drops the last hash brown wrapper into the bag and crumbles it into a white, damp ball, sailing the ball over his shoulder into the backseat: "Two points."

"Last night might have been the first time," I say. "Just because he smelled of pot doesn't mean he's a stoner." The more I think about this theory, the more I like it. "The other day he saw a bunch of war protesters and called them 'hippie losers.' You wouldn't say that if you were smoking, would you?"

"Hippie losers? No way. You'd say, 'Hail brother, well met.' Absolutely."

"You're no help."

"Hey, I grassed on him, what more do you want? Get it—grassed?"

"Not funny."

"No, it's not. And now I'm dragging you into this mess."

This mess. It sounds like a mess all right.

"What's the girl's name, anyway?"

"Her name is Samantha McCone. Sam."

"And what is Sam's story?"

"It's not a nice one. She ran away when she was in her early teens. Her parents were divorced, and her mom had moved her here. I don't know if drugs came into it before or after that, but she was missing for close to six months. Police brought her back. After that, behavior problems—you can imagine what it was like. I mean, how do you treat a kid who does something like that? But Sam got her act together in high school, graduated in May, and she was in my classroom three months later, bright-eyed and bushy-tailed. I've got a nose for it, and I didn't sense anything with her. She seemed like a good kid. She *was* a good kid."

"So what happened?"

"Same thing that always happens. You get weak, you get tempted, you relapse. Her mom says she started going into the city with these friends of hers, partying, not coming home until the next day. She didn't want to come down too hard too fast—Sam is hypersensitive—but before she knew it, the girl was gone. That was three weeks ago."

"When did she call home?"

"Sunday afternoon."

While I was with the Rent-a-Mob, feeling sorry for myself. "You talked to her yesterday? And she said she wouldn't go back."

"She'd run out of drugs over the weekend. Between Sunday and yesterday, she must have scored some more."

"And they let her stay in the halfway house?"

"It's more like an asylum. You'll see."

If your knowledge of Baltimore jumps from Edgar Allan Poe to *The Wire*, you have a distorted view of the city, expecting it to be hip deep in drugs, bullets flying through the projects, tattooed thugs eyeballing you as your car rolls through the corner. It's not that way, I tell people. Even the places that *were* like that are getting better all the time. There are Volvos parked along Patterson Park. Don't believe everything you see, I tell them. I'm from Baltimore. I should know.

But Gregory takes me to the Baltimore I'm not from, the city I don't know or even begin to recognize.

"This isn't such a great neighborhood," I say, watching two kids on a street corner bump hands, passing something back and forth. The closed store behind them is hidden under burglar bars, the glass underneath busted out.

"We're not in Lutherville anymore. Don't worry. If anybody gives you trouble, start sharing about Jesus and they'll give you a wide berth."

"I should have brought my fish."

Gallows humor. I really don't like the look of these streets. Long blocks of side-by-side row houses, every couple of facades boarded up and tagged with paint. Old sunbaked black men sitting on stoops, kids in long white muscle shirts running in front of the car with only a foot or two to spare, leaving Gregory to hit the brakes or run them over. At the intersections, lean young men in hoodies and puffed-out coats lean over for a look into the car.

"They're just checking to see if we're buying," Gregory says. "It's no big deal."

His calmness reassures me a little. This is the real world. What looks risky to me is everyday life for many of God's creatures.

"I envy your assurance," I tell him. "I shouldn't be a stranger to such places, after all."

"Why not?"

"Jesus ate with the prostitutes and tax collectors. I'm on his team, married to one of his official servants, and in theory my life is meant to be more like his. I'm supposed to aspire to this kind of thing. But it makes me uncomfortable all the same. I guess I don't have your affinity for the working class."

"This isn't the working class," he says. "This is flat-out poverty. I don't want any part of this, or the system that perpetuates it, any more than you do—" He breaks off. I sense there's more he could say, but for some reason he doesn't want to. He pretends to pay attention to the road. Finally, this: "In all honesty, I think my Marxism is about as theoretical as your Christianity. I want out of here as much as you."

"And Sam? How did she end up in a place like this?"

He shrugs. "How does *anyone* end up in a place like this?"

The amazing thing is, we'll pass a bunch of dealers hustling on the curb and one block up there's a parked police car. You'd think they would at least move their action farther down. But these are the front lines, I guess. You don't run away because the other side shows its head. If you're in a battle, you stand your ground.

The streets teem with kids. Teens. Grade-schoolers. Running alone or in packs. Dribbling basketballs, snatching caps off each other's heads and running down the block with them, their laughter incongruous to my ears given the surroundings, but natural enough to them. All of this must seem natural to them.

Eric Ringwald, Holly's husband, returned from one of his trips to Haiti telling after-dinner stories about the children there. "They have nothing," he would say, "absolutely nothing—and yet they seem so happy in comparison to us." He meant it sincerely, and I've heard the same thing from many others returning from short-term mission trips: middle-class Americans lamenting their own inauthenticity in comparison to the impoverished and joyous urchins they saw abroad. Maybe I'm channeling my brother's convictions here, but I can imagine Edwardian travelers returning from their gin-and-tonic-soaked holidays in Calcutta thinking much the same thing. I've never heard anyone come back from downtown Baltimore waxing poetic about the authenticity of poverty.

"Don't let it get to you," Gregory says. "We'll be out of here in no time."

Maybe it should get to me. What kind of person would I be if it didn't?

One rung above hell is how Gregory described the halfway house, and at first glance he appears to be right. Parking across the street, he unclips his seat belt, lets out a long sigh, and just sits there, working up the nerve to get out. This gives me a chance to look the place over. Mission Up sits at the end of a block of row houses, half of them boarded up and the other half looking like they should be. The tall, narrow facades make me think of a grade-schooler's smile: you run your eyes left to right and keep hitting gaps where teeth are meant to be.

Once upon a time, thirty years ago at least, Mission Up might actually have been a large boardinghouse, one of those seedy flophouse kind of places you see in old movies, with the creepy attendant behind the counter and the room keys dangling on wall hooks. After that, it must have been boarded up for a long time and only recently pried open and repurposed. Calling it a halfway house gave me the impression of something official. This is anything but.

"It looks more like a squat," I say.

But looking again, I notice some care has gone into this squat. The sign over the door is hand-painted in pink neon. The lettering is done with flair too, the *o* in Mission Up rendered as a smiley face. The trim on the ground-floor windows is picked out in the same bright pink. Even though the windows themselves are sheathed in what looks like chicken wire, if you give it a chance, Mission Up exudes a rude cheerfulness.

Gregory turns to me. "It's not going to be easy getting in. We'll have to talk our way past the nun."

"The nun?"

"You'll see. Just follow my lead."

Stepping out of the car feels at first like walking on the moon. But the ground under my feet doesn't give way, and the air is just as breathable as it is in the suburbs. By the time we're across the street, I'm thinking I can do this. I want to. Beth may hesitate, but Eliza, the girl whose eyes sometimes look back at me in the mirror, would charge ahead.

Gregory knocks on the door. Up close, I can see faded pink detailing on the inset panels, more evidence of life within. After a pause, he knocks again, glancing over his shoulder.

"She's a bit of a bear."

The door opens and I see what he means. A wide-eyed black woman about five feet tall and five feet wide looms in the threshold, her bosom and belly conflated into a single roll that pushes on the buttons of her shiny polyester shirt. The collar has a notch of white at the throat, just like the one Deedee's parish priest wears.

"What you—? Oh," she says. "The professor come back."

Not an ounce of hospitality in her voice. In fact, the way she says *professor* suggests the profoundest doubt that the man standing before her is any such thing. She says it with invisible quotes in the air, implying Gregory is an impostor.

Her eyes cut to me, glancing up and down in frank assessment. On her chest, a gold pectoral cross hangs, hugely out of proportion, its ends whirled with elaborate flourishes. It shines flatly and looks like spray-painted metal. She also wears a dozen or more tiny enamel badges of the sort men used to wear on their suit lapels. Knights of Columbus, a variety of crosses denoting holy orders I don't recognize, tiny Bibles, tiny Virgins, tiny saints of various sorts. Like a general's medals or a Boy Scout's badges. There's a lot of real estate to cover and she's managed pretty well.

"Sister," Gregory begins.

"Mother," she says, correcting him.

"Mother, that's right. Is it . . . Zacchaeus?"

His mouth has trouble tumbling out the syllables that emerged so smoothly from my own.

"Mother Zacchaeus," she says, fixing him in her small, cold eyes. "You know perfectly well."

"Well, look who I've brought!" He frames me with his hands, a magician's gesture. "This is Sister Eliza, a good Christian lady, and when I told her about your wonderful establishment here, she insisted on seeing it for herself."

"Hmm." Mother Zacchaeus looks me over again. "You a good Christian lady?"

"Absolutely!" Gregory says in a bright, loud voice, talking to the nun like she's hard of hearing or hard of understanding or both. It makes me wince to hear him condescending this way.

"We're here to see Sam?" I say, turning the end of the statement into a question.

"I know why you here, good Christian lady. And you not coming in."

Gregory leans into the threshold, and for a second I expect Mother Zacchaeus to deck him. Her torso twists and her hand cocks back, but at the last moment she merely grasps the edge of the door, holding it tightly. Short as she is, I have no doubt she could flatten my lanky brother, whose workout routine consists mainly of carrying a stack of books from his car to his office. Occasionally Deedee will tell me horror stories of the strict nuns of her Catholic youth, but those white-haired women had nothing on Mother Zacchaeus, I'm sure.

"You not coming in, and that is final, hear? This is a sanctuary, not a come-and-go-as-you-please."

"Come on, Mother Zacchaeus. You have to allow visitors."

"This isn't visiting hours."

"But Sister Eliza came all this way."

She looks at me again, a hint of uncertainty leaking into her glare. Gregory looks my way too, lifting his eyebrows for emphasis. *Help me out here, sis.*

"Please let us see her," I ask. "Her mom sent us to make sure she's all right."

She bites her lip. "For real?"

"For real!" Gregory insists.

I nod in confirmation.

Reluctantly, Mother Zacchaeus steps away from the door, allowing us into what looks like the main room where meals are served. Tables in three lines hold newspapers and books. Several street people are sitting on metal foldout chairs. Two play dominoes, while one sleeps with his head on his arms. A couple of women wipe down the serving tables. I see a thick metal bar about four feet in length leaning against the wall. When she shuts the door behind us, there's a kind of socket bolted into the wood. At night, the bar must go into the socket, in case some predator outside tries to force entry. Judging from Mother Zacchaeus's continued glare, she must be worried she's let the predators in without a fight.

At a desk to her left sits a man who dwarfs the woman. Clad in a bright-red track suit, he stands up. "Everything okay, Mother Z?"

"Aaron. Don't hover over me."

He shakes his head and sits back down at his post, muttering something under his breath.

"You follow me," she says, "and don't go wandering off."

Aaron shakes his head again. "You best be listening to her, that's all I got to say."

From the main room, a hallway extends into several rooms opening shotgun-style, one into another. I hear a television playing cartoons and children's murmured voices. A head peeks around the entrance: a teenage girl, making sure everything's all right. She disappears when I make eye contact.

We're not heading her way, it seems. Mother Zacchaeus mounts the creaking stairs, leading us past a tiny desk with a sign-out sheet on its surface and up to the second floor. Another hallway, much longer and just wide enough for a broad-shouldered man not to have to turn. Along one side, a series of doors, some of them still numbered in tarnished brass. Several are ajar, but no one is in the corridor. Through the walls, I can hear people moving, hushed voices. The place could be teeming with inhabitants, but none make an appearance. As I watch, one of the doors snaps shut. Everyone in Mission Up must be aware something unusual is going on, and they're keeping their distance.

Mother Zacchaeus pauses on the landing to catch her breath, then we begin the ascent up a third, narrower flight of stairs.

"You moved her," Gregory says.

She replies with a grunt.

I clear my throat. "How many people live here?"

"As many as need to," she snaps.

I get the impression she's not singling us out for harsh treatment. This is simply her manner. She's one of those people accustomed to putting her world in order and having it stay that way. Anyone coming along to challenge that order has to run the gauntlet of her hostility. Or maybe she just doesn't care for middle-aged white people turning up on her door talking to her like she's an idiot. It bothers me too.

The third floor is a mirror image of the second, though on a smaller scale. The hallway seems narrower, the doors smaller. Maybe it's a trick of the light, which comes entirely from a flickering fluorescent at the far end of the corridor. All the rest seem to be burned out. (I suppose I should be grateful there's electricity at all.)

Mother Zacchaeus leads us halfway down the hallway to

a room marked 3-9. The middle number, presumably 0, is long gone. She pushes through without knocking. Gregory motions for me to go first.

There are three mattresses on the floor, each with a mummy of sheets coiled in its center. Through the open window, the only source of light, I glimpse the rusted metal railing of an emergency ladder, then a patch of grass and busted concrete that must be what passes for the backyard. A girl sits on the mattress nearest the window, her hand propped on the sill, holding a cigarette with dainty grace between two fingers. She wears shorts and a nylon zip jacket, her long, smooth legs the color of caramel.

"Go take that outside, Aziza," Mother Zacchaeus tells her.

The girl takes a drag on the cigarette, then flicks it out into space.

"Go on, I said."

She seems to notice us for the first time. She glances over Gregory in a heartbeat, her eyes settling on me. Mother Zacchaeus flicks her hand and the girl rises to go. As she pushes past me, I get a whiff of smoke and cheap perfume. Up close, I am shocked how young she is. Surely not more than fourteen or fifteen.

"You awake?" Mother Zacchaeus says, kicking one of the mattresses.

The sheet mummy on the bed shifts in response. I hadn't realized anyone was there.

Gregory crouches next to the bed. "Hey, Sam, are you okay?"

He beckons me over. As I approach, the sheet falls back to reveal a sliver of face. A lock of sweat-matted brown hair covers one of Sam's eyes. There's so much eyeliner around the other it looks like someone tried to scratch over it with a black crayon. She cracks open an eyelid, testing the light.

"Leave me alone," she mutters.

Mother Zacchaeus kicks the mattress again. "You get up. Come on, now."

This coaxing tone is the closest thing to affection that's come out of the nun's mouth. Sam responds by propping herself up. I get a glimpse of bony shoulders crisscrossed in straps: white for the tank top, pink for the cami underneath, black for the bra straps. The side of her bottom lip is transected by a swollen cut. No, wait. Looking closer, I see it's a round piece of metal. A lip ring. Nice.

"Sam, get up. I brought someone to see you."

"What?" She rears back like a startled fawn, searching the room with panicky jerks of the head. Her black-rimmed eyes look comically huge. When she sees the expected someone—presumably her mother—isn't here, she slumps back on the bed. "I said, leave me alone."

The words aren't out before the nun's foot hits the mattress again, this time with so much force it scoots sideways half an inch. Sam sits bolt upright.

"Show some respect," Mother Zacchaeus says, pronouncing it *re-SPECK*. Leaving no doubt in my mind which of us she intends Sam to pay this respect to.

"Can you just ease up a little bit?" I ask.

Strangely, the nun reacts differently than I anticipate. Instead of lashing out to put me in my place—or worse, using that foot of hers—for the first time, Mother Zacchaeus favors me with a smile.

"Good," she says. "I guess we *all* want a little respeck."

I smile back, hoping we've gained a little trust.

Gregory isn't having any of that. He leans toward Sam,

clamping one of his big hands on her face, forcing her eyelid up to inspect her pupil. She twists away without much conviction.

"You've gotta be kidding me," Gregory says. He grabs her arm and wrenches it straight, exposing the socket of flesh inside her elbow. Turning it to make sure I can see the marks. "You call this place a sanctuary, Mother? From what, the cops? I knew the standards were pretty low here, but I didn't realize the liberties extended to letting your clients shoot up."

The hard, small eyes of Mother Zacchaeus narrow, but she doesn't answer back.

"I should call the cops," he says. "They'd run you out on a rail."

I put a hand on his shoulder. "Gregory."

"What?"

"You're just making things worse. Move out of the way."

Reluctantly, he trades places with me. I kneel beside the mattress, taking one of Sam's hands in my own. Her palm feels hot and clammy. She closes her eyes again.

"Sam, listen to me," I say. "You need to go home. Your mother is waiting for you, she loves you, and everything will be all right."

"She doesn't," Sam mutters. "She hates me."

"Nobody hates you, especially not your mother. She's worried sick about you, Sam. So is Greg. He's here to take you home."

Mother Zacchaeus says, "Nobody takin' this girl nowhere."

I ignore her. "Listen to me. You can't stay here, not like this. You know what'll happen just as much as I do."

Her head lolls back, but I can tell she's listening. On some level, no matter what's swirling in her veins right now, the girl can hear my voice. As I continue to cajole her, stroking her hand in a soothing rhythm, Gregory and Mother Zacchaeus step toward the window for a whispered argument.

"Where'd she get the drugs?" he asks. "Did *you* hook her up? Is that how you make your money, supplying the girls you keep locked up in here?"

"She ain't got no money when she come in here."

"Then how'd she score, answer me that?"

"How you think a girl like that pays when she got no money, huh? How you think?"

I try to tune them out, pulling Sam into my arms, pressing her flushed, sweaty face against my shoulder. It's no use. Their voices grow louder and the girl starts pushing away.

"Will the two of you shut up?" I ask, wheeling on them.

For a moment, they both stand frozen. Then Mother Zacchaeus stomps past me into the hallway, her face rigid but trembling with rage. She continues down the hall, her footsteps carrying. Gregory cups his hands over his mouth.

"What do we do now?" he asks.

"This girl's out of it. I don't think we're gonna get through to her. Not now. Not today."

"We have to."

"Just leave me alone," Sam moans.

We pause, staring at each other.

"Okay, fine." Gregory starts pacing. "All right. Let me think." I'm about to say something when he interrupts. "Tell you what, Eliza. You're probably right. Let me talk to her alone for a second, though. Just to be sure. In the meantime, you'd better go see what the nun is up to. I don't want *her* calling the cops on us. Go ahead, it'll be all right. Tell her you want to take the official tour or something. Keep her distracted so she doesn't cause any trouble."

"You know, if you'd just be a little more decent with people—"

"I know, I know. I just can't stand these petty tyrant types.

People like that know how to push my buttons. But you'll smooth everything over, Liz. Pretty please?"

I leave him with Sam and go in search of Mother Zacchaeus. As I descend the first flight of stairs, I can hear her steps a level down, slow and deliberate, like she's afraid of stumbling. When I catch up to her, she's crossing the main room to the front door, reaching for the metal bar against the wall.

Oh dear.

Irrational fear: I imagine her turning and clubbing me, the latent violence of our surroundings suddenly unleashing itself on my body. Broken bones. Coughing up blood.

But when she does turn, rod in hand, my presence there startles her. She jumps. The metal bar clangs to the floor. She clamps her hand down on the enamel pins dotting her chest.

"You scared me," she wheezes.

"You kind of scared me too," I say, nodding toward the rod.

She picks it up and leans it carefully against the wall, catching her breath. "You don't understand," she says. "Good Christian woman like you. What a good Christian woman doing in a place like this, huh?"

"Don't say that. What about you? You're a nun."

She touches the spray-painted cross dangling from her neck, as if to confirm that she is indeed what I said.

"I can't even imagine the things you see here. The things you have to deal with."

"What, here? Nothing to deal with here."

"I didn't mean—no, never mind." Casting around for another topic, I remember Gregory's advice. The official tour. "Listen, while I'm here, why don't you show me around? I'd be interested in seeing what goes on, if that's all right."

"For real?"

After a period of indecision, Mother Zacchaeus gives in. She conducts me through the main room. Along with the readers of the *Sunpaper,* I see the blaring television and the half circle of kids on the floor watching cartoons under the watchful eye of the teenage girl I spotted before. "This is a day care too," Mother Zacchaeus explains. In the next room, Aziza, the smoking girl from upstairs, is chatting with a couple of older women. They eye me warily at first, then ignore me entirely.

"Some of these girls, they turned tricks, some was on the pipe—"

"Same difference, most the time," Aziza says, making the others laugh.

The nun smiles, taking me into the next room. Here a heavily pregnant woman is fishing burnt slices of bread out of a toaster oven while a pair of toddlers circles her legs. The galley kitchen looks surprisingly clean, with canned goods stacked in back for storage. Through the back door we emerge onto the slab of cracked concrete I glimpsed from up above. There's a rusty grill near the edge of the slab. Then a narrow yard packed with a sun-bleached swing set and cast-off toys.

Mission Up, I realize, isn't run according to any particular plan. Whatever the needs are when women turn up on her doorstep, Mother Zacchaeus sternly improvises some plan to meet them.

"Are there other nuns who help?" I ask. "People from your order?"

She looks at me oddly.

"I'm sorry," I say. "I don't know the terminology. Nuns don't live in a monastery, but you don't call it a nunnery, do you?"

"You mean my convent?" she says, putting the same imaginary quotes around *convent* that she did *professor* when we showed up.

"Convent, that's right."

She ambles back into the building, seeming to lose interest in the conversation. "And nuns *do* live in convents."

So much for that.

I follow her back through the series of rooms, taking it all in.

"Did you paint the sign?" I call after her. "The one over the door."

"Nobody else did."

In the vestibule, the door stands open. Gregory is already waiting on the curb out front, looking at his watch. He sees me and beckons.

"Let's get out of here."

"Well," I say, turning to Mother Zacchaeus. "It was nice meeting you. I imagine we'll be back. If there's anything you can do to help convince Sam to go back to her mother . . ."

She lets the suggestion hang in the air. As I exit, though, she touches my elbow slightly, escorting me out, and for some reason I take this as acknowledgment. In her own way, she will do what she can.

"Thanks," Gregory calls to her. He turns to me. "Now let's get out of this hole."

"Please shut up," I whisper.

Before getting into the car, I give Mother Zacchaeus an apologetic wave. She nods imperceptibly, then closes the door.

"Greg," I begin, pulling the door shut, "you didn't have to be so rude to her . . ."

My voice trails off. As he pulls away, giving the engine some gas, I glance between the seats where he tossed the McDonald's bag earlier. A twisted mummy of bedsheets lies across the backseat, the matted brown hair and scribbled-out eyes poking out from one end.

"Greg," I say. "Go back."

"What?" He floors the accelerator. "A girl can't change her mind?"

"Have you completely lost your mind?"

"She's out of it, Eliza. And that place isn't safe. When she wakes up, she'll be happy we got her out of there."

He's right. I know he's right. But somehow it still feels like a betrayal of trust to me. I picture Mother Zacchaeus climbing back up those stairs to discover Sam gone, and she'll think we were exactly the predators she sized us up as to begin with.

But we're not, I tell myself. And that was no place to leave someone.

chapter 9

The Feast of St. Rick

Everything is under control. Sure, my husband has gone feral out in the shed. Sure, there's a nineteen-year-old junkie sleeping upstairs in my bed. Sure, Gregory has taken over the plans for Eli's birthday—such as it is—promising to collect both the ice-cream cake and the birthday boy. "You just relax," he says, "and take it easy. Everything is under control." If Sam wakes up I should call him, but otherwise don't worry about a thing.

I'm pretty sure this is all going to go wrong.

I am equally sure there's nothing I can do to stop it.

The world has gone crazy, and I'm along for the ride.

More evidence: Going outside for some air, giving the shed a wide berth, I find Roy Meakin snoozing in an Adirondack chair in the Smythes' English garden, over by the stone wall. He looks serene, hands folded over his paunch, a wisp of gray hair on his forehead shimmering in the breeze. I've never seen the chair here before, let alone caught Roy in the middle of an alfresco afternoon nap. I'm uncertain of the etiquette in such situations.

He must sense me gazing down at him. His eyes open. Casts disoriented glances left and right.

"Where'd she go?" he asks.

"Who—Deedee? I haven't seen her."

"She was right here. Painting. I shut my eyes for just a moment and . . ." He gets to his feet, shaking off a couple of flame-red leaves that fell on him while he was sleeping. He catches the last in his hand, holding it up for inspection, then tosses it to the ground. "This is embarrassing."

"Don't mind me."

"She was so excited," he says. "She's experienced something of a breakthrough. I was going to run her straight over to the church as soon as she'd packed her things here."

"I guess she went ahead without you. Maybe you looked too peaceful to disturb."

He laughs. "More likely she forgot I was here. That husband of yours is the only man she has time for anymore. She's become quite obsessed."

"With Rick?" I ask, remembering the offering of flowers.

"Oh yes. But don't get too worried. It's more of a religious fascination. The Catholic schoolgirl obsessing over Saint Whatshisname. If your husband's not careful, he might end up in Deedee's mural."

"That's just what I need."

Roy pats his pockets absently, making sure he has everything, pretending he didn't pick up on the acid in my tone. "Well, I guess I'd better get going."

"Wait a minute," I say, feeling guilty. "It's not a big to-do or anything, but today's Eli's birthday and after school we're having some cake. If you and Deedee are back around, say, three, why don't you come over?"

"That sounds nice. I'll let her know."

Roy passes through the garden and around the side of the Smythes' house, heading for his car parked on the curb. I follow him as far as the back steps that lead to the wraparound gallery, an exquisite Victorian gingerbread affair, though the detailed woodwork is missing a few dentals and could use a new coat of paint. I rap lightly on the back door. Loud enough for Margaret to hear if she's downstairs, and light enough not to disturb her if she is still in bed, which she often is these days.

"Why, look who's here," she says.

"Just wanted to check on you, Mrs. Smythe."

"Come in, come in."

Instead of swinging the door open, Margaret clutches the edge and walks a circle, carrying the door along with her. Then she takes a step toward the back of a couch, resting her hand on the wooden rib that protrudes from the cushions. She edges around to the front of the couch by resting her fingertips lightly on the shade of a side table lamp. Everywhere she goes, she's always reaching and resting and touching her way forward, which makes watching her progress slightly terrifying. I keep expecting her to take a fall.

She settles herself in an armchair with crocheted doilies draped over its back and sides.

"Won't you have a seat?"

"I can't stay long," I say, choosing the sofa across from her. "I wanted to invite you over for Eli's birthday party. He's turning sixteen."

"Sixteen," she says, her blue eyes widening. "I remember when I turned sixteen."

Margaret is a white-haired little pixie, cute as can be, with hunched, narrow shoulders and slender hips. She wears these knee-length dresses that zip up the back, covering her all the way to her neck, which is trimmed in pearls no matter the time of day or the occasion. The fabric of these dresses reminds me of old curtains. Although she's practically housebound, rarely leaving these days, even to attend mass, I have never seen her less than immaculate, her hair all done. She's a little bit Miss Marple, a little bit Queen of England. I just love her.

"You know, at sixteen I was already married."

"Really?"

She nods. "We had to fudge a little about our ages. It was like that, during the war. Life moved pretty slowly before the war, and pretty fast once the fighting started. I remember it all like it was yesterday. In fact, I remember it much better than I remember yesterday—which I don't remember at all!"

"If you think it would be too much," I say, "walking over to the house . . ."

She raises her hand, which shakes visibly. "Oh, I don't get out much anymore. I used to be quite a traveler, but I think I've traveled about as much as I care to."

It's charming, her idea that a walk next door would constitute travel.

"Maybe I'll have Eli come over and visit you."

"Don't take any trouble on my account. I'm sure a sixteen-year-old boy has better things to do with his time than come calling on little old ladies."

"Not at all. And besides, the boys love you. We all do, you know that."

"Do you?" she asks, leaning forward. "That's nice. That's very nice." Her eyes glisten in the lamplight. "That husband of yours, I've been hearing things, you know."

"From Deedee?"

She shrugs, as if to say, *Who else?*

"Well, I admit, it's a little strange."

"I don't think so," she says. "Not really. I remember when I was a girl, we had another man who lived out there, a handyman, I think he was. Worked for my daddy doing odd jobs, minding things. Name of . . . Bruce, I think. Adoniram Bruce, something ridiculous like that. Matter of fact . . . now, don't tell your husband this, but if I'm not mistaken, I'm pretty sure ol' Mr. Bruce passed away out there. From the flu, I believe. That must have been in thirty-nine."

She gazes around the room, perhaps imagining how it all looked when she was a girl. Not too different from how it looks now, I would imagine. Visiting the Smythes is a bit like walking into a museum, only the furniture isn't roped off and there's no charge for admission. There is, however, live entertainment. Especially if Deedee is home.

"Well, Mrs. Smythe, I'd better get going."

She starts to rise, but I motion her back down.

"Don't worry about me. I can see myself out."

"What a sweet girl," she says. "I do enjoy your visits."

Outside, the wind stirs the trees into releasing more leaves. They glide down into my path as I recross the yard. It's so tranquil here. I would be heartbroken to leave. After touring Mission Up and seeing how many people were packed in there, living in sunburnt and joyless blight, I'm sure Gregory must look at a place like this and think how unjust it is. Maybe he'd be right. But I love it all the same. There's enough ugliness in the world without having to feel guilty about the beauty.

Again I give the shed a wide berth. A feeling of presence emanates from the little building. The afternoon sun turns the windowpane into a mirror, so there's no seeing within, but the shed gives off the vibe of occupation. I sense Rick there. If I venture too close, I'll have to knock on the door and say something. How could I not?

Why wait?

Good question. He's in there now doing Lord knows what. There's no point in pretending otherwise. I don't want to see him, but I want him to know I know he's there. I want to remind him he still has responsibilities.

"It's your son's birthday today." I announce this to the backyard in general. "In your head, you might be on some kind of journey, but as far as Eli's concerned, you're just sitting in the shed, pretending none of us are here. I just hope it's worth it, that's all."

I wait to see whether he'll respond.

Nothing.

"Well, I'm not going to waste my breath anymore."

Pause. Still no answer.

I go back in the house, slamming the door loud enough to wake the dead. Uh-oh. Frozen in place at the foot of the stairs, I listen for movement in the bedroom. Nothing up there either. Loud enough to wake the dead, but not the deadbeat, apparently.

This house is full of crazy.

All I need is a few more inmates and I can give Mother Zacchaeus a run for her money.

*

The cake arrives first.

"You have to keep it refrigerated," Gregory says, as if this might not have occurred to me.

I slip it into the freezer. I've already cleared out the space.

"How's Sam doing?"

"Not a peep," I say. "Let's get one thing crystal clear: you can stay and have some cake, but then you're taking her home."

"I was thinking we'd drive back in the morning. It would be awkward bringing her over to Dad's for the night, don't you think?"

"She can't stay here."

"We don't have to decide anything right this second. I've got to get over to the school and collect Eli. I told him this morning I'd do the honors."

Then he's out the door.

Nice. He had a plan all along and didn't fill me in. That's obvious at this point.

At a quarter to three, Holly arrives, a present under her arm, here to lend me her moral support. Let me just say, the girl knows how to wrap. You can always tell who's never had kids by the effort they put into other people's children. She's used some kind of masculine-looking brown craft paper, with raw leather bootlaces in place of ribbon. Eli will take one look and think it's cool. The red-and-blue balloon paper I wound around the Nikes won't elicit the same response. I make a few admiring remarks about her wrapping prowess, then lower my voice to fill her in on the events of the day so far.

The more I talk, the wider Holly's eyes get. By the time I'm finished, they're about to pop out.

"You mean she's up there now?" she whispers, hand to her chest.

I nod.

Then a troublemaking smile crosses Holly's lips. "Beth," she says. "I want to sneak a look."

"Holly Ringwald, no you don't!"

But she's already tiptoeing up the stairs. I follow behind, just in case there's trouble. I've been dreading the moment Sam comes to her senses ever since we tucked her in.

Holly opens the door a crack to peer in.

"Don't wake her up."

She pulls the door shut. "It breaks my heart."

"You should see the place," I say. "It's like nothing I've ever seen. But at least that nun is trying to do something."

"I'm happy you made it out in one piece. Do you think it's safe, keeping her here?"

"She's safer, no doubt about that. I'm not sure about the rest of us."

As we descend the stairs, I hear the front door opening. Eli tosses his backpack on the front sofa, Gregory bringing up the rear.

"I told Damon he could come over."

"It's your party," I say. "You can invite anybody you want."

"It's not a party. We're just having cake."

"Suit yourself. And say hi to Ms. Holly."

For a non-party party, this one goes surprisingly smooth. Damon arrives, one of those teens who's inarticulate in the presence of adults but with his peers dominates the conversation. Not my favorite, but in our corner of Lutherville, age-appropriate companions are thin on the ground. It's older money in these parts, in every sense of the word. The boys go upstairs to Eli's room. I tell them to be quiet without explaining why. In the meantime, Holly and I lay the cake and plates out, light some candles, and discuss under our breath how to broach the topic of drug use with a sixteen-year-old.

Is it Damon he gets the weed from? If so, I'd like to wring the boy's neck.

Gregory floats on the outskirts, coming in and out of the kitchen as we set up, strangely tongue-tied. It's Holly's fault. Tall, attractive, and spoken for—that's my brother's type.

"So that's your brother," she says. "Now I see who Jed takes after."

Deedee and Roy appear at the screen door. He carries one of Deedee's paintings, a smaller canvas about two feet by two, keeping the image hidden next to his chest until he gets the signal to reveal.

"What have we here?" I ask.

"If you hate it, you just have to say so. Only I thought since it's the boy's birthday . . ." Deedee draws a circle in the air with her finger, the cue for Roy to flip the canvas.

"It's a study," she says.

"That's . . . nice."

"You do hate it, Elizabeth. I thought you might."

"No, no," I say. "It's just unexpected. I think Eli will love it."

Roy finds a suitable niche on the counter and props the painting with a jar of flour.

"Oh, I get it," Holly says, slapping her thigh like she's just understood the punch line of a joke. "The beard threw me off at first. That's *wild*."

Wild is right. Staring back at me from the counter is a sort of Byzantine icon depicting my husband, Rick, with a bushy, forked beard and an outsized halo. He's looking at me like I'm a great disappointment. Whatever sympathy I might have had for desert fathers dries up in the heat of that painted glare.

"If the boys miss him," I say, "they can feast their eyes on that."

Out of the corner of my eye, I catch Roy wincing. Holly touches my back as if to steady me. But Deedee, whom you might expect to take offense at this jibe, seems delighted. She comes around the island and gives me a hug. "You've got spirit, you know that?"

The thing is, silly as it is, knowing the kind of prices Deedee's artwork is supposed to fetch, I've always had this daydream of her presenting me with something. I have never collected art, but I do appreciate it. I don't go to museums because there's never enough time to do them justice, not because I'm a philistine. Moral of the story: be careful what you wish for.

Roy wasn't kidding about Rick ending up in the mural, I guess.

"This is really generous of you, Deedee. Thank you. I mean it."

"It's only a study, like I said, and I'm not sure I'm happy with the expression yet. But I'm getting there, Elizabeth. I have the germ."

Meaning, she has the idea, not some kind of virus.

Jed arrives. Eli and Damon come down. Instead of acting the part of graceless teen, Eli brightens when he sees the size of the audience, deciding to turn on the charm. He recognizes the subject of the painting immediately and thanks Deedee profusely. You'd think he had spent the last few days in agony, wishing he had a portrait of his father in the get-up of some medieval saint to hang over the mantel. The messenger bag from Holly is just what he needed too. He goes straight into the living room with it, emptying the contents of his backpack right into the new case.

Even I get the special treatment. He shucks off his old shoes and puts on the black Nikes right in the kitchen. "They feel like they were made for my feet."

"I'm the one who picked them," Jed says. "Mom wanted to get you Reeboks."

"You said he wanted Crocs!"

We all laugh, and I realize the non-party hasn't gone off the rails. Even the cake is tasty, good enough that I finish a whole slice.

The crazy has been contained and everyone seems happy. Holly winks, reading my mind. Sometimes the volcano smokes and doesn't erupt.

"Am I interrupting?"

Rick's voice. I turn toward the sound. He stands in the threshold, holding a plastic bag in two hands, several days' worth of stubble on his cheeks. He nods to everyone, edging into the kitchen, holding the bag out to Eli. Our son reaches inside, removing an open-faced cardboard display box with something shiny and brown inside. Eli's eyes light up with astonishment, a real reaction that gives the lie to his earlier act. He has to use scissors to cut the ties holding whatever Rick's given him into the box.

As he wrestles with the package, I study my husband, a familiar-looking stranger. He returns my look, then notices something on the counter. His eyes dart to the painting, then back to me. He does a double take.

"Dad," Eli says, "this is *amazing*."

"I'm . . ." Rick can't take his eyes off that painting. "I'm glad you like it."

And Eli does like it. He wrenches the final tie free and holds his present up for everyone to see. He might as well be clutching a trophy.

"That's nice," Deedee says. Then, turning to Roy: "What *is* it?"

"A Brooks saddle," Eli says. "It's the one with the copper rivets." He turns it over in his hand. "And copper rails!"

"It's a seat for his bike," Jed explains to a still-baffled Deedee.

Rick tears his eyes away from the painting. Dazed. He moves closer to me, close enough that we could touch if either one of us were so inclined.

"You see that, right?" he says.

"What, the painting? Deedee did it."

He exhales in relief. "I thought I was going nuts," he says, then shuffles away to Eli's side.

The party breaks up when Eli goes outside with Damon to replace the old seat on his bike with this gleaming new one. Jed is telling the rest of us more than we'd ever want to know about bicycle saddles. Suffice it to say, this is the best of the best. Rick must have gotten it when he took Eli's tire in to be repaired. I had assumed he would ignore his son's birthday entirely, while all along he'd planned on making this surprise appearance.

Deedee and Roy say their good-byes, taking a slice of cake home for Margaret. As they leave, Holly tries several times to rope Rick into conversation, but he shuts her down with one monosyllabic reply after another. Gregory leans in to inspect the painting closely, and I lose track of where Jed has gone. As for myself, I can't take my eyes off Rick. I feel like I should say something, only I don't know what.

Stay here. Don't go back.

"You have to admit it's pretty strange," Holly is saying. "I've never heard of anyone living in a shed for a whole month."

"Hmm," Rick replies.

"I wonder what this thing is worth," Gregory says. "You say she's a famous painter? How much do her pieces go for?"

Holly again: "At least have some cake. You haven't given up chocolate, have you?"

"Hmm, no."

Tidying up, I glance through the sink window. The shed door is ajar, and Roy is standing guard out front, holding Margaret's slice of cake. They didn't leave after all. Deedee is taking this chance to inspect the hermit's lair. Roy sees me and shrugs. As I watch, Deedee appears and the two of them creep home, leaving the shed door half open.

"Mom."

Jed's at my elbow, whispering in my ear.

"What is it?"

"There's a girl upstairs. I was going up to my room and ran into her in the hallway. She locked herself in your bedroom."

"That's Sam," I say. "I'll take care of it."

I leave Holly to interrogate Rick while my Marxist brother speculates on the value of art. Jed follows me up, breathing hard with excitement. First I go into his room, taking a pencil and paper from the desk.

"What are you doing?"

"Watch and learn."

I slide the paper under my bedroom door and use the pencil to push the old key out of the other side of the lock. It thumps to the ground. When I retrieve the paper, there's the key.

"Cool," Jed says.

"It's all right, Sam. I'm coming in."

I throw the door open, bracing for conflict. The bedsheets are rumpled, but there's no one there.

"Sam?"

I peer into the closet, then get on my hands and knees to check under the bed.

"Mom, the window."

Sure enough, the sash window stands open. I get there and lean outside just in time to see Sam shimmy to the ground and disappear behind the corner of the house.

"She's going round back. Come on!"

"Mom," he says. "Who's this Sam?"

No time for explanations. I call down to Gregory, then run into him at the foot of the stairs. Holly and Rick look on in astonishment.

"She's getting away," I exclaim, feeling ridiculous.

We pour out into the backyard, looking for signs of the escaping girl.

From the far side of the stone wall, Deedee calls out, "She went in there."

I follow her pointing finger to the now-closed door of Rick's shed. Of course. I head for the door, but Rick grabs my arm.

"Let me."

The first time he's touched me since the night the Shaws came.

I stop in my tracks, letting him go ahead. He puts his hand on the doorknob, pauses to collect himself, then pushes through. The door closes behind him.

The rest of us gather in a crowd, watching and waiting. Deedee and Roy come and rejoin us.

"What do you think's going on in there?" Gregory asks.

Jed leans toward me. "Who's the girl, anyway?"

"It's a junkie your mom brought home," Holly says, which earns her a caustic look from Gregory.

"Home to live?" Jed asks.

Deedee laughs out loud. "This place is getting more and more interesting!"

A minute passes. The others lapse into conversation. I try to tune out the nervous chatter. I can't even hear myself think. After five minutes, they fall silent again.

"It's been a long time," Roy says.

"You think he's all right in there?"

Gregory sniffs. "You think *he* is?"

The door opens. We wait to see who will appear.

Sam emerges into the light. She blinks at the sky, her arms tightly coiled around her body like she's cold. She takes a step toward us, recognizing Gregory.

"I want to go home," she says.

"Are you all right?"

"I want to go home."

"First thing in the morning," he begins.

"Not in the morning. Now. I want to go now."

"But—"

"You heard her," I tell him.

Sam walks through our little crowd, which parts to let her pass. Gregory follows her. "I guess we're leaving?"

"Call me when you get there, no matter how late."

When he's gone, I turn back toward the shed. The door is closed.

"I guess that's that," Holly says.

"The good thing is, she's going home. When I tried to convince her before, she didn't want to go."

Jed shakes his head, still trying to process everything. "I wonder what Dad said to her."

"I guess we won't get a chance to ask."

"So," Deedee says. "Let me get this straight. You couldn't get her to go home. She wanted to stay in some crack house downtown? And she talks to Rick for five minutes and he turns her completely around?"

"It's not a crack house—"

But she isn't listening. "His first miracle," she says to Roy. "And this is only the first week. Wait and see, I tell you. Wait and see."

They head back to the big house.

"Now, she's a hoot," Holly says. "'His first miracle.' And can you believe that painting? Are you going to hang it up over your bed?"

I see her lips moving, but I don't hear what she says. There's a high-pitched noise in my ear, a wiry tremolo. And like Rick looking around the kitchen to make sure he wasn't the only one who could see the painting, I glance at Jed and Holly, amazed that they can't hear the sound.

It's like Kathie Shaw's tinnitus, canceling out every other sound. A throbbing whine you were never meant to hear but cannot ignore.

chapter 10

A Night Visitor

Every morning a clump of fresh flowers lies at Rick's threshold, partly obscured under the falling leaves. I'm not sure where Deedee's picking them. Maybe she drops in on the florist each afternoon during her break from painting. Since the birthday party, we don't see her as much. According to Roy, she spends most of her time working on the mural.

"It's extraordinary the way she goes at it," he tells me. "The priest had the bishop over for a look, and he seemed almost jealous that she wasn't doing her mural for the cathedral. You really should go by and see it."

But I haven't visited the parish church. Why should I? I get an eyeful every time I climb the stairs. Without even asking permission, Eli drove a nail dead center in the upstairs landing and hung Deedee's portrait of his sainted father. Hauling clean laundry upstairs, I keep imagining myself tripping and falling backward. Landing at the foot of the stairs, my legs twisted at odd angles, the painted Rick staring down at me, thinking, *Serves you right.*

Days have passed and I still haven't confronted Eli about the marijuana. I make a point of sniffing him when he comes home. So far, nothing. Maybe Gregory got it wrong? I don't think so. More likely, Eli knows his uncle recognized the smell. He's taking more precautions now. This could be all in my head, but I imagine him on his guard around me, waiting for the moment I bring the subject up, ready with counterarguments.

So I'm biding my time, hoping to catch him off guard.

While cooking or doing dishes, washing and folding clothes, I remember the flat expression on Sam's face when she emerged from the shed. Resignation, I guess. What did Rick say to her? I imagine him giving some kind of Scared Straight speech, taking advantage of her disorientation. If life at Mission Up wasn't enough to scare her straight, though, how could Rick manage the job? Try as I might, I can't visualize that scene.

I've called Gregory several times to check on the girl's progress back home. After the joyous, tearful reunion—most of the emotion coming from her mother—Greg managed to get her into a drug counseling program. But she's depressed, he says, rarely leaving the house. She hasn't returned to class and probably won't anytime soon. I suppose Rick's miracle only went so far. From the description, it sounds like Sam is anything but healed.

"Is that how you want to end up?" In my imagination, I confront Eli with the question. And in my imagination, he breaks down and renounces pot in perpetuity.

I keep the key to Stacy's beach house on my nightstand. I'm still sleeping on my side of the bed. If I'm careful, I can turn the covers back and get a good night's sleep without disturbing the tucked-in side where my husband used to sleep.

*

"You can't drop out," Holly says. "You can't put your whole life on hold."

The phone feels warm in my hand, we've been talking so long. Talking in circles, rehashing the same themes.

"How am I dropping out?"

"What about last night? You missed the makeup party."

"That was last night?" Another one of the church ladies selling cosmetics on the side. The printed invitation is pinned to the fridge with magnets, half covered by another invitation to a party about cooking utensils.

"You're supposed to be my wingman at these things."

"Your wing-person," I say. "And I thought you were *my* wing-person."

"Ha, ha. It was funny the first ten times you said it. The point is, you're bailing on things. People notice stuff like that."

"I'm supposed to be on vacation."

"Yeah, but everybody knows by now that you're not. The boys are still showing up to school every day. People see you at the grocery store."

"Can't I take a break? Look at Rick. Nobody's giving him a hard time."

Which isn't exactly true. I keep taking messages from Jim Shaw, who doesn't understand why Rick never returns his calls. I leave Post-its on the bathroom mirror every morning, reminding Rick that Jim's waiting. I even go to Starbucks every morning for an hour, sipping coffee I could have made for myself at home, giving my husband time to sneak into the house, use the bathroom, and (hopefully) take a shower. He never leaves any notes in reply, even though I placed the stack of Post-its on the back of the toilet with a pen on top.

"Just don't forget about tonight," Holly says.

"What's tonight?"

"It's the book club, Beth!"

"The book club, right. Which book is it again?"

"You're killing me, you know that? Let's meet for lunch."

"I have plans for lunch."

"Really? What plans?"

"Plans," I say. "I have to go to Barnes and Noble, for one thing."

"To get the book." Her frustration escapes in a loud sigh. "I don't know what I'm going to do with you, Beth. I really don't."

Ninety minutes later, alone in the Barnes and Noble café between a neurotic-looking man doing what looks like grad school math homework and a table full of young mothers rolling strollers back and forth with one hand and holding caramel Frappucinos in the other, I sit staring at the back cover of tonight's book.

The two groups I belong to couldn't be more different. One of them, which Holly calls the Smart Girls, is mostly professional women, trying to keep up with all the books everybody is talking about . . . everyone who listens to public radio, at any rate. Despite the group's unofficial name, hanging with these overachieving ladies, I feel anything but smart.

The second group, the one meeting tonight, Holly calls the Bodice Rippers. The nickname isn't entirely fair. Yes, there are plenty of bodices in the books these ladies choose, along with corsets, bustles, and bonnets, but rarely does any of that dainty lace get ripped. Instead, the invariably strong-willed heroines keep their Brinks-level chastity belts locked tight. They find God and they get their man.

The Bodice Rippers read to escape, and the Smart Girls read to keep up. Holly reads to have a good-natured laugh at them both (though she enjoys the books on both sides immensely, whatever she may pretend to the contrary). And me? I guess I show up just to help. I'm always afraid that the night I don't show up, nobody else will come either. I hate to leave the organizers in the lurch.

If there's one thing I hate more than that, though, it's having to keep the two groups separated. The ladies are all from The Community. Most are at least acquainted with each other. But they run in different circles and turn their noses up at what the other group is reading. The Smart Girls pump me for ridiculous details about what the Bodice Rippers are reading, while the Bodice Rippers try to get me to agree that the Smart Girls only read so people will keep thinking they're smart.

At least with Pampered Chef, all you have to do is show up! There's not a three-hundred-page cover charge to gain admission.

The moms at the next table leaf through magazines and drop the first names of a bunch of celebrities as if they're people the women know. Whenever one of their phones pings with a new text message, the conversation lulls, but they talk straight through any noise that the various babies make. When the moms laugh too loudly, the math nerd on the other side of me gives them a stern look. Not that they notice.

"I can't hear myself think," he mutters, snapping his textbook shut.

But he doesn't leave. He digs through the satchel between his feet and finds a set of earphones. Soon he's cocooned in a buffer of preemptive sound, still looking perturbed.

On the front cover of my book, a nondescript beauty in black mourning holds a small bouquet of blood-red flowers. Over her shoulder, a rakish hero stands with his back to her, twisting his head around to give a view of his nondescriptly handsome face. They look like models in costumes, not historical people. I'm going to buy the book, but this cover irritates me.

Confession: I don't actually want everybody to be beautiful, not in that unlined, creaseless, symmetrical way. Android beauty, like it comes out of a test tube. Beauty without blemish or mark. Not only do I not identify with such people, I don't believe in them either. I don't even find them attractive. This is what makes watching television so hard: they don't cast actors anymore, only models. When they make the movie of *my* life, they'd better cast a character actor in the lead.

Don't try to tell me I'm not a character.

I have a balance on one of my gift cards, which takes the sting out of buying the book. Instead of retreating to the house, I drive around for a while and end up at Panera, where I hold down a table for the rest of the afternoon, flipping pages as fast as I can.

*

In the end, I lose my nerve. The thought of making an appearance in front of the Bodice Rippers is too much for me. They'll ask about Rick. If Stacy's there, she'll want to know why I'm still not in Florida. There will be too much explaining to do.

And then they'll ask me what I thought about the novel.

At home, I hole up in my bedroom. Eli comes and goes,

followed by Jed. At dusk, Holly starts calling. Probably to offer me a ride. After the third or fourth attempt, I switch off my phone.

"You're being stupid," I tell myself.

Snatching up the novel, I head downstairs, fully intending to go to the book club. What did I skim the novel for, if I'm not going to go? But I leave the book on the kitchen counter, pretending I'll pick it up on the way out, knowing I'm not going anywhere. Night falls and I curl up in an armchair, letting the clock tick down.

A funny thing about me: when I skip out, I also hide out. I don't cut one event to enjoy another. Instead I hunker down at home where no one can observe me playing hooky. "You might as well have gone," Rick will say, not understanding. Once the start time has passed and there's no chance of making it to the book club in time, I breathe a sigh of relief.

A knock at the door.

Jed and Eli don't knock, of course. They come and go as they please. So it must be Holly, driving over in person to call my bluff. Well, I won't give her the satisfaction.

Only it doesn't sound like Holly's knock. For one thing, Holly would pound on the door. *"I know you're in there. Your car is in the driveway. Come on out before I come in and get you!"* This knock is tentative, and there's no follow-up. A knock that's done its duty and is ready to give up.

Overwhelmed with curiosity, I go to the front window and ease one of the blinds up for a peek. The porch light is turned off. Whoever's at the door is standing too close for me to get a good look. But I can see the back of her profile—it's a woman, but not Holly. This one is smaller, thinner, with a wild explosion of hair. Goose bumps raise on my forearm. I think it's Sam.

I rush to the door. Before opening, I take a deep breath.

"Oh," I say. "Hi."

"If this is too weird, me turning up like this, just say something and I'll take off."

It's not Sam. It's Marlene. The dreadlocked girl from the Rent-a-Mob meeting. The one who used to be in Jed's youth group, who made such an impression on him. He'll be sorry he wasn't here.

"Come in, come in," I say, urging her inside. I reach for the wall switch, bathing the porch in warm, gold light.

This is perfect. If Holly complains about my nonattendance, I can tell her an unexpected visitor turned up.

"I'm sorry to just show up like this. I would've called, but I don't know your number."

"It wouldn't have made a difference. I turned off my phone."

"What happened the other day, it didn't feel right. It's kind of been chewing at me ever since. I still know some people from the church, so I asked how to get in touch. One of my friends told me you lived next door to that wonderful house. I've always loved that place."

"It is wonderful. The people who live there are wonderful too."

She nods. "I know Deedee Smythe—I mean, I know *of* her. I know her work."

Marlene's dreads are loose and free, and she wears an ankle-length tank dress, an old-lady sweater, and sandals, with an oversized fringed bag slung across her chest. She declines coffee and soda but perks up at the mention of tea, eventually choosing Darjeeling from the box of packets I hold out for inspection. Milk and no sugar. While I boil water, she looks around the kitchen, peering down hallways and up the stairs, her hands clutching the strap of her bag.

"I know it's strange to just turn up out of the blue—"

"Stop apologizing, Marlene. I'm happy to see you. If you look up those stairs, you can see an example of Deedee's recent work. She's painting a mural at the Catholic church just up the hill." I wait until she's had a few moments to inspect the picture. "You recognize who it is?"

"Oh," she says. "How funny."

"I'm not sure who he's meant to be. Not Judas, anyway, or he wouldn't get a halo, right?"

"Probably not. To be honest, I didn't realize she was still painting. The way people talked about her when I was growing up, I assumed she was retired."

"You grew up around here, then?"

She nods. "Over toward Loch Raven, on Chapelwood."

"Wow," I say. "Nice."

"They sold the house after the divorce, but I still drive by sometimes. It's strange to think of other people living there. But this place is really great. Did it used to be part of the big house?"

"Everything around here was. There's another carriage house kind of thing, and some outbuildings. The family has sold off bits and pieces over time. Deedee and her mother are the last of the line, I guess, and after Margaret's gone, Deedee threatens to move to California."

"I could never do that," she says. "No seasons."

"I know, right. This is my favorite time of year."

When the tea is brewed, Marlene clutches her mug in two hands, inhaling the steam. She's such a *cute* girl, really. If she'd take some of the metal out of her face, get rid of those awful dreads . . .

She notices the book on the counter for the first time. Sets her mug down to pick it up. As she flips the pages absently, I wither inside. Embarrassed.

"It's for a book club," I say, rolling my eyes. "I decided to skip it. I just couldn't get through the thing. You know how it is."

Now my cheeks feel hot. It's like the Jesus fish all over.

She sets the book down. "It's been a long time since I've gotten to read anything for enjoyment."

"They keep you busy in school," I say, wishing it had been a Smart Girls book on the counter. Why'd it have to be a Bodice Ripper?

"So, the reason I came . . . the thing is, your sudden exit really stirred things up. We had a good discussion after that, a lot of us. I guess you could say that I was deputized, though I did volunteer. Everybody wants to, like, apologize."

"Apologize for what?"

"I think you know. We kind of turned on you all the sudden. I feel kind of ashamed."

"Oh, don't say that."

"I do. And I apologize. You were going out on a limb even showing up, and we pretty much hacked the limb off. Chas was really bummed out. He would've come himself, but I thought it would be weird if a whole bunch of us showed up unannounced."

"Well . . . apology accepted. Thank you."

"There's more."

"I don't think I can take any more."

"We would like it if you would consider coming to D.C. with us. So we can make it up to you."

"The big demo? I don't know, Marlene—"

"Don't say no. Just think about it. You have no idea how much fun it will be. All those people together in one place, letting our voices be heard. It's liberating. Really. It's better than a concert even. And it's peace, Beth. It's not abortion or gay marriage or anything that might get you in trouble." She grins over her mug at me. "Everybody wants peace."

You'd be surprised, I think. I'll bet Peggy Ensign doesn't. Of course, last time we met, Marlene thought everybody was pro-choice too. It's surprising how much we can know, and still *not* know the world as it really is.

Eli comes in through the back door, carrying his new messenger bag. He stops in his tracks, looking at Marlene. Then he smiles. "You're not the same girl."

"This is Marlene," I say.

"Nice to meet you. I thought for a minute you were the junkie from the other day."

"The *what*?"

"It's an inside joke," I say. "Eli, have you eaten?"

He's already heading for the stairs. "Over at Damon's."

"My son," I explain. "He just turned sixteen. You were in the youth group with my other son, Jed."

"I remember. He's really tall."

"He's grown a lot since then."

As if on cue, Jed appears. He recognizes her at once, despite the facial jewelry and the hair. If anything, these changes make her more fascinating to him. He stands there, staring, answering my motherly questions in monosyllables. Marlene notices the attention and glances away bashfully. They are nothing like the couple on the book cover lying faceup between them, but I can't help seeing the similarities.

Oh, Jed.

"I was just telling your mom about this demo in D.C., trying to get her to come. A whole bunch of us are going down for it. You should too."

Jed clears his throat. "Okay. Sounds great."

"Awesome," she says, glancing away again.

My turn to interrupt. "You know, I haven't said *I'm* going."

"Mom," he says, managing to pack so much into the word. I'm embarrassing him just by being here, and betraying him by not going along with the plan.

Unlike Eli, Jed won't clear out. He lingers silently, which pretty much kills the conversation. Suddenly the age gap between Marlene and me seems a mile wide. She finishes her tea and apologizes again and practically begs me not to back out of the D.C. trip. Jed burns holes in me with his laser beam eyes as she makes the final appeal.

"I guess I'd better get going," she says.

"Let me write my number down, in case you want to call." I jot my mobile number down on a pad, then get her to write down hers. Then I walk her to the door, Jed following a few steps behind.

After she's gone, I turn to confront him.

"Now, don't get any ideas, my boy."

"Ideas about what?"

He doesn't stick around for an answer. Now that Marlene's gone, there's nothing to interest him downstairs. I return to the kitchen to clean up. I switch on my phone, now that I have an excuse to give Holly. When I reach for the pad to program Marlene's number in, the page is missing, ripped out, the perforated leftovers sticking out of the coiled wire.

"Oh, Jed."

*

After microwaving the last of my tea, I take the mug out back. Sitting in one of the outdoor chairs, I gaze up at the sky overhead, a soft throw somebody from church gave Rick for Christmas a few years ago around my shoulders. The moon and stars are hidden behind thick clouds, bringing heaven closer to earth, almost to the treetops, or so it seems from my seated position. As I watch, the cloud cover shifts. The wind pushes it gently from left to right. It's easy, watching this movement, to imagine the earth spinning, to imagine myself perched on the uppermost curve of the world. Some ancient, experiencing it the same way, would have mistaken this for a spiritual experience. I wonder sometimes how much of our understanding is based on what amounts to optical illusions.

The shed is dark tonight. What is Rick doing in there? I try to imagine and find that I can't. As near as the structure is, it seems more distant to me than the clouds above. Rick feels less present somehow. I no longer sense him out here the way I did at the beginning of his exile.

That's progress of a sort.

I could feel him everywhere once, during the first weeks after we met. I was a senior in college, pre-law, excellent grades, already on track for my stellar career. My parents loved the idea of a lawyer daughter, and I loved the thought that I could help people. Already I'd interned at a firm that did lots of pro bono work. One of the partners had even told me I had an affinity for the law.

All of that ambition turned fuzzy when I met Rick. It slipped into the region of memory where the distant past is stored. I spent all my time with him, and when I wasn't with him, I was thinking about him. He had a way of filling my life, always present. I could almost talk to him in my head.

I was lovesick, in other words, and he felt the same way about me.

My friends thought I was crazy. His thought the same about him. They told themselves it wouldn't last, that if it went on much longer they would have to intervene. So we dropped them, which left more time for each other. Time we put to use the way young couples obsessed with one another do.

The reality check arrived in the form of a plus sign on the pregnancy test. That's how I told him, by showing him the stick. He didn't take it the way I expected.

"I think this is a sign," he said. "It confirms what I've felt all along."

The sign said we should be together. The sign also said we should elope.

I graduated with honors, with a wedding ring (which I wore on a chain around my neck, since we hadn't told my parents yet) and with an eight-week-old Jed growing inside me, concealed under the flowing cap and gown.

For a long time after that, we were happy. I never felt like I'd given up my life in favor of Rick's. I never felt like the ministry thing was his career; I felt like we were doing it together, side by side. When we had Eli, we were thrilled. The first years at The Community were wonderful too. It was later that things started to change. After the church grew so large that most of the people there became strangers. After Rick accepted the job title that started to alienate him from himself.

He didn't understand any better than I did what a Men's Pastor was meant to do, but he was determined to be a great one. He had to take up golf, learn racquetball and handball. He had to follow sports in general much more than he'd ever done in the past. All the theology books from school went into boxes, replaced by the leadership handbooks, the best-selling self-help books, the guides to masculinity written by men who could only access the concept via cliché.

Ten years ago, even five years ago, Jim Shaw's instinct about Rick would have been right. He did have a voice that mattered. He did have something important to say. But the last few years have changed him, hollowed him out. Is it any wonder he feels less present to me, when he's hardly present to himself?

I'm not sure how much of this Rick could admit to. In the old days, I'd form a judgment on something only to find, when I shared it, that Rick saw things the same way. Now, not so much. He's trying so hard to live up to expectations that he can't admit to himself those expectations aren't worth living up to.

Of course, it's always possible I'm the one who's wrong. Not everyone sees him the way I do. Clearly, Deedee has a different take.

These offerings of hers really puzzle me.

For a woman who's lived her life alone, who has devoted herself to painting rather than a man, Rick's actions must look so different. What looks to me like a deadbeat, she interpreted right from the start as some kind of hermit saint. Why was she so quick to idolize him?

Does she see something of herself in him?

Or perhaps it's just the opposite. She sees something in him that is completely different, something utterly inaccessible to her imagination. A challenge.

You don't leave flowers for yourself, after all.

You don't appoint yourself to be your muse.

"You know what it is, Ricky boy. She admires you. Whatever she thinks you're doing, it's something she wishes she could do herself. But what that is, I don't have a clue."

I gaze at the shed, waiting for a reply. Nothing comes.

The last time I was outside enjoying the night, Gregory was walking with me. It's hard to remember the details of that walk—all the intervening drama has blurred them—but there was one thing he said that seemed important. How did he put it? *"Maybe this isn't Rick's time"*—it was something like that. Maybe this wasn't Rick's time, it was mine.

What would *my time* even look like? A bus ride to our nation's capital with a bunch of fruit loops and an infatuated son? A road trip down to Florida, maybe in a rented convertible, the wind whipping in my hair? Or something else entirely? Something I can't even begin to imagine?

I take my mug inside, pausing at the door.

"Good night, Rick."

A little wind, a little birdsong, leaves rustling across the lawn. But no reply from the shed. I wash out my mug, find room for the historical novel on the bookshelf, and retreat upstairs, full of the sense of possibility. Why shouldn't this be my time?

The only question is what to do with it. Not what I've *been* doing, I know that much.

On the nightstand, Stacy's key.

I really should have insisted on her taking it back. This key has become a symbol of derailment, the alternate autumn I was meant to live. It's a painful reminder.

I squeeze the floaty in my hand. Hard.

It smells of plastic, and when I drop the key, my hand smells of plastic too. But when I bring it to my face and inhale the scent of my skin, I pretend what I'm smelling is the salty, crashing sea.

chapter 11

Only Trying to Help

Blame everything on the dream.

Or rather, me waking up in the middle of the dream.

At five in the morning, stumbling down the hall from the bathroom, Jed or Eli (I don't know which) must have knocked something over (I don't know what). I hear the crash just as Mother Zacchaeus removes one of the enamel pins from her shirt to stick it onto mine. The sound startles her, and she drives the sharp back right through the fabric of my top and into my skin.

"Ouch," I say, only to find myself bolt upright in bed, blinking in the dark.

When your dreams run their course, you remember them the next day *as* dreams—assuming you remember them at all. When you wake up in the middle, though, the dream stays real. I can feel Mother Zacchaeus's presence in the bedroom with me, not to mention the pain in my chest from where she stuck the pin.

What had she been doing? Giving me an award for distinguished service.

"You saved that girl, Beth. You *are* a good Christian woman."

Disoriented, I switch on the lamp. It's strange not to find Mother Zacchaeus in the room. Then I remember that crashing sound. What was it? Swinging my legs over the side of the bed, I step into my slippers and creep into the hallway to investigate. My toe collides with something on the floor. Whatever it is, it's light enough to go skidding over the floorboards.

I switch on the light. From the ground, St. Rick stares up at me. The nail he used to hang from is there on the floor too. Eli must have pounded it straight into the plaster, which has a tendency to crumble, and at a right angle. The weight of the painting, though slight, would have been enough to work the nail out over time. I keep a lecture on file in my brain: the evils of not using the special plaster hangers to put pictures on the wall. But it's five in the morning. I'm not going to wake him up to go over the fine points of decorating.

Besides, no harm done. Not much anyway. I pick the painting up to inspect for damage and find one of the corners dimpled from impact.

I frown at St. Rick. "Serves *you* right."

The next morning, while I'm digging through the drawer where I keep the plaster hangers, Holly calls. Before she can give me a hard time for my no-show at the book club, I butt in with Marlene's unexpected visit.

"I'm a little worried Jed has a crush on this girl," I tell her. This makes it sound like I'm sharing because of Jed, not to get off the hook.

But Holly's not interested in my son's love life. I missed more than a bodice ripping last night. The book barely came up. The ladies were too busy talking about the latest scandal.

"It's probably better you weren't there," she says. "Apparently the drug-sniffing dogs at Eli's school found marijuana in a lot of kids' lockers. Including two who are in the youth group at The Community. Thanks to zero tolerance, that's an automatic suspension. One of the kids posted on Facebook that all of his friends do it, and it's unfair to single out only the people who got caught."

While she goes on, describing the reactions at the book club, all I can hear is the blood pounding in my head.

"Who are the kids?" I finally ask.

She mentions the names, but I don't recognize them. Eli knows them, I'm sure. And they'll know him too. I lean on the counter to steady myself. I feel physically sick.

"It's terrible," I say.

"I know, I know. But the way some of those ladies go on about it, you'd think they were never in high school themselves. Don't get me wrong. I'm not condoning anything. Still, you have to admit, there are worse things those kids could be into. Look at your houseguest from the other day."

"I feel for their parents."

"Yeah, you have a point there. They'll have a hard time showing their faces at church. It shouldn't be that way, though, if you ask me."

"No, it shouldn't," I say, too emphatically.

When I get off the phone, all I can think is, *That could have been Eli*. The bad part is, I've known for days and still haven't said anything. I wanted confirmation. I imagined him denying everything and then rebelling. Or worse, pretending to mend his ways only to hatch more sophisticated plans for deceiving me.

What he needs is a wake-up call. Maybe these suspensions

will do the trick. Then again, maybe not. There has to be something I can do, something to make sure he never touches the stuff again.

"You saved that girl," Mother Zacchaeus says. I feel the pain in my chest again.

"Thank you," I say aloud. She's absolutely right, and she's given me an idea.

So that's how the trouble started.

*

No Cool Mom sunglasses for me. I let Eli get a good look at my baby browns. Steely and merciless. Impossible to question. He puts his bike in the back, careful not to scratch his new Brooks saddle. When he slips into the passenger seat, he looks uneasy.

"What's going on?"

"You'll see," I tell him. "Trust me."

As we drive south into town, Eli's earphones come out of the bag. He cranks some tunes and starts slapping out the rhythm on his thigh. I smile. This show of absorption has the opposite effect of what he intends.

"You're trying too hard," I say.

He pretends not to hear me.

Soon enough, his hands go still. He tugs on the white wire snaking up his chest, popping the earbuds free.

He knows.

He knows I know about the marijuana. He knows the reckoning is about to come. And I'm pretty sure it's dawned on him where we're going. His brows furrow in concentration. No doubt he is working on his defense, trying to come up with the best strategy for dealing with whatever I have in store for him. He doesn't say anything, though, and neither do I. We're waiting each other out.

Finding Mission Up isn't easy. The first time I visited, I wasn't paying close attention to the route. Plus, this grid of huddled inner-city blocks all looks the same to me. Once I get us to the general vicinity, we cruise up and down the streets in search of the telltale pink accents and the hand-lettered sign. Eli keeps craning his neck at the sights.

"Did you see that?" he says as we roll through an intersection. "Those guys back there?"

"What's the matter? Never seen a deal go down?"

He laughs nervously. "Not out in the open like that."

I'm already past Mission Up before I realize we've found it. As I double back, Eli double-checks that the VW's doors are locked.

"We're not getting out," he says.

"That's where we're going, right across the street."

He shakes his head. "I'm not going anywhere. Are you crazy? Do you realize where we are?"

"I know exactly where we are. That's the place I found Sam, the girl who crashed your birthday party. Come on, Eli. Don't be afraid."

But he isn't budging.

"Come on," I say, popping the lock on my door.

He reaches across to grab my forearm. "Just stop it, okay? You're always pulling stuff like this, and I'm tired of it."

"Stuff like what, Eli?"

"Like this! Like the Rent-a-Mob thing. Whenever I say something you don't like, whenever I do something . . . you get this look in your eye and all the sudden, it's Scared Straight time."

I really shouldn't, but his anxiety makes me laugh. "Scared Straight?"

"You know what I'm talking about. You act like I don't know the way things really are, and you're gonna teach me by dragging me into some awkward situation—'Hey, son, let's go meet the hippies!' 'Hey, look, son! This is where the junkies shoot up! Let's have a look!' Stop laughing at me, Mom. I'm serious. You think you're making things better, but you're not. You're screwing them up." He slumps in his seat, arms folded. "Just like always."

Ouch. That wipes the smile off my face.

There are all these things you're not supposed to say to your kids, things that will demotivate and warp them, things that will make them grow up to be self-loathing axe murderers. But restraint seems to be a one-way street. A teenage boy in anger will say just about anything.

But I'm not giving in. "Let's get this over with, Eli."

"I'm staying right here."

In the end, I have to get out and go around to his door, which he won't unlock, forcing me to use the one power every mother possesses in such situations: shame. I start tapping on the window loudly, telling him not to be scared, and the power of humiliation does the rest. He may be afraid of the strangers on the sidewalk, afraid of what's waiting behind the scary pink door, but he's also sixteen and he will do anything to get his mom to stop embarrassing him in public.

"Okay, fine," he says, slamming his door shut. "Just be quiet, okay?"

He follows me across the street, eyes cast down. At the door, I pause before knocking.

"This isn't about scaring you, Eli. The fact is, you're scaring me. I just want you to see the world you're dabbling in. You need to decide if this is really the direction you want to go."

I'm proud of myself for that little speech, which acknowledges that I know about the weed without coming out and saying it. I'm proud, too, that he doesn't protest his innocence or try to argue. He hangs his head down, defeated. Maybe I'm getting through to him.

I have to rap on the door several times before there's any movement on the other side. Finally, I hear the bar dragging on the floor, the locks sliding open. When the door cracks open, it's not Mother Zacchaeus who answers. It is the girl who sat smoking in Sam's room. She is wearing a sequined tube top and cutoff shorts. Seeing Eli, she throws the door open wide.

"Well, well, what we got here? What your name, big man?"

Eli swallows hard but doesn't look up.

"Aziza, right? Is Mother Zacchaeus here?" I ask.

"Whatsa matter? Don't he talk?"

"Mom, can we just get out of here?"

"Ooohhh," she says. "This your boy? Come on in here and lemme take a look at you. Come on, now." She motions Eli through, but he doesn't budge. "He's shy, ain't he? Don't worry, big man. I ain't gonna bite you or nothing." She laughs, revealing a gold-framed tooth, then pulls a soft pack of Parliaments from her back pocket, offering him one. I wave the pack away. She pulls one free with her lips before tucking the cigarettes away, then fishes a purple plastic lighter out.

"Mother Zacchaeus?" I ask her.

She nods through a cloud of smoke. "She in the back. You go on."

I walk through, pausing for Eli to follow me, along with the girl's chuckles. She puffs smoke in his face as he passes her. Eli looks about as uncomfortable as I've ever seen him. As mothers go, I'm about as protective as they come. But this really couldn't be going any better. It wouldn't surprise me if he threw himself at my feet, promising never to touch marijuana again, if only I'd get him out of here.

I feel the footsteps trembling through the floorboards before I hear them. Eli steps back involuntarily. Then Mother Zacchaeus appears, stomping through the TV lounge from the kitchen, making her way straight for us. The way her eyes flash reminds me of a cartoon bull making its way toward the red cape. "Who's smoking inside?" she roars.

If Aziza didn't inoculate Eli against all future vice, this threatening nun is sure to do the trick.

"You?" Her eyes flash.

"I want you to meet someone," I tell him. "Mother Zacchaeus, may I present my son—"

Her hand flashes quickly.

I catch a snapshot of her open palm, then my cheek explodes.

The shock comes first. *She slapped me!* And then the pain, a hot, throbbing swell of pain. I double over, shielding my face with my hand, fully expecting my eye to pop out at any moment. There's embarrassment, too, because I can feel tears welling up.

"What's wrong with you, lady? You call yourself a good Christian. What's *wrong* with you?"

Mother Zacchaeus spits the words out over my reeling head. *What's wrong with me? You're the one who smacked me—what's wrong with you?* I can only answer her in my mind, though. My jaw has ideas of its own that mainly involve hanging there.

Eli edges forward to try to screen me from the nun. I see his feet, the new black sneakers exceptionally clean. *Don't*, I think. But there's no danger of Eli retaliating. He keeps inching forward only to move back again.

"You know what you is? You know? You a kidnapper, that's what. Aziza, why you open the door to this woman, knowing what she done?"

"*What* she done?" Aziza asks. "All she done is get that skanky little white girl outta here and she don't belong here in the first place. Shootin' up right in front of me like that."

"This lady a kidnapper," Mother Zacchaeus says loudly, proclaiming it to the heavens.

"Mom, are you okay?" Eli whispers.

I feel his hands on my shoulders, helping me upright.

"I'm fine," I manage to say, though the room is spinning. I face the nun. "Why did you hit me?" Clearly we've been dreaming at cross purposes. In my dreams, she pins a medal on me, and in hers the stabbing is intentional. "You seem to have completely misunderstood the situation."

Mother Zacchaeus cocks her head, like she can't understand me.

"We didn't kidnap Sam," I say. "We rescued her."

"Rescued her from what? From here? This here is a safe place. When you in here, nobody can come in and take you 'way. Nobody."

"She's fine now," I say. "She's back with her mother."

"Back with her mother ain't fine. Back with her mother is the problem. You don't know nothing, you know that?"

"Maybe not. But I didn't kidnap anybody. She went willingly."

Aziza, the smoking girl, laughs at this. "That man with you, he let her shoot up again and then he carried her out. That wasn't willing, that was unconscious."

This hits me harder than the slap. It makes sense, though. When I'd first spoken to her, Sam was growing more aware, more belligerent. When I saw her in the backseat of the car, she'd been completely out of it, passive and pliable. I remember Gregory saying once that the rehab counselors actually prefer when their clients check in high or loaded. It makes them easier to manage.

Eli tugs me toward the door. "Mom, let's just get out of here."

"Listen to the boy," Mother Zacchaeus says. "Get out before the police get here. 'Cause they coming to lock your kidnappin' self away—"

"Don't you get it?" I tell her. "We're on the same side. I was trying to help that girl, just like you. I brought my son with me to see what's happening here."

"Why, so he can laugh at us, like you doing?"

"No," I say. "I thought it would help."

She cocks her head at this too. "What you mean, help?"

I'm not going to elaborate. I'm not going to tell this woman my son's been smoking weed and I thought a firsthand glimpse of the bedlam that is Mission Up would freak him out sufficiently to get him to stop.

"How it gonna help?" she asks.

"I just . . ."

Eli pulls on my arm again. "Let's just go."

"No, wait," Mother Zacchaeus says. "The lady wanna help. Aziza, you hear? Go get the box. The lady wanna help us. She come down here for our benefit. She here to grace us with her presence. Go on and get the box."

Aziza disappears with a smile, returning from the lounge with a shiny pink shoe box. The top is taped down with clear cellophane and a jagged slot has been cut into the center. She holds the box toward me and shakes it.

"You wanna help, this is how."

I reach for the box.

"No you don't," she says, snatching it away.

Mother Zacchaeus shakes her head. "It's for putting your money in. Go on. You gonna help or what?"

"You just slapped me," I say. "I'm not paying you for the privilege."

She mulls this over, then smiles. This happened last time too, the sudden change of demeanor when I stood up to her. Mother Zacchaeus, I realize, is a bully. She only respects the people who stand up to her. If I slapped her back, we'd probably end up the best of friends.

But don't worry, I won't.

"You know, I think my brother understood this place and I'm the one who didn't. We're from two different worlds, I realize, but I left here thinking we were on the same side. Clearly I was wrong."

"Aw," she says. "Two different worlds. Now tell me this: in your world, you can just walk into the hospital and check somebody out? In this world here, it don't work like that. Here we don't let you just take somebody away. I don't know what side you on, but on *this* side, you gonna get yourself slapped upside the head doing things like that."

"Don't I know it. Anyway, you don't need my help, I can see that now."

She shrugs. "That depends on the kind of help. You can put

money in the box, if you want. You be surprised how much it cost, a sanctuary like this."

That word again, *sanctuary*. Glancing around, taking in Eli's wide-eyed stare, I can't help wondering how bad life has to get for a place like Mission Up to look like a sanctuary.

"Here," Eli says. He pulls out his billfold, a thick, duct-taped affair, and produces a wad of fives and ones. Aziza extends the box so he can wedge the money through the slot. "Now can we please just go? We don't belong in this kind of place."

"Amen to that," Mother Zacchaeus says.

Something clicks inside me, the same thing that clicked when I heard him say "hippie losers." "What do you mean, we don't belong? Why don't we belong?"

Eli shakes his head, like it's too obvious to explain.

"Why wouldn't we belong here? Are we too good for this place? Too rich? Too white?"

"Jeez, Mom, *shut up*."

"It's okay, big man," Aziza says. "We know you white."

Mortified, Eli leaves without me, pausing out on the curb where his uncle waited last time. Aziza chuckles and heads for the stairs. Mother Zacchaeus reaches for the row of enamel pins on her chest. She pulls one free, pressing the thumb of her free hand against her shirt to hold the back of the pin in place. Then she wriggles it toward the straining button placket until she can snap the pin together. That's a relief. I was afraid she would try to stab me with it.

"Come here," she says. "You know what this is?" She studies the tiny emblem on the front of the pin. "This is what they give for memorization. You take it. Go on."

I open my hand and she drops the lapel pin into my palm.

Sure enough, there's an open Bible inside a green border and the motto THY WORD HAVE I HIDDEN IN MY HEART.

"So you don't forget," she says.

How could I?

As I descend the stairs, the nun watches me from the door. Down the street, the *whoop-whoop* of a police siren sounds. Eli goes stiff, but the cruiser turns off at the end of the block.

"Don't worry about that," Mother Zacchaeus calls out.

We cross the street to the car. Before closing the door, she actually waves.

"That woman's nuts," Eli says, slamming his fist down on the door lock.

"You have to be a little crazy to be a nun."

"Is that what she's supposed to be? I don't think so."

"Well, she's something." Like Eli, I'm pretty sure Mother Zacchaeus has no affiliation with a conventional Roman Catholic order. But how do I put this? I've never understood the hierarchy of black churches—the bishops, apostles, and whatnot. They seem a little unconventional to me, but it's not like there's a rule book. At least, not a crystal clear one.

"And, Mom," he says. "I told you so. That was a disaster waiting to happen, and you walked us right into it, just like always."

I flip the visor down and check my face. Surprisingly, there's not a flaming handprint across my cheek. Shifting back and forth, I try to determine whether one side is puffier than the other.

"Eli, look at me."

He makes an inspection, then shrugs. "Wait and see. Maybe it'll bruise up."

"You'd like that, wouldn't you?" I turn the key in the ignition.

"No," he says. "I didn't like anything about what just happened."

"Well," I say, pulling away from the curb, "I guess it's time we had a talk."

He slumps against the door and sighs. "Whatever."

*

You should never use propaganda to teach kids the truth. For the last four years, since junior high, Eli has been indoctrinated by the school system with the goal of making him into a tolerant, non-bullying citizen who says no to drugs. Instead, like all the smart kids, he's adopted an ironic stance toward the virtues his leaders have so clumsily tried to impress onto him. His friends use the word *gay* as a synonym for stupid or lame. "That's so gay," I'll overhear them saying, or "Why do you have to be so gay?" They run in cliques, a social caste system, and while I'm sure Eli would never push anybody around physically, I don't have any illusions that the kid who spat out "hippie losers" really believes in his own superiority.

"You don't get it," he says.

"What's there to get? It's illegal, Eli. You can go to jail just for possession."

He shrugs. "A lot of things are illegal. Speeding is illegal, but look at you."

I glance down at the speedometer, and sure enough. I ease my foot off. "All I'm asking is that you'll promise me you won't do it anymore. All right?"

Nothing.

"Eli, come on. Just promise me—"

"I'm not going to say something I don't believe. I'm not going to promise not to, because what if I do? I'd be lying."

"You mean you're going to smoke more dope? You want to be a stoner, is that it?"

"Whatever. You're not even listening."

"Eli, I'm trying."

This isn't how I imagined the conversation going. I expected our visit to Mission Up to shake him up. Mission accomplished. I expected him to be cowed into submission. Not so much. Somehow, I had assumed that confronting him would do the trick. There would be tears, repentance, maybe some denial. I expected him to try to charm me, to reassure me, to do anything to win back my favor. Instead, he's defiant. Brazen.

"What you're saying is, you might want to keep smoking weed."

"Maybe," he says. "I don't know."

"What about the kids at your school who got suspended? You wanna end up like them?"

"Of course not," he says. "They're stupid."

"Because they got caught?"

He nods. "And anyway, it shouldn't be illegal. Pretty soon it won't be. I don't know what the big deal is. There are more important things in life."

"I want what's best for you—"

"Don't worry about it, then. I'm not stupid like those kids."

"No, Eli, I'm not saying I don't want you to be caught. I don't want you to be *hurt*. There's a difference."

"It doesn't hurt me," he says. "That's a myth."

I'm clutching the wheel with white-knuckled intensity, frustrated by the knowledge that I am losing the argument. That for all my waiting, I went into this unprepared. It never occurred to me that, confronted by the fact he was smoking marijuana, his response would be, "So what?" It's another slap in the face, a much more painful one.

"If you won't do it for yourself, then do it for me."

"You can't guilt me into something I don't believe in."

Oh really?

"All right, then," I say. "But I don't know what your father is going to think about this."

I hate the sound of that sentence, but it's out before I can stop myself.

"Well?" I ask.

Eli laughs.

"Stop that," I say.

"Are you kidding? Believe me, if you ask anybody in the neighborhood who in this family is smoking weed, they wouldn't say it was me. Look at you people! You're all crazy. You with your Rent-a-Mob. Dad holed up in his shed. He belongs in a strait-jacket, if you ask me."

Maybe we both do.

I feel like I'm going insane right about now.

chapter 12

The Reflecting Ditch

At the back of the bus, on a row all to myself, I study Mother Zacchaeus's lapel pin and contemplate rejection. First Rick rejected me—because abandonment is a form of rejection, and moving yourself into the backyard shed clearly qualifies as abandonment. Then the eccentric nun (*eccentric* is putting it mildly) rejected me—because slapping someone in the face and accusing her of kidnapping is also a rather obvious form of rejection. Eli was next. After our little talk, he shut down around me, restricting himself to monosyllables. When I tried to put a stop to his afternoon bike rides, he simply ignored me. The silent treatment qualifies as rejection, doesn't it?

At least I still had Jed. But now he's rejected me too, though in the gentlest of ways. After begging me to accept Marlene's invitation to accompany the Rent-a-Mob to the demonstration in D.C., coaxing me against my better judgment to remain open to new experiences, to go boldly where no man has gone before and so on, the moment we boarded Chas Worthing's chartered bus,

Jed detached himself from his mother and sat on the row just behind Marlene, never taking his eyes off her from the time we left Towson until we hit the gridlock around the Capitol Beltway.

"You're all alone back here," Chas says.

He plops down across the aisle from me.

"I'm fine."

"Everyone's glad you decided to come."

"Yes, I know."

They had all lined up first thing and let me know. Some apologies seemed genuine—Barber, for example, when he wasn't twizzling his mustache, appeared quite pleased to see me—and others, like Vernon, the gray-haired doctor, got through the procedure with a minimum of awkwardness. Even a few people who hadn't been at Chas's house that Sunday afternoon trooped over to say hello to me, as if they'd been instructed in advance to be especially welcoming. I imagine what I experienced was similar to what a newcomer at The Community has to endure when the professional greeters descend en masse to make sure they feel welcome.

"It won't be much longer," he says, glancing at the traffic through the window. "Since this is your first time, I'm looking forward to hearing what you think about it."

"For one thing, I think it's pretty extravagant, renting a bus like this to take thirty-odd people on an hour-long trip."

"It's the only way to make sure we get there in one piece. The MARC train gets you there, but half the group doesn't show up on time at the station and a few wander off once you're in Washington. This way, they know we're not leaving without them and they stick around for the ride back. Besides, I get a pretty good rate on the bus."

"If you say so."

"I like your son, by the way. Jed. He looks nothing like his brother, though, does he? I don't think there's much danger of him wandering off, as long as Marlene's around."

"They used to know each other," I say. "In the church youth group."

"So I heard. I never would have pegged her for a church-going type."

"You might be surprised at the kind of people who go to church, Chas."

"And you might be surprised at the people who go to a demo."

"I *am* surprised. I guess I'm one of them."

"I guess you are," he says, smiling broadly.

Once the bus reaches D.C. proper, Chas goes to the front and acts as tour guide, pointing out significant buildings and monuments to the left, then the right. I notice that Jed is no longer sitting on the row behind Marlene. Somewhere along the way, he moved forward to sit with her. Her neck cranes back and forth, following Chas's commentary, while Jed steals glances at her.

He's eighteen years old, a high school senior, and yet I can count on one hand the number of dates he's gone on—not the number of girls he's dated, mind you, but the actual number of outings. Most of these have been organized school functions. If it hadn't been for my coaching, he probably would have skipped out on those. More often than not, I've had to suggest names to him, girls he might like to invite to the Christian school prom substitute or the Spring Banquet.

He doesn't seem to need my prompting now. If you'd asked me before, I never would have imagined him being this confident around a girl, especially one who's in college. Tongue-tied and awkward, that's what I would have expected. That's what he *was* when he suddenly found Marlene standing in our kitchen. Not anymore.

And instead of feeling happy for him, I feel rejected. How do you explain that?

The bus disgorges us near the Washington Monument. As the Rent-a-Mob files out, pausing at the storage lockers in the flank of the bus to be issued painted signs, I am already overwhelmed by the throng of people all around. I'm accustomed to tourists packing the capitol sights, but the Square has become a staging area for chanting, shouting protestors. While the morning sun feels nice on my skin, the noise is deafening. I wish I could get back on the bus.

But there's no turning back.

"It's impossible, isn't it?"

I turn to find Dr. Vernon at my elbow, wincing at the noise. His sign is tucked under his armpit furtively, as if he might ditch it once Chas looks away.

"I should have brought my earplugs," I say.

"A lot of sound and fury, signifying jack squat. That's what I hate about these things. Oh, perfect, they brought the drums."

As he speaks, a group of tattooed young gypsies sashays around the bus, slapping a frenzied beat on their little Djembe drums. They leave a strong odor of marijuana in the air behind them, but even this gives Vernon no pleasure. I find myself warming to him all of a sudden.

"I try to tell Chas this isn't what it's all about. *This* doesn't change anything." He shakes his head. "But for him, this *is* what it's about."

As Chas leads us into the fray, I stick with Vernon near the back of the pack. The Square is packed shoulder-to-shoulder around the perimeter, but once we're farther in, there are pockets of open ground. The Washington Monument looms needle-like overhead.

"Everybody stick together!" Chas shouts, holding his sign aloft as a beacon.

Vernon keeps up a running commentary. "I mean, in 2004, absolutely. In 2006, all right. But now, this hardly makes sense anymore. It's like marching against slavery in 1870. It's over, whether people realize it yet or not. The damage is done."

"Let me ask you something, though. Why did you come?"

"Good question." He looks down at his marching feet. "It was a Saturday and I had nothing better to do. Plus, somebody has to be here to inject a voice of reason."

"Someone has to protest the protestors," I say.

"Exactly. I'm the gadfly, I suppose."

I nod, wondering how many of the others see themselves the same way. It's human nature, wanting to be the outlier. Drop me in the middle of the Bodice Ripper book club, and I want to be a lefty liberal. Drop me in among the war protestors, and I want to wave a flag.

Somebody's beat me to it, though. Once we've circled to the other side of the Monument, we pass a young man sitting alone in a wheelchair, strumming Lee Greenwood on his guitar, singing, "At least I know I'm free." He wears tan camouflage fatigues, with his empty pant legs folded underneath him.

"That's gonna end badly," Vernon says.

"What do you mean?"

"If he's not careful, he'll get himself roughed up."

"At a *peace* demonstration?" I ask, incredulous. "He looked like a veteran."

Vernon narrows his eyes at me, as if to say, *You've got a lot to learn about the world.*

Maybe so. But the mounted policemen worry me much more than the drum circles or the middle-aged militants. Even though the demonstrators try to give the horses a wide berth, the riders push in closer, hiding their gaze behind mirrored sunglasses.

It takes forever to work our way around the World War II memorial, and once we do, I lose my bearings entirely. In every direction, I'm confronted by a wall of backs, too close for me to see over them. I stick close to Vernon, afraid of being lost. He puts a hand on my shoulder. "You go ahead where I can see you."

Through the chinks between the people in front of me, I glimpse light ahead. Soon I hear Chas rallying the troops. Bunching forward, I find myself pressed against Barber and Jed.

"Wow," Jed is saying. "It's not what I thought it would be."

"What's not?" I ask, sliding between them.

And then I see it. We have emerged at the near end of the Reflecting Pool, opposite the colossal temple where Abraham Lincoln sits enthroned. Only the long rectangular pool doesn't reflect anything—no blue sky, no fluffy clouds, no wind rippling the surface. It's been drained. All that's left is a huge brown gash in the earth, a never-ending mud pit transected by a grid of wooden stakes. And without the water, there goes the illusion of depth. The pool turns out to be as shallow as a half-dug grave.

"The Reflecting Pool looks more like a Reflecting Ditch," Barber says.

Coming up behind me, Vernon chuckles. "Is that a metaphor or what?"

*

There are speakers (*oh, goody!*) lined up on a distant stage, their voices echoing and incomprehensible. They're all mad as hell, judging from the high-pitched shrill of their voices, and they're not going to take it anymore. Apart from the cluster of die-hards swarming the platform, the swirling sea of demonstrators seems indifferent. Despite the anger coming through the public address system, the atmosphere on the ground is celebratory. A surprising number of people have turned out with folding chairs, blankets, even coolers. There are cameras everywhere too: video cams, phones, SLRs with telephoto lenses. I can't turn around without ending up in somebody's frame.

Chas leads us toward an open patch of ground near the perimeter, seizing a park bench to use as a base of operation. Marlene enlists Jed to help pass around packed lunches. We sit cross-legged on the brown grass, having a picnic amid the chaos. Once the food is distributed, Barber huddles with Jed and Marlene, the three of them settling just to my right.

"This is Mob 1.0," Barber is saying, "totally old school. This kind of thing will be happening less and less. You can't get this many people to rally around anything unless you keep the principle so vague that it's practically meaningless."

Marlene nods. "This might look like a lot of people, but it's not. A few years ago there would have been twice this many."

As I chew, I glance around at the crowd, happy there aren't twice as many of them. The sun, which burned hotly an hour ago, hides itself behind the gathering gray clouds. Looks like rain.

"I wouldn't have come myself," Barber says, "except Chas

insisted. I'm much more into the flash mob scene these days. You know about that?"

"Like on YouTube?" Jed asks. "People showing up at the train station out of nowhere and singing a song?"

"And even that's gone a little stale for my taste. The thing is, we're a niche culture. Does anyone really want to identify with a cause that millions of other people support too?"

"Like peace?" I ask.

"Exactly. Generic peace can't even hold my attention. You have to drill down, right? What exactly are you against? All war in general? That's pretty broad. You can get a lot of bodies behind that, but it's not really unity. Narrow it down to, say, child soldiers. Less people turn up, but there's more passion. Narrow it down again to these particular child soldiers in this particular African civil war, and nobody knows what you're talking about—except the ones who do, and with them, you're like *this*." He twines his middle finger around his index finger. "Simpatico, right?"

"What does a flash mob have to do with child soldiers?" Jed asks.

"That's just an example. Like I said, even that scene's a little dated."

Marlene touches Jed's arm lightly. "The point is, the way to speak to the universal is through the particular. The broad message might appear to speak to everyone, but really it speaks to no one deeply. When you focus on the particular, even though it seems counterintuitive, by communicating just one thing to just one person, you say everything to everyone."

"Cool," Jed says.

I exchange a look with Vernon, who's sitting on my right. He smiles but makes no comment.

"Have you ever participated in a flash mob?" I ask him.

"Me?" He rolls his eyes. "I try to steer clear of anything that qualifies as a 'scene.' But like he said, Chas thought this was important, so here we are."

"You're like a family," I say. "Or a church."

"But with a lot less drama than either one."

"I don't know, Doc. Looking around, I wouldn't say that at all."

Much to my surprise, I am starting to enjoy myself. The clouds overhead, a cool breeze, the grass between my fingers, it's pretty much idyllic. After lunch, with the speakers still droning, we trek toward the Lincoln Memorial. As we reach the top of the steps, a fat raindrop bursts on the back of my hand. Then I feel them on my legs, see them popping on the marble at my feet. Just in time, we pass through the fluted columns and into the shaded temple, Honest Abe glowering down at us.

"The Great Emancipator," Vernon says.

"That's right," Chas replies in his tour guide voice. "But do you know what those tied bundles of sticks are in his armrests? Right there under his hands? Those are called *fasces*, the old Roman symbol for power—"

"Which is where we get the word *Fascism*," Barber says. "And it's no surprise, considering he suspended habeas corpus and assumed Guantanamo-like powers—"

"*But*," Chas says, cutting him off, "there's a significant difference here. Traditionally, the fasces would have an axe in the middle, but there's no axe here. Why not? Anybody?"

"If there was an axe," Jed says, "it might cut his hand."

"Good guess, but no. In the ancient world, when you entered Rome, you had to take the axe out of the fasces, in deference to the people. Symbolizing how the citizens trumped the state.

Even then, they understood that true power derives from a mandate from the people."

He goes on in this vein for some time.

I find myself wandering into one of the side chambers of the temple, where Lincoln's Second Inaugural Address is inscribed in stone. The letters themselves, deeply incised, have an aesthetic power. My eyes settle on one line: *Both read the same Bible and pray to the same God, and each invokes His aid against the other.* Things have only gotten worse sense then. From two niches (to use Barber's word), North and South, we've splintered into hundreds of thousands, a nation of tribes connected not by kinship or even creed. We're merely tethered together by the Internet, by our brand loyalties and shared consumer obsessions.

"What's wrong, Mom? You're not digging the history lesson?"

I give Jed a smile, surprised to find him alone. "Where's Marlene? I thought you two were suddenly inseparable."

A bashful shrug.

The rain has picked up, hammering the steps outside, making the vast cavern of marble seem almost cozy by comparison.

"It's really coming down out there, isn't it?"

He nods.

"So, you seem to be having a good time."

"I'm glad we came," he says. "It's really opened my eyes."

"Oh really?"

"I should be more involved in the world, don't you think? Marlene says there are a lot of meetings, a lot of things like this, just on a smaller scale."

"I bet there are. And the two of you would be getting . . . involved together?"

"You don't like her, do you?"

"Of course I do."

"You think she's weird."

"No, I don't. I'll admit, the hair is a little bit outside my comfort zone. All the metal . . . But, hey, we're pretty weird in this family, right? We're in no position to judge. The question is, what do *you* think about her?"

"Mom," he says, "I like her."

"That's what I thought. She's a little older, you know. I'm not sure how many college girls are into dating high school boys."

He frowns at the word *dating*, like it's a foreign, old-fashioned concept. Channeling Barber, I half expect him to tell me that dating's gone a little stale for his taste. But my son isn't jaded, just the opposite. He is flushed with the uncertainties of first love.

"Do you think she likes me, though?" he asks.

I start to say something humorous, then stop. He's asking in earnest. My late bloomer is finally taking an interest in girls.

"What do *you* think?"

"I don't know. That's why I'm asking."

"Well," I say, "my advice is to take it slow and see what happens. You don't want to come on too strong. Just be yourself and let her get to know you."

He nods, taking this in. I can see the wheels turning in his head.

"Don't overthink it," I say.

Another nod, even graver than the first. He is definitely going to overthink it. No question about that. Oh well, I've done my best, such as it is. I was never very good at dispensing romantic advice. Until now, I haven't been called on much in that area.

"There you are," Marlene says, joining us near the wall. She pauses to take in the gist of the inscription, then smiles at us both.

"The rain's not letting up. Chas thinks we ought to head back to the bus and call it a day."

Beside me, Jed looks crestfallen.

"So we'll be getting back to Baltimore early," I say. "You haven't made any plans, have you, Marlene?"

She shakes her head. "No, not really."

I give my son a suggestive look, then wander back through the columns to find the rest of the group. At the last moment, I see the light switch on in his head.

"It will be pretty early, won't it?" he says. "Maybe we should . . . ?"

He leaves the question hanging and I'm too far off to hear her reply.

*

The rain prompts a general exodus. As we descend the stairs, the masses have already thinned considerably, leaving bald patches on the ground. The speakers have stopped their rants and the bottom of the Reflecting Pool collects little puddles of standing water here and there.

"If this keeps up," I say, "it might fill with water again."

My drowned-rat hairdo keeps dripping down the sides of my neck. I keep peeling my damp shirt away from my skin, but there's really no point. We catch up to the last ranks of the nearest crowd, which brings us to a halt. The ground feels squishy underfoot.

Beside me, Vernon peels off his windbreaker and drapes it over my shoulders. I try to protest, but he pays no attention. Once again, he's wearing a cannabis T-shirt underneath, which makes me a little heartsick for Eli.

"Watch out for the horses!" somebody calls.

The mounted cops are weaving around the edge of the crowd, standing in their stirrups to see farther up ahead.

"What's happening over there?" Vernon asks, craning his neck.

"Do you see anything?"

"Some kind of commotion."

The problem is, the rain and mud make people ornery and combative. They want to be left alone. They don't want anybody crowding them. Thousands of people all leaving the Mall at the same time is bound to create some bottlenecks, and with the added pressure of the police . . .

Jed and Marlene draw closer to me.

"Something's not right," she says.

Instead of heading back the way we came, straight down the Mall, we drift leftward past a kidney-shaped pond until we're running parallel with the traffic on Constitution Avenue. The tree canopy offers some protection from the rain. Over the sound of the cars passing, the occasional blowing of a horn, I hear raised voices, then a loud wail.

I would stop in my tracks, but there are people behind us now. The mass moves forward under its own strength. I couldn't break away if I tried.

"This is getting scary," I say.

"There's a fight!"

I strain on tiptoes to see what Jed is talking about. No luck.

I can hear it, though: more shouting, some screams, horses' hooves.

Then, without warning, we are suddenly in the middle of it all. People are running in every direction, pushing others out of the way. A couple of horseback cops are trying to ride into a packed, writhing scrum.

It's not what I imagined, not the riot police breaking up the mob. Instead, the mob is fighting among itself. As I watch, a lanky kid with a black bandana wrenches a peace sign from an old man's grasp, dragging the man to the ground. More black bandanas surge through the crowd. Someone is blowing an ear-piercing whistle.

Everyone is running now. I see Vernon off to the side, fending off a bandana-wearing man with his sign. Jed takes my arm and hustles me around them. We stop suddenly as a horse gallops in front of us. Then Marlene takes my hand, pulling me forward, and Jed is ahead of her, using his height advantage to find a safe path through the fight.

"They must be anarchists!" Marlene yells.

I don't respond. I'm breathing too hard to talk. I can't remember the last time I ran for my life. Oh, wait, I never have. Until now.

A squat woman in a floppy hat barrels into me, trying to make her own escape. I lose my grip on Marlene's hand and go wheeling sideways. I glimpse another mounted cop—maybe the same one who nearly trampled me a moment ago—dragging a bandana-wearing man by the shirt collar, using the momentum of the horse to literally lift the man into the air. Chas and Barber appear behind the horse, holding Vernon between them. A stream of blood pours from just above his eyebrow.

"Come on," Marlene says, seizing my wrist.

The fight is behind us now, but we keep moving. Jed leads the way, crossing Constitution when there's a gap in the traffic, putting distance between us and the Mall. I motion for Chas to follow us. He waves me forward and mouths words I can't make out.

We finally stop for breath outside a pristine marble building that looks like a miniature White House with the front of the Lincoln Memorial slapped on front. This turns out to be the Daughters of the American Revolution Museum. I plop down on the steps, wheezing like a three-pack-a-day smoker. Jed doubles back to help carry Vernon.

"Can you believe that?" Vernon says. The marijuana leaf on his shirt is now speckled with blood. Between the Mall and here, he's managed to tie his wound with one of the black bandanas, which he managed to liberate during his struggle.

"It's terrible," I say.

"Terrible, yes. But exhilarating. Did you see me thrashing that kid?"

"You were amazing," Chas says, helping ease Vernon onto the steps. "He didn't know what hit him. And you got yourself a souvenir too."

"I feel alive," Vernon says.

Above him, Jed laughs. He, too, feels alive. His eyes are shining from the adventure. Marlene regards him with a dazed expression, and he doesn't even notice.

"Beth, nothing like that has ever happened at one of these things before. I don't want you to get the wrong idea."

"Don't worry about me. What about the others?"

Chas glances down the street toward the tree line. "They all know where to find the bus. I guess we'd better start making our way over there."

The six of us, now a band of survivors, wander northward in search of a cutover, finally turning on E Street for an unexpected glimpse of the White House across the south lawn. We pause at the gates and smile like tourists. Jed takes out his phone and makes me snap a picture of him and Marlene with the White House in the background. The farther we get from the fight, the more Vernon seems to want to relive it. He makes Barber and Chas both recount his exploits as they'd witnessed them, then explains everything to me in heroic detail. A kid in a black bandana tried to grab his sign, so he walloped him upside the head. When the kid ducked under and tackled Vernon to the ground, the doctor reached out and grabbed a handful of nose, twisting as hard as he could. The kid yelped and scrambled to his feet, disappearing into the fray, leaving Vernon in possession of his bandana.

"I didn't even feel this," he says, pointing to the cut on his forehead.

We're the last ones to reach the bus. Barber pauses on the steps. "A fight broke out at the peace rally. Sounds like the setup for a joke."

Chas waves him inside, then funnels the rest of us through. As Jed and Marlene ascend, I notice her hand clasping his. I'm the last one to get on apart from Chas.

"Well," he says "are you glad you came? Would you do it again?"

"Would I do it again? Probably not. Am I glad I came? It's been quite an experience, so yes, I suppose I am."

As I walk down the aisle toward the back, Marlene rests her head on Jed's shoulder. All the anxiety he expressed in the Lincoln Memorial seems to have vanished. He smiles up at me, confident. I give his shoulder a squeeze. Not every surprise your children throw at you is a disappointment.

You have surprised me, Jed, but so far, I like what I see.

chapter 13

Bad Habit

Sounds like you had quite a time," Holly says. "You should have invited me along."

"I'm not sure you would have enjoyed it."

"Why not? Am I not cool enough for your new friends?"

"Honey, even I'm not cool enough for them."

We're sitting by the window at one of our favorite lunch cafés, watching the rain pelt the outdoor furniture on the patio where we usually sit. The weather has taken a turn. It's wet and cold outside and people are finally reconciling themselves to the end of a long Indian summer, wearing sweaters and scarves and raincoats as they dash from the parking lot into the restaurant. Holly sports a tailored tweed jacket, looking very equestrian, and this morning I dug out my favorite thrift-store find, a beat-up double-breasted leather coat from the seventies, hip-length and nipped at the waist.

The waitress brings our salads, more bread, another tea for

Holly, who keeps sucking them down. "They put too much ice in these things," she says once the girl is gone. "Anyway, I'm sorry things didn't go better with Eli. I should have warned you. Kids these days? They're all libertarians. They don't want anyone telling them what they can or cannot do. As long as they're not violating anybody else's freedom, the government—and their parents—should just butt out."

"Now you tell me. Are they libertarians, or just teenagers?"

"You think there's a difference?" She smiles. "Don't tell Eric I said that. He's been testy ever since he got home."

"Is it serious?"

She seesaws her hand. "Kinda, sorta. We go through phases. I guess that's normal, right? The thing is, ninety percent of the time, the two of us are in sync. We're not navel-gazers, Beth. We don't psychoanalyze our relationship. That's how my mother was, and I couldn't stand it, always badgering my dad about his feelings, upset that he didn't share enough. Me, I look at marriage differently. I want it to be a source of comfort, not anxiety. The best way to get that is to leave the scabs alone."

"That's not always easy. I've been picking at mine."

"*You* have an excuse. I mean, I can hardly complain to you about Eric, can I? It's not like he's living in the backyard."

"So what is he doing?"

"Little things. For example, he was giving me a hard time about my hours at the church. Every time we reclaim another section of that warehouse, he gets hit up for another donation. Usually, he likes it. The thing about Eric is, he wants to give money away. He loves doing it. He loves being able to help. And if he doesn't have the money, he'll go out and find it. All of a sudden, though, he's complaining about getting calls from the pastoral staff. He's acting like it's my fault, like I'm trying to drain him by adding on to the building."

"You're the one trying to put the brakes on the crazy spending."

"I know, right? They'd have gold thrones on stage if it wasn't for me." She laughs. "Okay, maybe that's an exaggeration, but you know what I mean. Every time it comes up, I get the silent treatment. That, or he goes into this spiel about how I don't understand."

"Don't understand what?"

She shrugs. "Finance. The way the world works. Take your pick. It's like my dad telling me money doesn't grow on trees. 'It doesn't? For real? Well, where does it come from?' Duh. There's some other stuff too, but it's all trivial. He's just picking a fight, and I don't know why."

"You are happy, though? Overall, I mean."

"Sure, Beth. Of course we are. I'm certainly not unhappy."

"You're getting what you need from the relationship?"

She pauses, fork in air. "What does that mean?"

"Just . . . I don't know. Sometimes you seem a little lonely. We have that in common."

"Lonely." She weighs the word on her tongue. "Look, you know me. I don't subscribe to the philosophies of the marriage-industrial complex. I'm not looking to a man to fulfill me completely. That's a lot of pressure to put on anyone. I like my space. I like having my own friends. I like to be alone sometimes, but that's not the same as being lonely."

"I realize that—"

"You feel lonely, Beth?"

"Of course I do. Like you said, my husband lives in a shed in the backyard. If I didn't have Deedee's painting, I'd have forgotten by now what the man looks like."

"Seriously, though. Before Rick went nuts. You were lonely? That makes me sad."

"It makes *me* sad, Holly. I don't want to be this way."

"What way? You're great just how you are. There's nothing missing about you. You know that, right?"

"I think there is. I'm not like you. I didn't stick it out in school. I didn't fulfill my promise. I was all set for law school and then I got pregnant with Jed. The first half of my life pointed one way, and the second half pointed the opposite direction. All the things I intended to do—to be—none of that ever happened. I know it's my fault. Nobody forced me to give up anything. But still . . . I miss it. I miss what I should have become."

"It takes a village, Beth. A husband can't give you everything any more than you can give him everything. But you have your kids, you have me. You're not alone, and you're anything but a failure. Are you kidding me? That's crazy talk."

I smile wanly. "It runs in the family these days."

"You're depressed because of Eli. Look, if it will help, why don't I take a crack at him? He might be able to shrug Mommy off, but when Aunt Holly sinks her teeth in, that's another story."

"It's not because of Eli," I say. "But you're welcome to talk to him. I'd love that, actually. It's not like I can ask Rick to help."

Whenever I spill my guts like this, I always feel sick afterward. How much of what I said do I actually believe? To be honest, it's hard to tell. Sometimes, when you process out loud, you say things you don't mean at all. I'm not sure this is one of those instances. These existential complaints of mine, they all ring true in my ears. If that makes me superficial, the victim of midlife regrets, then what can I say? Guilty as charged.

"At least eat your food," Holly says. "I can't have you lonely and starving. That would be too much on my conscience."

*

Some people have dessert after a meal. Holly likes to window shop. When she's really in a funk (there's that word again!) she starts trying things on, modeling new outfits in the mirror until I give her the thumbs-up or thumbs-down. This afternoon, as she disappears into one changing room after another, my head churns with conflicting ideas.

I don't know what to do about Eli.

I'm afraid Jed will have his heart broken.

My cheek still stings from the slap Mother Zacchaeus gave me—not literally, but I can't stop thinking about it. Something's unsettled there.

"Is that a metaphor or what?" Vernon's words keep coming back to me, the soundtrack to a confused crosscut of mental images: the worship team projected on-screen, Rick looking at the painting of himself as a saint, the Reflecting Pool casting no reflection of the stormy sky above. The square opening in the roof of a Quaker meeting hall that can never be found again, no matter how often I retrace my steps. Everything means something, only I'm too dim to make the necessary connections.

In my pocket, I carry the enamel pin with the image of the open Bible. I work the raised letters with the edge of my thumbnail the way an old Catholic like Deedee's mother, Margaret, frets the beads of her rosary.

"What do you think?"

Holly stands before me in diaphanous silk, a decadent, clingy show-dress only appropriate for the kind of events I never find myself invited to. She looks good in it too. She should. While I ferry kids back and forth and do grocery runs, she meets her personal trainer for an hour of body sculpting. Whatever that is, it sounds like a lot of work.

"When they give you the Oscar, that's the dress you should wear."

She studies her reflection. Bites her lip. "So that's a no."

"Your uniform works for you. Why change it up?"

"Just so you know, I'm not leaving here with nothing. There's one more outfit."

While she's busy, I wander through the shop, casting an eye on the shimmering dresses on their plush hangers. Behind the counter, one of the shopgirls is busily texting while the other rambles on about her Halloween costume from last year, and how this time she intends to go all out.

Halloween already?

Holly comes out in a strapless metallic number.

"You're not serious," I say. "Are you going to the prom on Jupiter or something?"

"You don't like?"

"I was just thinking, we're past the point of no return with Rick's retreat. Closer to the end of October than the beginning."

"He's held out longer than I ever expected." She turns in the mirror to get a look at the back of the dress. "You're right. I'd never wear this."

"Gregory said maybe this was my month, not Rick's. It's halfway gone, though, and what do I have to show for it? Some loose teeth from getting slapped."

"And some civil disobedience."

"And a stoner son. It's not enough. I want to *do* something."

Holly swishes toward me, eyes alight. "Something like what?"

"I don't know—"

"You've still got Stacy's keys, right? That's what we should do. Serve our husbands right."

"Not something like that," I say. "I want to make a difference somehow."

"Hold that thought."

While she changes back into her tweed and denim, I head to the front of the store, gazing idly through the rain-streaked windows. In my pocket, the back of the pin works loose under the pressure of my thumb. I push the pad of my index finger ever so slightly forward, just enough to feel the point break skin. In the glass, my reflection stares forlornly, looking trapped. Not to mention transparent.

We have to run to Holly's car to keep from getting soaked.

"I think I know what it is," I say, pulling my seat belt on.

"Your meaningful thing?"

I nod. "The only problem is, if you go along with this, you might annoy that husband of yours."

"Is that right?" she asks. "Tell me more."

*

Eric Ringwald sees us through the glass wall separating his office from the secretary's desk. He jogs over, smiling, then holds us up on the threshold to give Holly a kiss.

"Where have you girls been? Out shopping?"

"Don't worry, I didn't drain the bank account. It's a good

thing too. Beth here thinks it's time for you to whip out your checkbook."

Eric raises his eyebrows. "Oh boy. Maybe we should sit down."

This is only the second time I've visited Eric's lair. From the tour during my first visit, I recall that all the surfaces are exotic hardwoods, that the pictures on the walls are not reproductions, and that the little bronze head on the pedestal behind him is by a Frenchman named Minaux (which Eric pronounces like *minnow*) and was a gift from a famous international diplomat, whose name I would certainly recognize if only he were at liberty to say it aloud. Not that Eric is a great appreciator of art. "I'm not," he insisted, "not at all. It's the stories that matter to me, not the pieces themselves."

Nevertheless, there are plenty of pieces.

Before I sit in one of Eric's chairs, I pause to consider that it probably cost more than my car. (What am I talking about? Of course it cost more than the VW!) A scientist somewhere engineered the cushions to make people entering this office in search of donations especially uncomfortable. The back tilts too far to the rear, and there are no arms. If I don't exert abdominal strength to hold my body upright, I'll be staring at the ceiling.

"I was surprised to get your call," Eric says to Holly. "Surprised and intrigued."

"I'll let Beth explain."

They both turn toward me.

"I thought about you the other day," I tell him. "Remember your trip to Haiti? When you came back, we all went to dinner." I pause long enough for him to nod at the memory. "You were talking about the children. How they had nothing, but still seemed so happy."

"It's true," he says. "I'll never forget those kids."

"I met a kid not long ago. Not a child, a young woman. I found her in a place that seemed terrible in my eyes, an unimaginable place. But if she hadn't been there, I believe she would be dead today. It's here in Baltimore, this place. It's called Mission Up, because I think it used to be one."

"I've never heard of it," Eric says. He presses his fingertips together thoughtfully. "Tell me more about the girl."

Starting from the moment Gregory arrived on my doorstep on the eve of Eli's birthday, I recount the whole story of our visit to Mission Up. I tell him about Sam and about Mother Zacchaeus, pulling no punches along the way.

"This nun sounds like a real harpy."

"Eric went to Catholic school," Holly says. "He harbors some resentment toward the nuns."

He smiles and raises a finger. "Only Sister Magdalen."

"The thing is," I say, "I feel like this place was dropped in my lap. I had no idea it even existed. The first time I saw it, I wished it didn't. But the more I think about it, the more I realize that Mission Up needs our help. It needs my help. Of course it's not what it should be. Of course it's sketchy. That woman is doing the best she can with what she's got, and she's all on her own. The good guys evacuated that neighborhood a long time ago. Mission Up is all that's left. But even as it is, in all its squalor, that place is still a sanctuary."

"And you want me to find some money for it?"

I nod.

"How much?"

"I have no idea. All I know is she needs some help."

"Is there a nonprofit? A foundation?"

"There's a fleabag hotel full of recovering addicts, battered women, ex-prostitutes, and their kids. I'm pretty sure there's nothing else, nothing official. Does that make a difference?"

"It could."

"But, honey, not everybody who needs help has nonprofit status. Those kids in Haiti—"

"True, true," he says, holding up a hand to silence Holly. "Tell you what, Beth. Let me make some calls. Let me see what I can do. I like this thing. It appeals to me. It would make a change to do something like this instead of adding another wing to the church building, right?"

Ouch.

"This is the real deal," he says. "No, really. I like it. Leave it with me."

He holds Holly back for a couple of minutes. I spend the time chatting with his secretary, an older Hispanic woman who idolizes her boss and thinks his wife walks on water too. I enjoy her company. To borrow Eric's line, it makes a change.

Out in the parking lot, Holly tells me I did a great job.

"You hooked him. I can tell."

"What about the part at the end, about the new wing of the church?"

"I don't think he was joking. He'd love to tell them the money's all tied up in inner-city projects, just to see the looks on their faces. He'll come around, though. He always does."

"I feel funny. This is the first time I've ever asked someone for money."

"You're not bad at it, Beth. Maybe you've found your purpose in life."

She's joking, of course. That doesn't mean she's wrong.

Maybe I *have* found my purpose.

Like Jim Shaw told me, you don't need a law degree to make a difference.

*

That night I light some candles on top of the TV set and uncork a $5 bottle of Shiraz, pouring until I hit the halfway mark on my plastic juice glass. We don't drink thanks to Rick's employment contract, and even before that I never had much taste for wine. At least, I had no taste for cheap wine, which was the only kind I ever tasted. I'm celebrating, though, so tonight's an exception. Before taking a sip, I run upstairs and fetch Deedee's painting, propping St. Rick against the television screen.

"Who's the saint now?" I ask, raising the juice glass to my lips.

Five-dollar Shiraz tastes like grapes and lighter fluid. I finish what's in the cup on principle, then pour the rest down the sink.

Still, a good day's work.

When Eli comes home, I make a point of going up and sniffing him. He takes it in stride and sniffs back.

"Mom," he says, "have you been drinking?"

Two hours later Jed slips through the back door. He crouches in front of the refrigerator in search of something to eat.

"Where have you been?" I ask.

"With Marlene."

"Of course you have. That's every night since we got back from Washington. Aren't you taking things a little quick?"

"We're just hanging out," he says.

"Then I guess everything is going well. She likes you?"

He shrugs. In the freezer he finds a bag of fish sticks. "Mom, do you mind?"

"Anything for you."

While I'm heating up a tray of fish sticks, he goes into the living room and switches the TV on. "What's this? Some kind of shrine?"

"If your father's in the way, just move him."

The smell of fish sticks brings Eli down the stairs, even though he's already eaten. I bring a heaping plate in to the boys, who have their feet on the coffee table as they watch a reality show about a gun shop where they're always blowing things up. I sit and watch with them, even munching on a fish stick or two.

"They're kind of burnt," Eli says.

"They're not burnt," I tell him. "They're caramelized."

Just as I'm starting to enjoy myself, an evening of normalcy in front of the TV with my sons, the telephone rings. It's Jim Shaw. I take the phone into the kitchen.

"Look, Beth, I'm getting pretty worried here. Has something happened to Rick? I keep leaving messages and never hearing back. It's been two weeks now—no, *more* than two weeks. I gotta tell you, this is really throwing me for a loop."

As he speaks, I go to the sink and look through the window. The light inside the shed is on.

"It's nothing to worry about," I say.

"How can I *not* worry? I offer the man a job, he says he'll get back to me, then nothing. If he's not interested, Beth, then he should at least have the decency to say so. Unless . . . Beth, he is all right, isn't he? Has something happened up there?"

This is silly. Jim and I have had this conversation two or three times since his visit at the end of September. I'm getting tired of giving him the runaround. It's Rick's problem, not mine.

"Nothing's wrong," I tell him. "Jim, he's out in the shed. I'll take the phone to him, okay? Just hold on a second."

When I turn to go out, Jed is standing in the kitchen doorway. "What's going on?"

I clamp my hand over the receiver. "I'm taking the phone out to your dad."

"You want me to do it?"

I shake my head.

"Is everything all right?"

"Everything's fine."

The night air chills me. As I cross the lawn, I notice a heap of dried flowers at the foot of the shed door. He's stopped bringing the offerings inside. Maybe Deedee will take a hint and stop bringing them.

"Rick?"

I stop a few feet from the shed, waiting for a reply.

"Rick, are you in there? I have Jim Shaw on the phone."

Nothing.

"Just hold on a second, Jim."

I hold the phone up to my eyes, find the Mute button, and press it down. Then I walk right up to the door and lightly knock.

"Rick? Are you asleep?"

Inside the shed, Rick coughs. The sound sends a tingle up my spine. This is the first sign of life he's given since the birthday party.

"Can you open up a sec? I have Jim on the phone."

Silence.

He hears me. He knows I'm waiting. But still he doesn't come to the door.

"I'm done playing games," I tell him. "I'm tired of making up stories. Here he is. You need to talk to him. Or if you don't want to, then you tell him yourself. I'm through."

I knock again, shaking the door on its hinges. There's no way he doesn't know I'm here.

He clears his throat and says something inaudible.

"What was that? I can't hear you."

"I can't talk," he says. His voice sounds strange, low and scratchy. "Tell him that for me, Beth."

My name. Hearing him say it has a strange effect. I want to push through the door and see him. I want to touch him. I want to tell him to pull the plug on this insanity and come back inside. All that from hearing his choked voice utter that tiny syllable.

"I'm not going to tell him anything," I say. "I'm going to leave the phone right here. If you don't want to see your wife, that's fine. I'll leave it and go inside. Is that what you want?"

Silence again.

"Okay, then." I push the Mute button again. "Jim, he'll be right here."

Then I set the phone down and back away.

After a moment, I turn and run.

Inside, with my back against the kitchen door, Jed appears again, his hand clamped over his mouth. "What's wrong, Mom? Why are you crying?"

"I'm not," I say, wiping my eyes. "In five minutes, I want you to look outside, and if the phone's still by the shed door, bring it inside."

"What about you?" he asks.

"I'm going to bed."

At the top of the stairs, I find St. Rick hanging on the wall again. Eli must have brought him back up. I pull him down again and take him into the bedroom, intending some kind of desecration. In the end, I prop him against the lamp on my nightstand. With the light off, a faint luminescence remains in the room, enough to detect the shine of the painting's surface.

"Who's the saint now?"

*

"The sad fact is, you're being taken for a ride."

"I don't understand," I say.

Across the exotic hardwood desk, Eric Ringwald fixes me with his benevolent gaze. The summons was unexpected. I would have called Holly except I thought she would be here already. Instead, I'm alone across from Eric, who's been doing his due diligence and has some news to report.

"I know some people in the Baltimore Police Department, so I made a few calls. This Mission Up place, it's a blight on the neighborhood. If they could shut it down, they would."

"I know it isn't pretty—"

He holds up the silencing hand. "And this nun of yours, Mother Zacchaeus? She's not a nun at all."

"I had a feeling she wasn't in an order or anything like that. I'm not familiar with how things work in other churches. Besides the Catholics, I mean. Not that I'm familiar—"

"What I'm saying is, she's not a nun. Not a Catholic nun or any other kind. Her real name is Rosetta Harvey, and she's got a rap sheet down to here. Possession, dealing, prostitution, you name it, going back more than twenty years. This is not a good person, Beth. She is not at all what she seems."

I open my mouth to reply. Nothing comes.

"When she slapped you, you're lucky that's all she did. She's done time for assault too. The guys I spoke with, they couldn't make it any clearer. This is not somebody you want to get yourself involved with. You're lucky you got that girl out of there when you did."

The kindhearted secretary comes in with a tray of coffee. I pour cream into mine, no sugar, stirring slowly with the little spoon provided.

"I don't know what to say."

"The world is full of these people, Beth. Trust me, I deal with them every day. They're out to get something for nothing, cheat the system, feed their ego, whatever. She's got herself an evil empire down there, a captive audience to rule over. I don't know what the scam is, and I don't want to know. Neither do you, quite frankly. The depth of evil in this world would shock you, believe me. I'm just happy I was able to help this time."

I sip my coffee. I'm sure it's good, probably carried by hand from the dew-swept mountains of Jamaica. But I can't taste a thing.

"I gave Holly a call and asked her to come over," he says. "I thought you might need someone to talk to. And let me just say, I hope you don't let this get to you. Just because this lady turned out to be a fraud doesn't mean your instinct to help wasn't sound. I'd never forgive myself if I thought you might walk out of here hard-hearted. The world needs more people who really care. Hold on one second." He lifts the phone, which has just begun to chirp. "Beth, I'm gonna have to take this."

I take my coffee into the lobby. The nice lady asks if I'd like a refill. I shake my head.

"It would be wasted on me."

I don't know what to make of this. My head is reeling. Of course she is a fraud. The ridiculous getup, the passive-aggressive manner, the bullying, a whole host of red flags. It's not like I missed them. I just didn't connect the dots. I let my newfound sense of purpose get ahead of me.

"I feel stupid," I say.

"You know what," the secretary says. "I feel that way every time I walk out of there. That man has a head on his shoulders, don't you think?"

I put the coffee cup aside and wander into the corridor in search of a restroom. In the mirror, I appear remarkably composed. Not a hair out of place. I wash my hands out of habit, ball up the paper towel, and then look at myself again. Turn, then back. Turn, then back. But no, she's never there. It's always Beth in the mirror looking back at me.

Plain old Beth.

Who's the saint now?

*

Before Holly shows up at the office, I decide to go.

I have no desire to talk.

I feel thwarted. Tricked. Like my good intentions have been thrown back in my face.

Maybe that's what I deserve. Was this about helping people in need, or was I just trying to make myself feel better? Taking advantage of their need to meet a selfish need of my own? As my friend, Holly will feel duty-bound to reassure me. I don't want to be reassured.

When I reach home, there's a panel van in front of the Smythes' house. The name of a local courier service is stenciled on the side. Curious, I park the VW and walk next door. The front door is open, and I find Margaret Smythe in the parlor, hands clasped, clearly agitated.

"What's going on?" I ask.

"It's my daughter. She's gone insane."

"Where is she?"

Margaret lifts an open palm to the sky, as if to say Deedee could be anywhere. At the top of the broad winding staircase, a couple of men in work boots and zip-front overalls appear, carrying a large, bubble-wrapped canvas between them. They start down the stairs, backpedaling with care, the wood creaking under their weight. Then Deedee leans over the rail.

"Elizabeth," she says. "You're just in time."

"I don't see why you want to do this!" Margaret declares.

"Oh, Mother, don't vex me. You simply cannot understand. Don't mind her, my dear. She can't help pitching her little fits."

Being trapped between mother and daughter is always awkward. Deedee treats the eighty-something Margaret as if she were a child sometimes. And to be honest, the fine old lady does have an impish quality to her. More than once I've seen her stir up trouble for her own amusement. Not to mention mine.

"I am not having a fit. I just think you should be committed. It's never a good sign when a person starts giving away all her treasured possessions."

The movers are trying to focus on the bend in the stairs, but I can tell the women are making them nervous. Deedee follows close behind them. The sound of her voice seems to speed them forward. They reach the ground floor with a sigh of relief, propping the wrapped canvas against one of the balustrades.

"Is it going to fit through the door?" one of them asks the other, eyeing the front entrance with suspicion.

"How do you think it got in here to begin with?" Deedee asks.

The bubble wrap obscures the canvas. I already know what's underneath. Margaret showed the picture to me once, not long after we moved in next door. It was the first of Deedee's paintings I ever saw, back before I realized she was so accomplished in the art. She had led me up the stairs into a wood-paneled room that had once been her father's study. There was a fireplace fronted by green glazed tile, and over the mantel this breathtaking painting.

"What do you think?" Margaret had asked.

"She's beautiful," I said. "Is it you?"

"Oh no. That's Deedee. She did it when she was twenty-five. It's the earliest painting of hers we have, and the only self-portrait. I keep it in here because she doesn't like to see it. Deedee never comes in here."

At twenty-five, Deedee's thick, honey-blond hair hung heavily upon her shoulders. She looked out from the painting with cool, penetrating eyes, the expressionless expression of a young woman studying her own face in a mirror. The scale of the piece seemed immense, maybe six feet by six feet square, the whole of it dedicated to her face, her throat, the top of her shoulders. Deedee's way of flattening things out hadn't emerged by this point, it seemed. While the picture was as realistic as a photo and even more minutely observed, there was a depth to the contours of her face, a dimensionality that was to disappear later as her style progressed.

"I couldn't imagine having a painting of myself at twenty-five," I said.

That impish grin of Margaret's appeared. "She was always very vain."

Now the self-portrait is bundled up and being manhandled out the door by a couple of jumpsuited movers, much to Margaret's displeasure. As they clear the door, Roy Meakin appears in the threshold.

"Deedee, you can't be serious," he says.

"Of course I am."

"If you have to sell it, then let me buy it. I'd be happy to pay whatever price you name."

"I'm sure you would, Roy. But I won't have you gawking at my younger self."

He turns to me. "Maybe you can stop her. The rest of us can't seem to get through."

"I don't even understand what's happening."

"What's happening," Deedee says, "is a new period in my work. I'm done with the old. It's time for the new. And that one especially has to go."

"Why especially?"

"It's an affront, that's why. A painter painting herself, painting her own reflection, obsessed with her mirror image. Look what happened to Narcissus, so obsessed with himself." She takes me by the shoulders, very intense. "The trick is to see through the glass, not to be distracted by the image it bounces back at you. You see what I mean?"

"Not really, no."

"This thing goes to the gallery or the trash heap, one or the other."

She follows the movers out, catching up just as they're making the descent down the steps to the sidewalk. Despondent, Roy looks on. Margaret hobbles over, touching the wall for support until she reaches his side.

"Do you know which gallery?" Roy asks under his breath.

"I have it written down," she says, passing him a folded slip of paper.

He inspects the paper, frowning with determination. "I'll take care of this."

Margaret directs a stern look in my direction. "You understand Deedee is not to know? This isn't the first time we've had to save her from herself."

"My lips are sealed."

Leaving them to their conspiracy, I walk outside to see the canvas loaded into the van. Deedee stands on the sidewalk, arms folded in satisfaction, like she's just pulled off a remarkable feat.

"They think they've outsmarted me," she says. "But I told Mother it was going to the Annandale, when it's really heading for Rooney & Gill. It's not the first time they've tried to match wits with me and failed."

I make a mental note of the name Rooney & Gill so I can pass the information along. The painting's better off down the street at Roy's than hanging in some stranger's living room, surely. My promise to be the best neighbor ever is occasionally put to the test. This time I have a feeling Margaret's the one to side with.

The van pulls away. Roy ambles our way, a hangdog expression on his face.

"Don't pout, Roy. A man your age?"

"You don't always know what's best. Even for yourself."

He heads down the sidewalk in the same direction as the van. Holly's car passes him, pulling up to the curb near the mouth of my driveway.

"It's that friend of yours," Deedee says. "The loud one."

She retreats to the house before Holly can catch up.

"I heard the bad news," Holly says.

"Let me borrow your phone."

Intrigued by the request, she hands it over. I punch Roy's home number in and make the call. His voice mail picks up. "She didn't send it to the place she told Margaret about. It's going to something called Rooney & Gill. Good luck!"

"What was that all about?" Holly asks, dropping the phone back into her purse.

"Favor for a friend."

"I'm glad to hear it. That's the reason I'm here. To do a favor for a friend."

"What kind of favor?"

We walk as far as the driveway, pausing next to her car.

"You've been holding on to the key to Stacy Manderville's beach house for something like three weeks. I've had enough. We're going."

"I can't leave now."

"We are going to do this, Beth. Me and you. It'll be an adventure."

"Holly, I can't afford the plane tickets, and I'm not having you pay for everything."

"Not a problem. You said it yourself. Florida's just a day away. We'll have ourselves a road trip, two girlfriends on the open highway. It'll be like *Thelma & Louise*. Minus the Brad Pitt, of course. Come on, Beth. You *need* this. If you stay around here, you're going to end up going batty."

"No," I say.

"That's settled, then."

"Holly, no."

"Remember to pack your bikini."

"Yeah, right. Now you're dreaming."

chapter 14

Thelma & Louise

Remember the scene in *It's a Wonderful Life* where George Bailey is looking for a suitcase to take on his travels, one that's big enough for a thousand and one nights with room for labels from everywhere from Italy to Samarkand? And the guy behind the counter pulls one out and says, "It's yours." George's old boss, Mr. Gower, is footing the bill. The suitcase even has his name inscribed on it.

Miss Hannah was a big fan of *It's a Wonderful Life*.

In addition to serving as a doctor in Korea—which was nothing like *M*A*S*H*, she was always quick to point out—she was a world traveler, having trekked through Southeast Asia at the behest of various charities and aid agencies throughout the sixties and early seventies. Under her influence, I imagined myself taking similar journeys. When I graduated high school, she presented me with an old-fashioned Hartmann suitcase, tan leather with fancy dividers inside the compartments, and my initials underneath the handle.

I find the suitcase up in the attic collecting dust. Bringing it down the pull-ladder, I wipe away the accumulated age and open the thing up for the first time in years. Inside are some of my old notebooks, the letters and cards Rick wrote before we were married, an old term paper with a red "A" inked on the front.

"You're bringing that?" Jed asks in surprise. "What about Dad's suitcase, the one with the rollers?"

He's trying to help, but he doesn't understand.

"No, this will do."

After cleaning it up, I sniff the lining. A little musty, but not too bad. My clothes are already folded on the bed, along with a zippered plastic bag full of makeup and toiletries. Once everything's inside, there is still plenty of room. I'm tempted to stick the painting in before closing the lid. Bad idea. The whole point is to pack light. Don't take anything you'll later regret.

Since Jed keeps hovering, I put him to use. "Go get my sunglasses out of the car. I'm going to need them down there."

I think it flattered Miss Hannah, the thought that I was her young protégé. By the time she came back to the States, her parents were gone and her only sibling, a younger brother suffering from his son's suicide, needed her. Because she'd been so close to my grandmother, her college roommate, my mother pretty much adopted her. She was in her late sixties when I knew her, but not at all frail.

There's a reason they make suitcases out of nylon these days. The old Hartmann weighs a ton. Wrestling it down the stairs, I have to lean left to compensate. Jed meets me by the front door with my white sunglasses, which I stick on my head.

"Are you going to miss me?"

"It'll be kind of strange."

"If anything happens, you know your father is out back. Don't feel like you can't disturb him. You can call my cell phone if you need me, and I put the number where we'll be on the fridge too."

"It'll be fine. Don't worry."

"And, Jed, I want you to keep an eye on your brother."

He nods gravely, making me wonder how much he knows. I would ask, but if he doesn't know about the marijuana, I would just as soon keep it that way. No point in giving him ammunition to use against Eli in their next fight, which is exactly what he would do. Boys will be boys.

"I asked Deedee if she would look in on you, so don't be surprised if she drops by."

"Nothing's gonna happen," he says.

"And, Jed, if you bring Marlene over here . . . be a gentleman, okay?"

"Mom!"

"Stay downstairs and don't hole up in your room. Try to think about appearances."

His cheeks flush red and he starts to push me out the door. The sunlight blinds me for a second, until I can flip my sunglasses down. Holly pulls up behind the wheel of Eric's convertible, giving the horn a tap.

"Give me a kiss," I say. "Tell Eli to call me."

Before I'm down the driveway, he has already closed the front door. Holly bounces up and gives me a hug. She smells of suntan lotion and perfume.

"We're gonna have a blast," she says.

In the trunk, there are already three expensive-looking cases, the kind you see in glossy magazines being carried by models who travel in private jets. "You said you were packing light."

"What?" she says. "I had to bring a *few* things."

I slide the Hartmann in on top, trying not to leave any scratches on Holly's bags, which probably cost more than the chairs in Eric's office. Before I get in the passenger seat, I shrug my leather coat off too. The last thing I want is to catch a rivet or buckle on that plush interior. The door shuts with an airtight seal. Everything is quiet in our little bubble.

"Am I really doing this?"

"Yes, you are. Do you have the keys?"

I reach through the seats into my coat pocket, producing the yellow floaty from which dangles the beach house key.

"Let's do it!" She pushes a button to start the engine. On the dashboard, a big control screen lights up. I've never been inside a car this nice, let alone taken a road trip. I bet it has power steering and brakes that work too.

"I feel like I'm abandoning ship."

"You need a vacation, Beth. This is gonna be great."

As we roar down the street, I watch my little house disappear in the side-view mirror. Remember: you're traveling light, leaving the baggage behind. No shed, no weed, no St. Rick staring at you in your sleep. No guilt about leaving either. No pseudo-nuns slapping you down just for trying to help. No big church with big screens. No mirrors with strangers looking back at you, strangers who used to *be* you.

Ahead of you, there's a long strip of sand and a blue-green infinity, crashing waves that come not from a sleep machine but from the actual crash of actual waves. Sun on skin and long hours of doing absolutely nothing. Two women who are lonely in their marriages but not alone, escaping from the world that won't give them everything and won't let them feel content with what they have.

"Wait," I say. "I forgot my swimsuit."

"Seriously? Never mind. We'll take care of it along the way."

*

Fifteen hours is a lot of time on the road. An hour to D.C., just settling in. Two more hours to Richmond, where we stop for lunch and end up talking about Jim and Kathie Shaw, and what it would be like if Rick did take the job and we moved down here. "You claim you'd keep in touch," Holly says, "but the Shaws said exactly the same thing." We hit the outlet mall on the highway for a swimsuit. Resisting Holly's peer pressure, I go with a one-piece. More resistance: I refuse to try it on and model for her. Not my thing.

Somewhere in North Carolina, six hours in, things take a turn for the silly. Holly confesses to having a crush on the Archbishop of Canterbury.

"Ever since the Royal Wedding," she says. "That voice. Those eyebrows."

"You do have a thing for older men."

Say what you want about air travel. There's something liberating about the open road, whether you experience it by bus, by ancient Volkswagen, or riding shotgun in the übercool car of the future. Midafternoon in Fayetteville, North Carolina: Holly stops for gas and pushes the magic button that folds the convertible top away. For nearly an hour, we blast eighties music and let the wind whip our hair—mine practically blinding me when I don't hold the tangles back, Holly's so short it can barely tickle her cheek. By the time we reach the state line, the wind has battered us into temporary submission. She puts the top up and in the silence that follows, we both look at each other like we're nineteen again.

"This is fun," I say.

"What did I tell you?"

Stacy's beach house lies on the Atlantic coast of Florida somewhere between Jacksonville and St. Augustine. The GPS screen on the dashboard counts down the miles, updating our time of arrival, ensuring that during every moment of the journey we have a sense of forward progress.

Through South Carolina, we rehash the events of the past month, with Holly telling me once again how sorry she is about the results of Eric's investigation into Mission Up.

"It's the kind of thing we *should* be doing," she says by way of encouragement. "We're always sending people on short-term mission trips halfway around the globe, taking up collections to sink wells in Africa, and right on our doorstep, right under our very noses . . ." She throws her hands up, stumped by the inexpressible depth of need all around us. "Not that those things aren't important. I know they are. But what does it say about us that trouble abroad elicits our sympathy while trouble at home just makes us want to lock our doors?"

Not knowing how to answer, I somehow find myself telling her about Miss Hannah, something I've never done before.

"She spent most of her life halfway around the globe," I say, "but for her, it wasn't about the distance as much as just doing something."

"Was she a medical missionary?" Holly asks.

"Not so much a missionary. It wasn't about winning converts, more like patching people up. We never talked about it, but I imagine she would have considered 'saving souls' as above her pay grade. She was there to stitch up the wounds."

"That's important too."

I know it's important. That goes without saying. The fact that Holly feels the need to say it aloud reflects how warped, how disoriented we have become.

Let me be honest. On the subject of my pre-evangelical past, I tend to be tight-lipped, even with Holly. Originally embarrassment kept me from talking. After meeting Rick, I'd come to see the worldly piety of my youth as insincere. How can you care for a person's body, his physical needs, when what's important is the soul? The goodness of someone like Miss Hannah, who made people well without thinking to rescue them from hell, became problematic for me. I felt like this was obvious to the real Christian, and was ashamed it had taken me so long to realize it.

Now, though, I keep my counsel for different reasons. All I have to do to make Rick's eyes roll is mention my Quaker upbringing. I stay quiet because I don't care to hear the criticism anymore. Even Holly's need to assure me that Miss Hannah's work had value gets on my nerves.

"Let me ask you something," I say. "Why is it that we talk about the importance of bodily resurrection, then act like our greatest bliss in life will be to shuffle off this mortal coil and float around like disembodied ghosts? Just because the body and the spirit aren't the same thing doesn't mean they aren't intertwined. If our bodies didn't matter, why'd God give them to us in the first place?"

"So we could buy clothes?"

"I'm serious, Holly. How can we talk so spiritualistic and be so materialistic? What's the verse about the poor person coming to the door, and instead of giving them food, you say, 'God bless you'? I think that's what we do more often than not, and to feel better about it, we make donations or build a Habitat house."

"Or try to, anyway."

"Exactly."

"You're preaching to the choir, sister."

"I'm preaching to myself. I'm guilty of this. What you said the other day about marriage, I think it's right. You want a stable relationship, and you don't get that by constantly nitpicking it, scrutinizing every little thing. But that's exactly what we're taught to do with God, isn't it? Scrutinize the relationship, make sure it's good enough, make sure we're doing everything that's expected and getting everything out of him that we want. If you spend all your time on that, what's left over for the rest of the world?

"That's the problem, isn't it? That's what keeps us cloistered in our little groups, insulated, always going deeper and deeper inside ourselves and finding less and less there. That's what drives a guy like Rick into the shed and cuts him off from his wife and his kids. Thinking he'll find God if he can just shut the world out. But what if God's waiting . . . not in here"—tapping my chest—"but out there?"

"I've never heard you talk this way, Beth."

"That's because I never do."

"You should," she says. "I like it."

*

In Savannah, we switch drivers. I'm petrified at first, but the car ends up working more or less the way they all do. As long as I don't touch anything on the center console or the dash, confining myself to holding the wheel and pushing on the gas or brake, I figure I'll be fine. My voice is scratchy from talking, and Holly's worn out, so she takes a nap while I listen to the radio. Eventually we leave the station's range and I listen to static instead, afraid to delve into the mysteries of channel changing.

We reach the beach house just before midnight, stopping along the way at a convenience store for groceries. While Holly sleeps, I run inside, grabbing juice and snacks, a box of swimsuit-unfriendly donuts, extra suntan lotion, some Diet Cokes. I try for some bottled water, but the store is sold out. Not surprising. The shelves are half empty as it is, like there's been a run on fat-filled, carcinogenic treats. The guy behind the counter looks as worn out as I feel. He stares right through me, communicating in nothing but grunts.

I let Holly sleep until we're at our destination.

Confession: I've never been to a beach house before. I always imagine them up on stilts, overlooking the sand and maybe a bonfire. During the past few miles, I've observed what look like condominiums along the oceanfront, stoking my sense of disappointment. Spending a few days in what amounts to a modern apartment block by the water . . . well, it's not very romantic, is it?

Stacy's beach house does not disappoint. For one thing, it's a tiny place, freestanding, separated from the road by a weathered picket fence. There's no garage, just a corrugated carport, the back end open to the glistening, moonlit ocean. No houses on either side, so there's plenty of privacy. We're on a small ridge overlooking the beach, and Stacy's place seems to be nestled on the one spot amenable to construction. The ground on either side slopes precipitously down to the beach. The lights of the nearest neighbor are about a mile down the road.

"Wake up, Holly. We're here."

Her eyes pop open. She sits upright. "This is it? I thought it would be bigger."

When I get out of the car, a balmy wind hits me full in the face. My clothes ripple against my body and the smell of salt fills my nostrils. True to my fantasy, I can hear the white noise of waves churning onto land. I'll sleep tonight with the window open, listening to that sound.

Holly opens the trunk only to have it snap shut, blown back by the force of the wind.

"Kind of windy, huh?"

She has a stupid grin on her face. I look at my reflection in the window. I have the same stupid grin on mine.

chapter 15

A Little Rain Must Fall

For breakfast, it's convenience-store donuts and French press coffee on the tiny back porch of the beach house. In the light of morning, I find that Stacy's beach house isn't as modest as it seemed last night. While small, the house reeks of luxury, from the frosted glass blocks that enclose the shower to the marble tile that covers all the floors. Staying here is a bit like I imagine living on a yacht would be.

"I could get used to this," Holly says.

On the refrigerator in the compact kitchen there's a laminated set of house rules. It's not unusual, according to her, for rich people accustomed to loaning out properties like this to post rules for their unsupervised guests. It seems a little strange to me, though.

"Beth, what are you wearing?"

Holly's closet, unlike mine, extends to the resort wear category, thanks to which she sports a gold-fringed wrap over her two-piece and massive designer sunglasses. Meanwhile I'm turning heads with an oversized Ravens T-shirt of Rick's, liberated at the last moment from the laundry pile (the clean pile, I'm pretty sure).

"Hey, I'm not trying to impress anyone."

She smiles. "Mission accomplished."

A strong wind blows over the ocean, chopping the waves. It's an overcast morning, and there's no one on the beach in either direction. The sand looks grayish white.

"Is it weird to you that nobody's at the beach?" Holly asks.

"To tell you the truth, I prefer it that way."

"And I guess you prefer it without sun too?"

I shrug. "You have to be careful with porcelain skin like mine."

"Spoilsport." She lowers her glasses and gives the beach a hard look. "Beth, seriously. I have a bad feeling about this."

I lower my white plastics. "Looks like rain. So what? The ocean is full of water, so you're bound to get wet one way or the other. Don't worry about it."

"Hmm," she says, snapping the big sunglasses in place.

While I finish my coffee, she goes inside and tries to figure out how to turn on the flat-screen TV in the little sitting area adjoining the kitchen. There are about a thousand buttons on the remote, and I gave up fiddling with them. Besides, I don't mind a few dark clouds and a little rain. I've never been a sun-and-surf sort of girl. Anything that keeps the beach crowd-free is a plus in my book. I had enough of crowds at the D.C. demonstration to last me a good long time.

Off to the left, a path of wooden steps descends down the slope to the beach, hemmed in on either side by weather-beaten rails. At the foot of the slope, there's a sort of grass hut straight out of a 1950s tiki lounge. Taking my mug with me, I go down to check it out.

"Beth, come look at this," Holly calls, but I'm already down the steps.

"In a minute."

I'm sure the original plan for the tiki hut included stainless steel grills, slabs of granite, and a fancy outdoor shower, but erecting the structure was as far as they got. Under the grass roof, there are a couple of folding lounge chairs, but that's it. The wind whips at the corner of the roof, stirring the grass like the fringe on Holly's wrap. I like it down here.

"Beth, really. Come here."

I climb the steps and join her in front of the television, where a local newscaster is talking over some storm-tracker satellite images.

"Guess what?" Holly says. "It's hurricane season. Can you believe this? We drove fifteen hours to get to the beach just in time for a hurricane. Are we the stupidest people in the world, or what?"

Thinking back to the convenience store, the missing water and the empty shelves suddenly make a lot of sense. The guy behind the counter could have been a bit more forthcoming—but then, he probably assumed everybody knew. According to the weatherman, mandatory evacuation orders were issued overnight to a variety of locations, but my knowledge of the Florida geography is too sketchy for me to know whether we're affected or not.

"How does the Sunday school song go?" she asks. "'The house on the sand went *splat*.'" She slaps her hands together on the last word for emphasis. "I knew something was wrong."

She settles on the edge of the small couch, the remote in her hand, staring wide-eyed at the coverage. I have to smile. The storm is just outside. If she turned her head a little to the right, she could see the black thunderheads on the horizon, the churning gunmetal ocean, the occasional swooping gull bright white against the backdrop. Instead, she's glued to the screen, watching a meteorologist's commentary on some time-lapsed images of what's happening before our eyes.

Meanwhile, I feel strangely energized by the coming storm.

By energized, I mean that my skin starts tingling from the feet up. I begin to feel pent up in the little house, so much so that I have to go onto the porch just to feel like I can breathe again. The humid breeze, though hardly cool, raises goose bumps on my flesh, visible tremors of anticipation. I imagine towering waves crashing down, sandstorms whipped into the sky, fat raindrops breaking like hailstones on the roof, even though the actual scene is relatively calm: just darkness in the distance, an empty stretch of sand, and a preternatural brightness to everything, as if the ground is somehow giving off light on its own.

"Beth, you shouldn't go out there."

"I'm just going to have a look."

I go back down the steps, past the tiki hut, my bare feet sinking in the smooth, fine sand. It must be high tide. The frothing waterline seems so near the edge of dry ground. The first wave to hit my feet sends cool spray up my legs. A thrilling sensation. I walk a few feet farther out, until the waves reach my knees. The whole idea of people throwing "hurricane parties" suddenly makes sense to me. We're so accustomed to nature as a passive backdrop, something to look at or build on or destroy. When wind and water and sky rear up and announce their presence, we're either afraid (like my friend) or weirdly intrigued.

Something within us speaks to something in the storm, saying, *It's nice to know you're there.*

When I wander back to the house, the sand now plastered to my wet skin, Holly opens the glass screen door with a flutter of relief.

"Thank God you didn't get sucked in," she says. "I thought for sure you were gonna be swept out to sea, Beth. And I thought Rick was the crazy one in the family!"

"You should go out there. It's exhilarating."

"The good news is, it's been downgraded. It's not a hurricane anymore, just a tropical storm. It'll touch ground farther down the coast, but we'll still get a bucketload of rain." As she relays the news, disappointment creeps into her voice, the same disappointment a panicked housewife might feel having to report that the escaped inmates from the prison have all been rounded up. Fear, too, can be exciting. People are funny that way, prone to regret, even when the thing we regret is the aversion of disaster.

"If it's just a storm," I say, "then you ought to come out. There's a little grass hut at the bottom of the steps. You can at least venture that far."

She looks dubious at first, but after leaning over the railing to examine the hut, she finally gathers some glossy magazines, a Diet Coke, and a tube of sunscreen (just in case). We pad down the steps and settle into the lounge chairs.

"Let's at least drag them onto the beach," I say.

But she prefers the dubious shelter of the grass roof, so we leave the chairs where they are. While the wind whips the pages of her oversized magazine, snapping them like sails and wafting sample perfume fragrances through the air, I recline the back of my chair, enjoying the calm before the storm.

*

Before I met Rick, before law school was more than a dream, before my parents divorced and my brother's drinking almost wrecked his life, when I was a college freshman with just a semester under my belt, I went on a journey. No, not a journey: it was more of an odyssey. Not an odyssey so much as an obsession. Grief must have played a part, though I remember at the time feeling very calm, very detached. Finding the Quaker meetinghouse where Miss Hannah had taken me, the one with the square hole in the roof, appealed to me as an intellectual puzzle.

At least that's what I told myself.

Never much of a navigator, I asked my father for help with the map. He had a road atlas, but the page devoted to Maryland offered too little detail, so we went to the service station for a foldout of the state. He opened it up on the curved hood of my old Beetle—that thing couldn't outrun a lawn mower and the paint was so flaked you couldn't tell what color it was meant to be, but I adored it anyway.

"Now let's have ourselves a look," my father said, smoothing down the map. "You think it was somewhere up north?" He traced his finger up the line of I-83 past Cockeysville all the way to the state line. "How long a drive was it? You wouldn't have gone as far as Pennsylvania, I don't suppose."

I shrugged. "Maybe an hour? We were on the highway a little while, then on some country roads. There were a couple of little towns. We were talking the whole time, and I wasn't really paying that much attention."

"That'll make it hard. What were you talking about?"

"My future. How I need to make something of my life. That kind of thing."

"Like she made something of hers."

I detected a note of irony in his voice. "Well, she did."

"Yeah, I know. She never let anybody forget about it, did she?"

I'd always known Dad didn't care too much for Miss Hannah. He'd never warmed to anybody on my mother's side of the family, or their associates. When it was time for holiday visits, he always came down with a mysterious illness or had to work a few hours late. In Miss Hannah's case, however, he was particularly annoyed. I sensed this throughout my teens, but never understood why.

"You didn't like her, did you?" I asked him.

"I wouldn't say that. I felt sorry for the old broad."

"You felt *sorry* for her?"

I found the idea deeply shocking. In my eyes, Miss Hannah had always been a woman to admire. She was certainly no object of pity. She would have laughed at the very notion.

"Look, one day you'll understand. She could've had a life, that lady. A husband and kids, a family. She could have done all right for herself, being a doctor. She wouldn't have had to be alone."

"She wasn't alone," I said. "She had friends like me."

"Good. I'm glad you feel that way. All I'm saying is, when you catch the do-gooder virus, you lose a lot more than you ever gain."

"Do-gooder?" The term sounded so old-fashioned, it made me laugh.

"You know what I mean. You couldn't be around ol' Hannah for ten minutes without her sizing up your life, weighing you and finding you wanting. 'Nice house,' she'd say. 'Nice kids. Nice car.' And then she'd let you know that that house, that car, they cost ten little orphans their lives. You chose the house and the car, she chose the orphans—it was a zero-sum game with her."

"There should be more people like her," I said stiffly. To be honest, I was ashamed of my dad at that moment, for saying such unkind things about such an amazing person.

"If there were more like her," he said, "the world would end. There'd be no more children born, just orphanages to put them in. No more living. No more being happy."

"That's ridiculous."

"Is it?"

He leaned down as if to study the map, but I could tell he wasn't paying it much attention. My father never liked getting into deep conversations. Not with me, at least. A knock-down-drag-out fight with Gregory was more his idea of fun.

The truth for my nineteen-year-old self ran something like this: Miss Hannah, by her very excellence, made men like my father uncomfortable. Not only had she made something of herself, but her accomplishments outshone his and made him feel small. Accepting a woman as an equal he had no problem with. As a superior? Not so much.

I'd never heard Miss Hannah say anything unkind or judgmental. Maybe I come by the art of projecting myself onto others honestly.

That afternoon he drove up I-83 with me, veering off toward Monkton, then doubling back in the direction of Hampstead, always asking whether anything looked familiar. Nothing did.

"Are you sure it was north? Maybe she took you out toward Reisterstown, more to the west? There's a meetinghouse out in Westminster, though I never heard of it having a hole in the roof."

The next day I tried again, following his advice. I didn't take him along, though, not wanting him there when I discovered the place. He was bound to try to ruin it.

When I found the meetinghouse in Westminster, a white plank structure, I was filled with disappointment. Fortunately, in the greasy spoon across the street, I ran into a couple of old-timers who knew the area quite well and took an interest in my quest. They argued over the map and put a half dozen *Xs* in various spots from Manchester to Taneytown, New Windsor to Walkersville.

Gas was much cheaper back then, and I used plenty of gallons. Over the course of my Christmas break, I acquired a frustratingly good knowledge of central Maryland. I went to every Quaker-related site within fifty miles. The search proved hopeless.

On Christmas Eve morning, I planned a quick drive northeast to Jarrettsville, where a librarian who'd helped me look up possible locations had said she remembered a brick one-story church that looked a little like a dentist's office. Could that be the one? I had to sneak out early because my mother had given an ultimatum the night before: the quest had to end or it would spoil her Christmas.

As I started up the Bug, the passenger door opened and Gregory slipped in. He wore dark glasses and a denim jacket with a hoodie underneath. I heard a sloshing sound as he settled himself, liquid shaking in a bottle. I'd seen him the day before with a flask-shaped bottle of brandy, and now he must have had it hidden inside his coat.

"Where are you going, Eliza? What's the deal?"

"I'm not going anywhere until you get out."

"Come on, I know what you're up to. Take me with you. I promise I'll behave." Before I could protest, he added, "If you don't, I'll tell them you're leaving."

"Fine," I said.

The whole way, Gregory needled me about the search. I

could tell from his breath that he'd been drinking. Hair of the dog, I figured. Strange as it sounds, I never made the connection between his drinking and him being an alcoholic. I was a college student. Everybody drank. And compared to some guys I knew back at school, he seemed to have it under control.

"Why are you so obsessed with finding this place?" he asked. "By now, it's bound to be a disappointment. You've built it up way too much."

"I just want to find it," I said. "If I can."

"You should have paid more attention to where you were going."

"No kidding. At the time, I didn't know she was going to die."

Saying it out loud: a bad idea. Tears started to stream down my cheeks. Even in his state, Gregory could see it was no good for me to drive. He made me pull over so he could take the wheel.

"It's all right, Liz. Don't cry. She lived a full life, you know. It's not like she went before her time."

"I just wish I could have been there."

"I know you do."

Neither one of us was surprised when the Jarrettsville lead turned out to be a bust. All the one-story brick buildings we could find that looked like dentist's offices really were dentist's offices. Once again I had failed in my quest.

"I'll help you out if you want," Gregory said. "I'll ask around. Maybe some of Mom's friends might know . . ."

"There's no point. It's over. Let's just go home."

Wheeling the car around, he reached over and ruffled my hair, like I was a little kid. I swatted him away half-heartedly. He squeezed my jaw, trying to make me smile.

"Come on," he said. "It's not so bad. You're gonna be all right."

And even though we hadn't found what I was looking for in Jarrettsville, the farther we drove away from it, the more I felt I was leaving something behind. Even if I could have talked to Gregory about spiritual things, I wouldn't have opened up to him that day. What I was leaving wasn't just my childhood or my happy memories of the departed Miss Hannah. I was pulling away from the closest moment I'd ever had to a physical experience of the divine.

When you get older, when your memory starts to slip, you look back and realize that all the years you spent in anticipation were in fact your best years. While you were looking forward to better things, they were already the best, and from now on life would only go downhill. That's how I felt at that moment.

Giving up on the search meant surrendering the most profound intimacy I'd ever known in my nineteen years of existence.

From here on out, I believed, I could only grow farther away.

*

I must have nodded off on the beach.

When I open my eyes, I'm staring at the sky through a bald spot in the grass roof, a gap that wasn't there when we arrived. Holly's chair beside me is empty. One of her magazines lies face-down on the sand, anchored by the Diet Coke bottle. Her fringed wrap is coiled around one of the chair legs. She must have gone back up to the house—but no, sitting up on my elbow, I see her down by the water, kicking the waves with child-like abandon.

"You finally caught the bug," I mutter aloud.

The dark clouds loom closer, but the sky above burns especially bright in compensation: a pure, clear blue. I shed my sunglasses, taking in the stretch of hot white sand. I feel comfortably lethargic.

Sinking down, I gaze at the sky through the gap in the grass hut's roof. Around the edges, a few stray blades shimmer in the breeze. As I watch, a bird flashes past, too quick for me to make out anything but the blur of a wing. Every strong gust seems to push the gap a little wider, exposing another inch or two of sky. It's the movement that keeps my attention, the intermittent expansion. Otherwise I would have looked away already.

Instead, I keep looking. My attention shifts from the edge of the hole to its center, to the impossibly clear blueness of the sky. It's not natural to really look at something. The urge to glance away is hard to resist. If you discipline yourself, though, if you relax into the gaze, things that ordinarily wouldn't hold your interest for more than a second can reveal extraordinary depth.

I lie there, feeling the wind blow the hem of my Ravens T-shirt wide, feeling the dry sand on the soles of my feet flake away, more aware of myself, of my body, of *the fact of my embodiment* (I don't know how else to say it) than I have ever been. The blue sky is textureless, infinite, throbbing in the familiar way of my youth. I lie before it the way Miss Hannah sprawled on the wood pew, submitting to the vision.

The longer I look, the nearer the sky is. And it changes on me, losing its innocent hue, darkening and deepening. Sometimes it appears so abstract—unmediated color—and then a bird will streak past or a bit of gray cloud will pass along the edges, shocking me into the realization that the sky is much farther away than I fancy.

Then the cloud is gone and I'm floating again.

Sometimes the sky looks liquid too, and I imagine that instead of looking up I'm gazing down into a bottomless, swirling sea of bluish-purple black, and the only thing preventing me from falling is a kind of reverse gravity that pins me to the roof of the world.

You're crazy, you know that? I tell myself.

And though I don't speak the words out loud, I hear them as if I had. As if I'd whispered into my own ear. Apart from my voice, there is nothing but silence: no wind, no wave, no sound of Holly on the beach. No drums beating or crowds howling, no resentful *whatevers*, no evasions or lies. No smack of hand on cheek, no nothing, no noise.

But oh, this silence isn't empty, not at all. The silence is very full.

It was always there, I realize, from the moment Miss Hannah first showed me until now. I'd searched and searched for it, but it hadn't gone anywhere. It was never so far that, with a little looking, it couldn't be found.

If only I had searched in the right place.

A low rumble fills the air, a physical sound (again, I don't know how else to say it), a sound I feel on my skin. It is not a voice. It is not saying anything. Or if it is, the message is merely this: *I am here. I am present.* Then the rumble grows a throaty, ragged edge and I recognize it as thunder. Through the gap, the sky is molten gray. I sit up and see Holly, her water-freckled skin gleaming in the last light, running toward me with a smile on her lips, her hands held over her head as if to fend off heaven.

"You're gonna get soaked if you stay down here!"

She snatches up her things and rushes toward the steps. I throw a leg over the side of the lounge chair, forcing myself up. The hiss of rain fills my ears, the drops speckling the ground all around me. I imagine what it would be like to peel off the T-shirt and run into the surf, alone and sylph-like with the storm.

But then I really would be crazy, right? Instead, I follow Holly up the stairs, arriving soaked and laughing as she slides the glass door shut behind me.

"Is this wild or what?" she says. Meaning the two of us, not the storm outside.

"You got wet. I told you so."

"If our husbands could see us now, huh? They'd pretty much freak out. What am I saying? I'm freaking out. This isn't my idea of a holiday at the beach."

"But it's good," I say.

"Yeah," she says. "I think it is."

As we stand dripping on the marble tile, towels clutched around our shoulders, I tell Holly that I don't want to stay.

"I need to get back," I tell her.

Whatever I was looking for here, I just found it. And there's something waiting for me at home. I didn't get a sign under the hut or anything. I didn't hear a voice. By why should I have to? Why should God have to speak for me to know what he is saying? Couldn't he also be present in silence?

Just by looking, I was suddenly able to hear, and now I think I know what needs to be done. My father had been wrong—he had to be. It isn't a zero-sum game. Having a family doesn't mean I can't help. There's something I can do, and I intend to do it.

"Okay," she says, processing. "But can we at least wait out the storm?"

"There's no rush," I say, not believing it at all.

Inside, I know I won't rest until I'm back.

chapter 16

Home at Last

Holly's side of the argument, which runs from still-drizzling Jacksonville to the sunny edge of Glen Burnie thirteen hours later, can be summed up in two words: nothing's changed.

And my answer, equally succinct: *I* have changed.

It's not easy to explain. Spiritual awakenings never are. Enlightenments, realizations, burning-bush experiences—none of the ready-made categories seem up to the challenge, particularly when nothing happened to me that didn't happen to her. I looked at the sky, that's all. I looked and I had a feeling.

"The trick is to see through the glass, not to be distracted by the image it bounces back at you." Deedee's words, and now I begin to understand them.

Whether I've changed or not, the facts remain the same. Mission Up is still what it is and Mother Zacchaeus is still really Rosetta Harvey with a criminal record. I'm still a middle-aged white lady from the suburbs who doesn't know what she's getting herself into and has no business anyway butting into things she can't comprehend.

"Eric won't change his mind, Beth. When it comes to charity, everything has to be aboveboard. People don't open their wallets these days if they think they're being scammed."

"Nobody has to open their wallet. That was my mistake, thinking Eric could fix things, thinking the answer was to turn on the spigot of money. Like the thing that hurts *us* would help *them*, like it's just a question of pointing the hose in the right direction."

"Now you've lost me."

"It doesn't matter. I know what I have to do."

"Then explain it to me."

"I don't think I can. I just know."

I can tell something's slipping, the bond between us is stretching thin. The sisters-on-the-way-to-the-beach soundtrack skips to its end. The reality of everyday life looms ahead, darker than storm clouds.

"I really want to understand," Holly says. "If what you're looking for is some kind of service project, there are better things to invest yourself in. Safer things."

"I'm not looking for anything. It was looking for me."

"I wish you'd stop talking like that," she says.

"Like what?"

She shakes her head, but I know what she means. Talking like I've drunk the Kool-Aid. Talking like a woman on a mission, a true believer.

Which is what I feel like. Nothing's changed, she's right.

But a hole opened up in the roof.

*

It's past eleven, half an hour from Lutherville, and there's no answer on the home phone or Jed's cell. I hate to disturb Deedee this late, but call her anyway, looking for reassurance. No answer there either.

"I don't know what's going on."

"At least you know where Rick will be," Holly says. "That's something."

When we pull up in front of the house, there are no lights on. Next door at the Smythes', too, everything is dark. It's as if our corner of the street has lost power. No sign of occupation.

"This isn't right," I say.

Without bothering about the luggage, I get out of the car and rush to the door, fumbling with the keys until Holly comes up behind me, telling me to calm down.

"I'm sure they're okay," she says. "Maybe they went out."

"Everyone together? They're all gone?" I shake my head at the impossibility of the idea.

Then I'm inside, calling Jed's name, calling Eli's, switching on lights as I move through the house. Up the stairs, into their empty bedrooms, down the stairs and through the empty kitchen. Out in the backyard the shed looks dark too. I burst through the back door, crossing the distance in a run, grabbing the doorknob and opening the shed.

Empty.

All the furniture in the little outbuilding has been pushed against the walls. On the floor, where I'd seen Rick stretched out the first night, a bedroll is hastily piled. The books pilfered from the shelves are stacked on the open rolltop desk, which is pushed against the fireplace. The topmost volumes lie open, anchored by an empty Nutella jar. I go for the lamp and, in my frantic haste, tip it off the side table.

"Beth, are you okay?" asks Holly.

"He's not in here. Where are they? Something's wrong."

I head across the lawn, past the stone wall, and onto the back steps of the Smythes' wraparound porch, with Holly trailing behind me. Despite the late hour, I rap on the door and several of the ground-floor windows, expecting a light to switch on inside. Nothing.

"Try calling them again."

I dial the Smythes. On the other side of the glass windowpane, I hear the phone ringing. No one answers. I try Jed's number. Still nothing.

"What about Rick? Try him."

I dial and hold the phone to my ear. In the distance, a faint electronic chirp. Following the sound, we end up back at the shed, where Rick's phone is plugged into the socket by the desk.

"Holly, I don't know what to do."

By now, my sense of spiritual calm is shattered completely, just a heap of menacing shards at my feet. We return to the house for another fruitless search. Maybe there's a note? Maybe a message on the voice mail? I even go to the computer and check my neglected e-mail inbox.

"Anything?"

I shake my head.

Then the doorbell rings and we both jump.

I wrench the door open, expecting Jed or Eli, even Rick. Instead, Roy Meakin stands there with an apologetic look on his face.

"I know it's late," he says, "but I saw the lights and thought I'd come over and check. Is there an update? I haven't heard anything since they left."

"We just got here, Roy. I have no idea what's going on. Where is everybody?"

He frowns. "You don't know? They're at the hospital. There was an ambulance, paramedics, the whole shebang."

I'm looking down at the dark sky again, with nothing to pin me in place. Falling into black despair. First thought: Rick being hauled out of the shed, dead from hunger. Then I think of Eli and some freak weed-related accident, or Jed . . .

"Rick," Roy says.

My knees go weak. I put my hand out to steady myself.

"He saved her."

"What?"

"He saved her. Margaret. If it hadn't been for him, she wouldn't have made it. That's what Deedee said. We were at the church when it happened. Just pulled up and saw the flashing lights."

Holly's beside me, her arm around my shoulder is all that's keeping me up. Relief floods in, sucking the life out of my fear. He's okay. The boys are okay. And then I remember Margaret. Rick saved her life? What happened? I need to get to the hospital, whichever one they're at.

Ahead of me, Holly asks, "Where did they take her?"

Roy looks at her, then back at me. "Tell you what. Let's *all* go."

And just like that, the three of us go marching off into the night.

*

"They just left," Deedee says. "I sent them home. There was no point in them staying all night. He's done enough already."

She stands in the hallway outside her mother's ICU room, speaking in a soft undertone. The nurse who went in to fetch her still hovers off to the side, ready if needed. In the car on our way to St. Joseph's in Towson, exhaustion overtook me—the storm, the long drive home, talking in circles, the sudden panic of the last hour. Now I feel revived.

"You probably passed each other on the road," she says.

I reach out and give her a hug. "How is your mother doing?"

"Under the circumstances, very good. It was her heart, Elizabeth. You know she's had problems. She had an attack, a stroke, and she fell. It was Rick who found her and called for help. I was . . . I was working." She holds her paint-flecked hands out. "I wasn't there."

"*Rick* found her?"

Deedee's eyes light up as she tells the story. "He said he heard something. A voice. He followed the sound and found her in the house, at the foot of the stairs. Elizabeth, if he hadn't been there, she would have lain on the ground for hours. She would have died, I'm sure. She couldn't get up, she'd hurt her leg."

"She was calling for help and he heard her? All the way in the shed?"

"Isn't it miraculous?"

"It's pretty . . . amazing."

"And he came up here to check on her, brought the boys. You're right, he was absolutely amazing. I'll never be able to thank him."

At this moment, I have an overwhelming urge to see this amazing husband of mine.

I suppress it, though. We've only just arrived, and Deedee could use some comforting.

The four of us head down the hallway to a lounge, where she

and Roy fill in some of the details between them. They'd been at the church, where Deedee was nearing the final stage of her mural. ("It's wonderful, really wonderful," Roy insists.) When they arrived and saw the ambulance, Deedee flew into a panic. Rick calmed her, explaining that Margaret had fallen—he didn't know about the stroke yet—but seemed to be all right, though very shaken. Then the paramedics had taken her out on a gurney, which was almost more than Deedee could bear.

"She was able to grip my hand," she says, her voice husky with emotion. "And she whispered to me not to worry. But really, how could I not worry? I should have been there."

"You can't blame yourself," Roy says.

"He's right, Deedee. And anyway, Rick *was* there."

The words sound strange in my ear.

By the time we've reassured her, it's well past one. Roy tries unsuccessfully to coax her to come home, but Deedee is determined to spend the night in her mother's hospital room. In the end, we leave her with promises to check back in the morning. We drive back to my house, where Holly unloads my suitcase and takes her leave.

Roy says good night, crossing the street toward home.

"By the way," he calls out. "I never thanked you. I made a visit to Rooney & Gill, and everything's taken care of."

"That's good to know."

I slip inside, locking the door behind me. Once again all the lights are off.

That rankles. They should have realized when they got home and found all the lights on that I'd been here. They ought to have waited up, or even called. I check my phone, just in case, but there are no missed calls. I'm miffed.

On the drive back, I imagined myself heading out to the shed, asking Rick about what had happened. Just talking to him again.

But finding the lights off hardens me to the idea.

I leave the heavy suitcase at the foot of the stairs, not wanting to lug it up in the dark and risk knocking something over. I feel my way past the bathroom to my bedroom door, closing it behind me. The curtains are drawn, but through the gap a shaft of moonlight bathes the room in a grayish haze. I creep to the edge of the bed, kicking my shoes off, pulling my T-shirt over my head, peeling off my jeans and leaving them in a little puddle on the floor. Then I lift the covers and slide inside.

I'm not sure how long I lay there before I realize I am not alone. A breath in the room, a sound—I don't know what it is, but suddenly, I'm not by myself in the bed. I sit up, I turn. In the hazy darkness, I can make out the shape under the covers. The broad plane of his back, the peak of his shoulder. He faces away from me toward the wall, his breathing heavy and regular. Asleep.

My husband is in bed beside me. I'm not sure what to do.

I slide my hand along the mattress. Without touching him, I edge forward until I feel the heat of his body on my fingertips. That's close enough to reassure myself he's really here.

Okay then.

Rick is here.

Will he be here in the morning when I wake up? Will he wake up and be shocked to find me here? Will he retreat back to the shed?

I turn away from him, resting my head in the pillow. Still, I can feel his presence. My eyes won't close. I'm not tired at all. I stare into the gloom, tracing the shape of the nightstand, the trunk of the lamp, and . . . something's not right. I reach out my hand, feeling my way over the top of the nightstand. There's something there I don't remember from before. It feels like a shallow wooden box, rough around the inner edges. *What is it?*

I grasp the edge and lift slightly. The face of St. Rick stares back at me. What I was feeling was the painting, turned facedown by my husband. He couldn't sleep with it looking at him.

I roll toward him and throw my arm over his broad shoulder. In his sleep, his warm hand moves upward to rest on my arm.

*

The next morning, when I wake, Rick is propped up on one elbow, looking at me.

"You're back," he says.

I smile, suppress a yawn. "So are you."

He doesn't say anything.

"Are you?" I ask.

"I think . . . yes. I am. Did you have fun in Florida?"

"There was a big thunderstorm. I didn't even get a tan."

"Is that why you came back, the storm?"

"Sort of," I say.

It's too early, too soon to get into any of that. There's so much between us that is unresolved, so many open questions. This is not the time for them. Having him back is enough. I'm afraid of doing anything, saying anything that might drive him back into the shed.

Jed and Eli are already downstairs. Their surprise at seeing their father come down from the bedroom is matched only by the double take when I follow behind him.

"I thought you were in Florida," Jed says, bafflement in his voice.

"Boys," Rick says. "What do you want for breakfast?"

Rick ends up flipping omelets while I brew coffee and pour orange juice. Over breakfast we act like a normal family—by which I mean, we pretend. Apart from the occasional glance, you'd never think anything strange had been going on in our lives the past three weeks. Eli goes to school first, leaving Jed alone with us. He doesn't seem uncomfortable around Rick—they would have talked last night—but being around both of us is clearly overwhelming. He keeps checking the time on his phone.

"I tried to call you last night," I say. "Quite a few times."

He glances at the screen. "Oh."

Nothing more, just *oh*. All my maternal anxiety reduced to a single syllable.

He leaves five minutes early, relieved to get away.

"Well," Rick says. "He's off. Alone at last. And we have plenty to talk about."

"Yes, we do."

He sits on one side of the breakfast table, silent. I sit on the other, staring down at my coffee.

"Who's gonna start?" I ask finally.

"I guess it should be me."

chapter 17

The Everything Fast

He starts at the beginning.

The thing that drove him out to the shed was Jim Shaw's promise of a megaphone. At The Community, Rick always struggled for more of the coveted "stage time," exposure in front of the whole church, under the spotlights for everyone to see. And the larger the church grew, the less of a role he seemed to have up front. There were people who'd attended The Community for months, for years, who did not even realize he was on staff. Only the men got to know the Men's Pastor, and even then, just a fraction of them.

At Jim's church in Richmond, the stage would be Rick's. His voice would be the one people heard every Sunday. Instead of shrinking, his reach would extend mightily.

"That was the problem," he says. "Somebody puts a megaphone in your hand, and you better be sure you have something to say. I didn't know if I had anything. Jim put me on the spot in a big way. Was I ready for that? To be honest, it scared me."

One of the leadership blogs Rick kept up with had recently run an article about something called a "digital fast." You unplugged your phone, stopped checking e-mail, shut down Facebook and Twitter. The idea being, we're so bombarded by these media and feel so much pressure to stay on top of them that our focus becomes second-by-second instead of eternal. I remember him talking about this, though at the time I wrote it off as yet another trend-of-the-month. But Rick took it seriously and decided to go one better.

"I didn't want to make this decision on my own. I wanted to hear from God. And to do that, I thought, 'I need to unplug.' With all the noise coming in, I was afraid I'd never hear him if God did try to talk to me. So I started with the idea of a digital fast, and the more I thought about it, the bigger the idea grew. I went out to the shed thinking I would keep a vigil, that I would wait until I heard the answer. I laid down on the floor, Beth, and I started praying."

"I know."

His eyebrows raise. "You saw me?"

"Honestly? I thought you were praying, but you were really asleep."

"Ah." He ponders this. "Can I level with you? I'm being completely transparent here. I'm not sure I know how to pray, not really. Up on stage, under the lights, I can spin a prayer out as long as anybody, but when I tried that night, I just ran out of words. They dried up on me, and that made me more scared. How could I be talking to people about God if I couldn't talk *to* him?"

As he speaks, a well of sympathy springs up inside me. I never told Rick about my own struggles with prayer because I thought he wouldn't understand. The first time I saw him, he was deep in prayer, and ever since he's always been quick to chat with God like they were best buds, like they were brothers in the same fraternity. Now I know better, and it makes me love him a little more.

"When I woke up that morning," he says, "I knew the vigil wasn't enough. You thought I was crazy, and maybe you were right, but when the idea came to me, I had to do it. If I'd gotten anything from God, that was it. Not a digital fast, but an *everything* fast. That's what I called it in my head, the Fast."

Rick's Fast wasn't about abstaining from food, though that was to come. It was about abstaining from life, other people, the outside world. The satellite dish, to get reception, must be perched on top of the roof. In the same way, Rick had to elevate himself, get above things, if he was to receive the signal he wanted.

"The thing is, I never expected it to take so long. You were pressuring me about the birthday party, about Florida, and in my mind, I kept thinking all of that might still happen. If I could get this Fast done with, hear from God, and make the decision, then life could go on as normal. I wasn't expecting the Fast to change things permanently, not like they have."

So things have changed permanently? I let that hang in the air for now.

Not being the reflective type, Rick wasn't sure what a Fast like this should look like. At first, he imagined an intensive self-improvement course. He would read books, he would watch videos, he would fill himself with influences in the hope that something would flow out of him in prayer. The first couple of days, he tried his best. He stayed up reading until his eyes hurt, but at the end of a two-or-three-hour stretch, he could remember almost nothing from the books. He started writing things down—"I have a notebook out there full of quotes"—and then, as a form of prayer, he'd read them back aloud, sharing them with God.

"What about the birthday party?" I ask. "I didn't expect you to show up."

"I planned ahead. I bought the saddle when I got Eli's tire fixed. I knew there'd be people there, and you'd feel awkward having to tell them what was going on. So I came. Then I saw that painting. It really messed with my head, Beth. I don't know what that was all about, but when I spotted it, at first I thought I was going insane. You'll think I'm an idiot, but I honestly wondered if I was the only person who could see it."

"That was Deedee's idea of you," I say. "St. Rick."

He nods slowly. "I saw it in the bedroom. You were sleeping next to it?"

"Not really." My cheeks flush. "Just the once. It fell off the wall and—"

"The *wall*? You hung it on the wall?"

"Eli did. You must have seen it when you snuck into the house."

"I guess I didn't notice."

"How could you miss it? That thing was staring down at me every time I went up the stairs."

"Do you think it looks like me?"

"You mean, do I think you're a saint?"

"No, that's not what I mean. I just . . . it took me a second to realize who it was supposed to be. Then I thought, maybe it was the sign."

"Yourself reflected back at you?"

"Stupid, I know. And then I went back to the shed and that girl was there."

"Sam."

He nods.

"What did you say to her, anyway? She came out of there and wanted to go straight home. Deedee thought it was a miracle."

"Maybe so, but it wasn't me. I don't remember exactly. I think I said something like, 'You can't stay here,' or 'You don't belong here.'"

"It must have been a miracle," I say, "or maybe she was still high."

He smiles, and again I feel something opening up inside me, pleasant and painful at the same time. Just talking to him again fills me with awkward joy. Don't let it end. Don't let me say anything to spoil the moment.

"There was something else," Rick says. "The flowers."

"That was Deedee too."

"I thought it was you at first, then I realized it wasn't and didn't know what to think. Deedee, huh? The funny thing is, I had this feeling I wasn't alone, that someone was watching me. I wanted to believe it was God, though, not the next-door neighbor."

The daily offerings added something to the Fast. Until then, he had imagined his struggle taking place in private. Now, the larger world was involved. A secret watcher who seemed to be rewarding him for his persistence, encouraging him to go further. When his food ran out, he decided he would go without. And apart from the Bible, he stopped reading the other books. He had already let his phone battery die, but now he unplugged the laptop and let that lose power too. No more YouTube motivational videos, no more sermon podcasts. He denied himself the use of the fireplace and moved his bedroll to the hard floor.

As he confides all these privations, I remember what it was like when Gregory came out of rehab and started talking about his addiction for the first time. Hearing the other side of so many of our family stories, the explanation for things that had never made sense before. Because he'd lived through it, he could narrate the tales with a certain amount of detachment, even highlighting the humor in situations that were, for me, utterly harrowing to hear about. The time he wrecked his car while drunk and wandered off and got lost in the nearby woods. The time he blacked out in the back of a cab and woke up in the emergency room. There were so many, each one more terrifying than the last.

And now Rick is telling the same kinds of stories, sounding like a man fresh from some kind of spiritual rehab. This might be hagiography in Deedee's ears, the lives of the saints, but for me it's heartbreaking to think of what he was going through just a few yards away in the backyard.

"You look terrible," he says. "Do you want me to stop?"

I shake my head. "Of course not. But what happened with Margaret? You heard her calling for help? That's what ended the Fast?"

"Not exactly. See, I felt like I'd had a breakthrough. What Jim was asking me, really, was to be a big voice in the church. He remembered all the talks we used to have, all my theories, and he said the guys like me are the ones who ought to have the platform. And I agreed with him, Beth. All I wanted was some assurance from God that if I stepped up to the plate, I'd hit one out of the park. When I didn't get it, *boom*, the ground collapsed underneath me. All I could do was double down. If God was gonna hide from me, I had to go after him harder.

"And then it struck me, the problem I was having. The big voice, the megaphone, all this envy over stage time. It was ego, Beth. It was Self. I couldn't hear from God because I didn't even speak his language anymore. That was the revelation: I'm not going to be a big voice. I don't even want to be. What I need to be is 'the still small voice.'"

That familiar phrase. The still small voice. It's from the Old Testament, the story of the prophet Elijah. When God reveals himself, there's a great wind that rips the mountain up, then there's a mighty earthquake, and then there's a fire. But the Bible says God isn't in the wind, or the earthquake, or the fire. No, after all that drama has concluded, in the ensuing silence, Elijah hears a still small voice, a low and gentle whisper.

"God wasn't giving me a megaphone. He was telling me to shut up. To be still and know."

Confession: I'm a little disappointed. I was hoping for more. Let me try to explain. You remember the Tom Hanks movie *Castaway*? The guy's plane goes down and he ends up trapped on a desert island like Robinson Crusoe for years and years. I loved it right up until the end, when he makes it home and realizes life has kept going without him, and Tom gives a little speech that encapsulates the lessons learned. They should have stopped the movie before that part, because what he says then, his Life Lesson, turns out to be something sappy and sentimental he could have learned by staying home and watching *Oprah*.

After all the suffering the man went through, you expect him to learn something amazing, something he couldn't have fathomed any other way. Instead, you get cliché. Stop talking and listen. Be still and know. Was it really all for that? The weeks of insane isolation, what he put himself and his family through. He could have saved us all the trouble. His spiritual self-help books are chock-full of that kind of thing.

"What's wrong?" he asks.

"Nothing."

"No, really, Beth. You've got this look on your face."

"Never mind my face, just keep going."

"Seriously."

All righty, then. He wants to know, so I tell him. I give it to him with both barrels, including the Tom Hanks reference, knowing the whole time this is exactly what I didn't want to do. I'm ruining the moment. Spoiling our first communion since he went into that ridiculous shed.

Only he doesn't react as I expected.

He grins a little. Nods. Rubs his chin, which is clean-shaven. No mountain man beard, no designer stubble. He must have taken care of that before he took the boys to the hospital.

"I know it's not much," he says. "I didn't come back because I learned something profound. Just the opposite, really. While I was having this great revelation, how God wanted me to be the still small voice, I went back and looked up the passage. It's in 1 Kings 19. And I realized I'd gotten it wrong. God's not telling Elijah to go out and be the whispering prophet. It's the way God speaks to him, not the way he's supposed to speak. And anyway, Elijah just brags about how dedicated he is to God, until God has to explain to him that there are, like, seven thousand other guys in Israel who are just the same.

"The point being, I wasn't listening. Instead of being the small voice, I wanted to hear the small voice. That was the real breakthrough. I want to hear. And I did, Beth. The moment I had that thought, the moment I tried to listen, I heard something."

"God?"

"No," he says. "It was Margaret. I didn't know that at the time. I just heard *something*. So I followed the sound. When it took me next door, I followed, still not realizing what it was. I went inside and only then, only when I saw her there on the floor, did I recognize her voice. All that time, I still thought it was a kind of signal, some kind of sign. But it was Margaret on the floor yelling for help."

"That was the message."

"I didn't get a message, Beth. The ambulance came, and afterward I was sitting out in the shed and suddenly, it dawns on me: what am I doing here? Just like that, I can't even remember why it seemed so important, why I thought there was no other way."

He reaches across the table and takes my hand. It's the first time we've touched, really touched. Intentional, eyes fixed on each other.

"I'm sorry, baby, I really am. I basically abandoned you. Abandoned the boys. And I can't sit here and tell you there was any good reason. All I can tell you is, I am sorry."

I squeeze his hand. "You saved her life."

"Not because of the Fast."

"You wouldn't have been here otherwise. We'd have all been in Florida instead of just me. And don't forget about Sam. Whatever you said, it made an impact on that girl—"

"You're sweet," he says, "trying to make me feel better. But I'm a big boy. I can admit when I've screwed up royally. All this, and I'm still back at square one. I still don't know what to tell Jim."

"Did you talk to him at all? I left the phone out there . . ."

"I told him I was still prayerfully considering it. Those are the exact words: 'prayerfully considering.' You can take the man out of ministry, but you can't take the ministry out of the man."

"Out of ministry?"

"I'm not saying that, Beth. I'm not saying anything. To be honest, I don't know what to say. But tell me you forgive me, or at least tell me you'll try."

This is a big ask, whether he realizes it or not. Part of me wants to melt, wants to make everything okay again, or at least pretend. But if we start acting like the last three weeks didn't happen, we'll be picking up where we left off. We were miserable then. I don't want to settle for a lesser misery just to avoid a greater one. I'm ready to be non-miserable. Easy grace won't get me that.

"Beth?" he asks, imploring.

"You promise not to do it again?"

Too easy, I think.

"Never."

"All right, then."

He leans over and tries to kiss me. His hip catches the table, which scrapes across the tile and pushes into my ribs. *Is that a metaphor or what?*

"Oops," he says. "Sorry."

He's gonna give up. Before he can, I reach for his T-shirt and pull him to my lips. He tastes clean, his breath fresh, not at all like a desert father or a crazy hermit. He tastes like himself.

It's the first time Rick has ever told me he was sorry.

Confession: I'm going to let that cover a multitude of sins.

chapter 18

Mural, Mural on the Wall

Once you've resolved to reconcile, the hardest part is telling the people who've supported you during the separation. I go over the speech to Holly in my head, even practicing a few lines in the mirror. She'll understand, naturally. She'll be happy for me. But I worry that, under the mask of outward joy, I might detect a note of disappointment in her face. *You're weaker than I thought, Beth. You gave in to him so easily. How do you know he won't do it again?* Nothing's changed, after all.

The boys prove a challenge for Rick.

"Eli will be all right," I warn him, "but I'm not sure about Jed. You should know, while you've been out there, he's found himself a girlfriend."

"Yes, he told me."

To my surprise, father and son seem to have bonded on the day of Margaret's fall. Maybe Jed sensed a change in his dad, or maybe being in love has rendered his teenage anger moot. Rick knows all about Marlene, though he doesn't remember her from The Community. He has even reconciled himself to the piercings and dreadlocks.

"There's something appealing about that to a boy," he says, opening the window into the male psyche a little too far for my taste. "It's . . . exotic."

The real trouble comes from Eli, Dad's favorite. He won't fall into line with the restored family relation. Whenever Rick enters a room, Eli walks out. At dinner, if he shows up at all, he's sullen, answering all his father's attempts at conversation with pointed silence. When I get him alone and try to talk to him, he blows up. "This is how it's going to be? You're just going to pretend like nothing happened?" Either that, or he grows paranoid about the prospect of me telling Rick about his use of marijuana. "Just do it," he'll say. "Get it over with. I dare you."

But I don't say a word about the smoking to Rick. We're already taking on water and listing to starboard. The last thing I want to do is capsize the family.

Eli worries me. For now, I have to leave it at that.

*

"So it's over?" Holly asks, incredulous.

"That's what he says."

"And the job in Richmond? Is he going to say yes?"

"That's still undecided."

"Still?" she says, packing a lot into the word.

It's Sunday and we're having coffee in her office between services. Rick stayed home, and so did Eli. I left Jed pacing in the lobby, waiting for Marlene to show. Somehow he persuaded her to give The Community another try, and in return he's agreed to spend the afternoon at Chas Worthing's, painting signs with the Rent-a-Mob.

There's a lot more Holly wants to say. I can see it. But she swallows the words, forcing a change in subject. "What about Margaret? How is she doing?"

"That's a miracle," I say. "Seriously. She could have broken her hip in that fall. For that matter, she could have broken her neck. All she's got is the fracture in the forearm, which is plastered up, and the side of her face is a little lopsided—but she can talk." Every day since the first night, I've visited the hospital, and every day Margaret seems a little more herself. Her speech is a little slurred, her right side seems stiff, but the doctors appear optimistic apart from the fact that they're holding on to her for observation. "Fortunately, she doesn't seem to remember much about the accident."

"And Rick? What does he say about it?"

"Just what you know already. He heard her calling and went to help." I don't feel comfortable going into greater detail. That is Rick's story to share, not mine.

"What about your big plan? Have you shared that with him?"

My big plan. The morning of the storm seems so far away, the silence under the shifting sky, the sense of purpose afterward. The long, excited drive back, countering all of Holly's common-sense arguments with a vague but hopeful optimism.

Once Rick had recounted his weeks in the shed, I told him my own side of the story. He listened intently, especially when I told him what my brother had said about this being my time and not my husband's. "Maybe he's right," Rick said, latching onto the idea. I held nothing back, even rewinding to my meetinghouse epiphany with Miss Hannah, so he'd understand what had happened to me at the beach and why it meant something.

I expected him to dismiss it all as Quaker nonsense and say that I was once again "letting the process of spirituality get in the way of the content of faith," a line of his from way back. But I suppose he was in no position to judge, not after inventing his own wacky process. So he took it all in. The respect he showed for the experience frankly surprised me.

Maybe he didn't find enlightenment in that shed. But he certainly changed.

None of this is fit for Holly's consumption. Not yet. She's not going to accept my rehabilitated Rick without more time to get used to the idea.

"Recent developments have kind of thrown me for a loop," I say. "The past couple of days, we've been learning how to be a family again. Trying to, anyway."

"Oh, Beth, I'm sorry." She puts her coffee down, comes around the table, and gives me a hug. "Here I am peppering you with questions, when you barely know which way is up."

Over her shoulder, the monitor flickers. The praise team is on stage, lighting into their first set. Without any sound, it's hard to guess what they're singing. The camera cuts to the audience. From the hand-clapping and the syncopated swaying, it must be a jaunty number. When the camera cuts back, I can see the band playing and, on the screen behind them, a flash of audience close-ups.

"Hey, look," I say.

She turns toward the screen. "It's Peggy!"

Sure enough, there's Peggy Ensign, projected on the big screen—rather, we're watching her on a small screen that projects the big screen for us. She's in the crowd of worshippers, hemmed in on every side by half-seen, moving people. Her own claps, her awkward jerking motion from side to side, is always a little bit out of step, a little behind the people around her.

"Oh dear," Holly says. "They really shouldn't stick people up on-screen like that. But, hey, people like it. They get to see themselves larger than life."

As she speaks, Peggy realizes she is on-screen. A big, fulfilled smile breaks out on her face, then the camera cuts to one of the praise team beauties, her eyes tightly shut in passionate praise.

"How was the sermon this morning?" I ask.

"New series, Beth. Secrets of a Happy Marriage."

"Good. I'd better take notes."

This time I stay for the service, sitting with Holly in our usual spot on the far right-hand side of the auditorium with a flanking view of the stage. The hissing speaker overhead doesn't bother me, and I pay very little attention to the huge projection screen in front of us. I retreat into myself, thinking of the grass hut on the beach, the Quaker meetinghouse I could never find again, and whether all this time I could have re-created the feeling just by looking at the sky, which was always there. At one time, I had imagined my life as a straight line extending before me, sometimes a pathway, sometimes an arrow. Now I look back and find a twisted coil, as if the once-taut rope of my life was severed at some point and dropped to the floor in a long series of random loops.

As if I've been living in circles. Which is a bad thing, if there's somewhere you need to get. Not so much if you're already there.

Jed finds me in the lobby afterward, threading his way through the exiting crowd. He's alone. I brace myself to deliver some encouraging words, but he cuts me off by announcing that Marlene is waiting outside. "I thought we could all go to lunch."

"How did she enjoy the service?"

He seesaws his hand. The gesture reminds me how much he resembles Gregory, who's fond of doing the same thing. "She said it would have been better if Dad was speaking."

"See, you should be proud of him."

"Mom, I am."

Something *has* happened between them. Something big. "You and your dad have made peace, huh? I can tell there's something different."

"I don't know. We just talked, I guess. Everything I hate about this"—he sweeps his hand to encompass the whole of The Community—"I think he hates it too, in his own way. I couldn't tell him apart from the church. Now I can."

"You hate it, but you invited Marlene."

"She wanted to come," he says. "It's not like I twisted her arm."

For lunch Jed takes us to Bertucci, the brick-oven pizza place, where he has a good time acting the part of the grown-up. For church, Marlene took out half her piercings, tamed her hair into a jutting ponytail, and dressed in a girlishly demure button-front dress shapeless enough to have originated in her mother's closet, or possibly her grandmother's. Her sweater makes up for this by looking like it came straight from the *Mad Max* wardrobe room. The two of them seem very cozy in each other's company, sharing the same pizza, scooting close enough that their elbows touch.

"So, how was it being back?" I ask.

Marlene shrugs. "Just like I remember."

As critical as I am, the thought of her mental censure makes me feel defensive. I want to stick up for The Community a bit. I suppress the impulse.

"So, you're going to the Rent-a-Mob this afternoon?"

She nods. Most of the conversation goes like this, me beginning the sentence with *So . . .* only to watch it fall to the ground.

"This will be your first time," I say to Jed, stating the obvious.

"If you don't count D.C."

"That was quite a fight."

Marlene chomps her pizza, still nodding. "You know, I've been thinking about what Barber was saying, and it pretty much sums up where I am. With the whole Rent-a-Mob thing, I mean. It's a lot of time to invest, and really, it's not like any of it makes, like, an impact, you know?"

"It's more about the experience, Chas would say."

"Yeah, but that's Chas. I always wanted it to be *for* something."

"So what's left? Flash mobs?"

Jed lights up. "I think they're cool. I've been watching the videos—"

"Maybe a mob isn't what I need," Marlene says.

"No, right," Jed says, changing course without missing a beat. "That was crazy in D.C., just wild."

"Maybe it's a relationship, you know? Like, a real relationship."

It scares me a little, hearing her talk this way. Too much, too soon. I look at Jed, my little boy, and worry that a girl this intense will swallow him up. Then I remember how I felt the day she told me about her youth group connection, as if we'd failed her—as if I personally had let her down. This is what it's like, letting people into your life. They don't just give, they also take. And a relationship, a real relationship, means opening yourself to that.

I hope I've taught Jed these things. I hope I've learned them myself.

"Anyway," Marlene says, "I think the fight really scared some people off."

"You think?"

In the parking lot, as we part ways, Jed talks about maybe giving the Rent-a-Mob a miss, maybe going down to the mall, checking out what's showing at the movies. Marlene warms to this right away, and I find myself conflicted. Eliza wants to shout at them, "Go change the world." Beth says, "The world can wait." Whatever they choose, I leave them to it, content that at least one leg of the family table, Jed's, doesn't seem to be in immediate danger of falling off.

*

I forget how out of touch Rick has been. When he comes back from the shed, books in his arms, cleaning up after steering a wide berth around the outbuilding the past few days, I notice an expression of anxiety on his face.

"What's the matter?"

"Roy Meakin's out there. Him and Deedee. He was having trouble with the grill, so I went over to try to help."

"That's nice of you."

"Beth," he says. "Do you know about this mural?"

"At her church?"

"There's some kind of mural," he says, ignoring me. "Deedee's painting it, and that picture she gave Eli, that's part of it. The way they were just talking, this mural . . . it's inspired by *me*."

"That's my understanding."

"You *knew* about this?"

I nod. "Part of Deedee's obsession. She was killing herself over that painting, not knowing what to do, and suddenly you did your thing." I snap my fingers. "Just like that, she's hooked."

"Roy said I was her muse."

The way he says it, lips curled downward in dismay, makes me laugh. "Rick, you're embarrassed, aren't you? Don't be. She'll make you famous. Everybody in Lutherville—all the Catholics, at least—will stop you on the street for an autograph."

"Stop."

"It's nothing to be ashamed of, Rick. It's art."

"Have you *seen* it?"

"I couldn't bear to. Don't take this the wrong way, but I was angry. It was bad enough having to live with St. Rick."

"St. Rick? That's what you called me?"

"No," I say. "Don't get worked up. St. Rick is what I called the painting. You're fine. It's him I don't like. St. Rick is the scapegoat. They all have special powers, these saints, and that one's his."

"St. Rick," he says, loading the words with every kind of disgust. "And you haven't seen the mural?"

I shake my head. "You think we should go check it out?"

"I'm afraid to, Beth. What has she done? We have to *live* here. Has she ever considered that?"

"Not likely," I say, encouraged that, in Rick's mind, we are staying in the neighborhood and need to worry about what people might think. "Anyway, Deedee thinks you walk on water. She wouldn't have done anything to embarrass you."

"The walk-on-water thing embarrasses me. That's a little too close to being worshipped."

"Now, don't let it go to your head. Listen, you inspired her mural, you gave her a reason to lay flowers at your door, you even saved her mother's life. I don't think you have anything to worry about as far as the mural is concerned."

"Are you sure?"

"Absolutely," I say, not believing it.

"So we should go and look?"

"Absolutely," I say, wanting to do anything but see that mural, to be reminded of the crazy man who, for the last three weeks, took over my husband and made my life miserable. Miserable, daring, surprising, and full of possibility, that is. Most of which is snuffed, now that St. Rick is gone.

"You're sure?"

"Absolutely we should. Maybe Roy and Deedee will go with us. Why don't I go over and ask?"

*

The church is very still and cool inside, with a smoky sweet, crypt-like smell. Deedee leads the way, enchanted at the thought of Rick's reaction, while Rick brings up the rear of our little party, arms crossed, his mouth a nervous flat line.

"Are you sure this is a good idea?" Roy whispers.

I raise my eyebrows in reply: *It wasn't my idea, believe me.*

The scaffolding is still up, the sheets of plastic, cloudily translucent, draping the mural off from view. Deedee pauses at the opening and turns.

"The work is finished, more or less, but I'm keeping it screened off until the official unveiling on All Saints' Day. That's the day after Halloween for heathens like you, Roy. Now . . ." She pauses to draw herself up to her full height. "Prepare yourselves." She turns and parts the curtain, holding it open for the rest of us to pass. "Roy, you've seen it, so let Elizabeth go first. Rick, are you ready for this? I think you'll be amazed."

I duck through the plastic, mindful not to bang my head on the scaffold. The wall is profusely, minutely decorated. Deedee switches on the work lights, and suddenly the shapes come to life. I take a step back, banging into the scaffold I was so careful to avoid.

"Wow," I say.

Rick edges up beside me. His jaw hangs open. He leans close to examine the figure at the very top of the mural. St. Rick perches high atop a stone pillar, a sort of fluted Greek column with just enough space on top for his toes to curl like a gargoyle's over the edge. I have to go on tiptoes to see. This St. Rick doesn't glare like the one at home. He gazes down from the heights with a faint, beatific smile.

Underneath him, in the same flatly photo-realistic style I recognize from Deedee's other work, the streets of Lutherville extend like two sides of a triangle. At the far right, the Smythe house anchors the mural. On the far left, the redbrick face of Eli's school. Not every landmark is there—none of the more, *ahem*, commercial properties have made the cut—but the resemblance remains striking. And the warren of streets crisscrossing the wall are far from empty. Crowds of people fill them, passing back and forth, going about their everyday lives under the gaze of St. Rick.

These people, the inhabitants of Lutherville, are not represented in Deedee's usual way. This is what gives the painting its breathtaking strangeness. They dress in ancient styles, flowing robes with gilded trim. Their long, grave faces have a Byzantine quality, their skin like old frescos blackened over time by cooking fire, their features medieval and jagged. As if each person stepped out of an icon onto the streets of Lutherville.

And above every head, every one without exception, square halos float like crowns.

"Why are they square?" I ask.

"A square halo means the person depicted is still living," Deedee says.

"Mine isn't square," Rick says. "Mine has arms coming out like a cross."

"Yours?" Deedee chuckles, her low voice reverberating. She jabs her finger up at St. Rick. "You mean his?"

"Okay. His. St. Rick's."

"St. Rick?" She laughs louder, not having heard the nickname before. "My dear, *that* is Simeon Stylites, desert father extraordinaire. Though really it's not Simeon Stylites at all—it's Christ. To get a cruciform halo, you have to be part of the Holy Trinity."

"Well, he *looks* like me."

"He has to look like somebody. Everybody does—even Judas Iscariot. But don't read *too* much into that."

Something dawns on me. I have my inner double. Now Rick has a troubling alter ego too, not staring at him in the mirror, but from the wall. St. Rick is his Eliza. Or even stranger, maybe St. Rick is his Beth, the person he is becoming rather than the person he once was or could have been. Perhaps we have more in common now than I realized.

Roy comes alongside me. "What do you think, Beth?"

"It's marvelous."

He turns to Deedee, whose eyes narrow in pleasure.

She starts walking the length of the mural, talking about the old icon painters, the techniques of gilding, how challenging it was to translate the vision in her head onto the wall. I quickly lose the thread, absorbed in the scene. Crouching at the lower right corner, I examine the Smythe house. The level of detail is extraordinary. Even the minuscule details of the Victorian dental molding are suggested in the way the eaves are shadowed. Within the frame of an upstairs window, a halo glows, presumably Margaret. Our own house is there, and just behind it the shed, which seems to radiate ever so slightly, burning brighter than its surroundings.

On our street, which forms a border to the bottom of the mural, a family of saints. A bearded man. A woman. Two smaller men. Their features don't resemble ours particularly—apart from St. Rick, none of the faces look familiar, whatever Deedee says about everybody having to look like somebody. They all resemble one another, however. And it's not what they resemble that matters, but what they represent.

Rick's eyes travel the wall, taking everything in. I can tell from his expression that he's overwhelmed. But he seems to be processing, making some kind of connection in his head. He stares, but not blankly. That stare is full of meaning.

"The bishop," Deedee says, "was a little taken aback. He started off enthusiastic enough, but that was before the streets were populated. Once the saints came marching in, he had some doubts."

"What does it all mean?" Rick asks.

Deedee's about to speak, but Roy interrupts, laying a finger against the side of his nose. "That's the question you can never ask—not of the artist, anyway. You'll get a different answer every time, and what they all amount to is this: what it means is already there. It's telling you what it means."

"He's right," Deedee says. "I can no more 'explain' it than you can. There it is. Interpret away."

She flings this out dismissively, as if it concludes the topic. My husband, however, takes the invitation seriously. He turns back to the mural, squinting hard, and I can tell he's working on an interpretation. I feel a bit panicky all the sudden, afraid of what he might say. So far we've avoided any friction. Instead of reading that as a good omen, I take it as proof that there's a catastrophe around the corner. A big one.

"This is great, Deedee," I say. "Really wonderful. Thanks for giving us the sneak peek. Right, Rick? Honey? We'd better get back . . ."

"I think—" he says, pointing at the mural. His arm bobs a little, so that the pointing hand reminds me of a dippy bird, one of those toys that bends down to sip water from the glass with its beak. "I think it's saying that the world is full of souls. Not just human animals, not just living things, but . . . people. That there's something—I'm not sure what to call it; a divine spark?—inside of us. The world is full of this holiness, this enchantment that we don't see . . ." His voice trails off. He nods, still looking at the mural.

I glance at Roy, who raises his eyebrows. I raise mine in reply. I don't know who just said that. It didn't sound like my husband to me.

"It's good," Rick says finally. "It's very good."

With that, Deedee beams.

chapter 19

It Takes a Village

The day of Margaret's return from the hospital, Rick keeps the boys home from school to help him with a project. No matter how hard I pry, he won't give me more information than that. Instead, he urges me to get out of the house. "Call your friend Holly," he says. "Go shopping."

"I want to be here when Margaret gets home."

"That won't be for hours. I checked with Deedee and they're not even going to release her until after lunch."

"You talked to Deedee? The two of you are like best buds these days. Ever since you liked her painting. Should I be jealous or what?"

"What you should be," he says, "is out of the house."

As I'm sitting in the driveway, waiting for the VW to stop its start-up shimmy so I can put the transmission in gear, something flashes out of the garage, passing on my right. Craning my neck, I catch Eli's back. He's standing on his bike pedals, pumping away for maximum speed, disappearing in the direction of school. Not a surprise, really. Eli hasn't given an inch since Rick moved back into the house.

Rick comes out of the garage, gazes at the horizon, and shakes his head. I crank the window down. "I guess that's one helper down."

"We'll see. He might calm down and head back."

"Maybe."

This is as good a time as any, I think.

"Hey, Rick, there's something I should tell you."

He walks around to the driver's window, arms crossed. There's bound to be a better way of doing this. Sitting in the driveway with the engine running doesn't seem ideal. But I've waited so long already without finding the perfect moment.

"It's about Eli," I say. "There's a problem. He's been experimenting with marijuana. I don't know where he's getting it, or how much he's smoking, but when I confronted him, he didn't back down. He doesn't think there's anything wrong with it. He said he isn't going to stop."

As I speak, the same expression comes over Rick that I remember from his examination of the mural. That overwhelmed but processing look. He doesn't say anything at first. My words hang in the air, sounding much more matter-of-fact than I'd intended: Cool Mom doesn't freak out about a little weed. Cool Mom takes things in stride, hoping for the best.

"All right," he says.

"All right?"

He nods. "Leave it with me."

"And what—you'll take care of it? Rick, like I said, he's really digging in his heels on this."

"You've had to carry the load by yourself since I checked out.

Time for me to pick up the slack. Leave it with me and I'll figure something out. Promise me you're not going to worry about it."

"Oh, I can't promise that," I say. "But, Rick?"

"Yeah?"

"Did I mention that I love you?"

"I don't remember. I don't think so, no."

"Well, I love you."

"Thanks," he says. "I love you too."

"Don't think you have to become St. Rick on my account."

"St. Rick?" he says. "Who's he?"

*

As soon as I reveal where the idea came from, Holly's interest in shopping evaporates.

"He said that? 'Go shopping'? Of all the misogynistic, pig-like things—"

"Now, now. You do like to shop."

"Not anymore, sister." She pauses, then: "Although . . . there is one thing I was just thinking of trying on."

After lunch, she insists on accompanying me home, following in her car, either to chew out Rick or see Margaret safely home, I'm not sure which. Although she's never actually met my elderly neighbor, going to the hospital that night instilled a sense of duty. We arrive just as Deedee is walking her mother up the front steps while Roy fetches luggage from the trunk of his Rolls.

"Can we help with anything?" I ask.

Seeing us, Margaret insists on coming back down the walkway. Deedee holds her arms out to corral the old lady, who seems frailer than before and stooped from the weight of the sling that supports her cast. Still, her blue eyes shine impressively, alight with intelligence, undimmed by age.

"Thank you so much," she says, patting me on the hand. Then she turns to Holly, thanking her as well, already informed that one of my friends had visited the hospital that first night. "It's good to be home, and I don't want anybody troubling over me."

"Well, we're *going* to trouble," Deedee insists.

"It's no trouble," I say. "I was thinking it would be nice to drop in on you, just to see how you're doing."

"I would enjoy the company."

"Mother, you'll have a nurse. I told you already I'm hiring someone."

"A *nurse*," Margaret says to me in a confiding tone. "Like I am some kind of invalid. Me. Tell me this: how many women my age could take a fall like that and not break a hip? Not very many, I can assure you. A nurse—a real nurse"—she raises her voice to make sure Deedee hears—"told me I was as strong as an ox. But really, I doubt many an ox could survive a fall like that unscathed."

Deedee taps the cast with her fingernail. "This is what you call unscathed?"

It's hard to believe Margaret had a stroke last week. She speaks as clearly as ever, and the lopsidedness I noted to her face back in the hospital seems to be gone. A complete recovery, so far as I can tell, apart from the cast on her arm.

"I have something for you," I say, turning to Holly.

Since I don't haul around a purse, Holly obliged me when the thought occurred on the way home. I chugged into a convenience store, only to strike out. We had to hit two more before finding what I was after. Holly reaches into the bag slung from her shoulder, producing the familiar red-and-yellow package.

"A Zagnut!" Margaret coos. "Thank you, thank you."

Deedee gives me a hard look. "It's a candy bar, Mother, not a brick of gold from Fort Knox."

"*You* always forget."

"Maybe you'd prefer to have Elizabeth take you inside?"

"Don't be silly. If you wipe that frown off your face, I'll share."

They go inside, Roy hovering as always. Holly and I stand on the sidewalk and watch them. Margaret waves before Deedee shuts the door. I turn to Holly and smile.

"In another life, that could be us."

"Ha," she says. "I've got dibs on the mother."

*

We head next door, finding the house empty. Last time we did this, panic ensued. Now I shrug off the absence. "They're probably out back." Leading the way into the backyard, I run straight into a pile of furniture: the couch and chair from the shed, the rolled rug, the bookshelf, even the rolltop desk.

"What's up with this?" Holly asks.

"I don't know. I guess it's part of this project of Rick's."

The shed door is open. We find Rick inside, working a mop up and down the wooden floor. In the early afternoon sunlight, the planks are gleaming. Behind him, Jed is scrubbing too, fretting the grout lines in the fireplace with a newly bought wire brush. I step inside, my lungs filling with the aroma of pine-scented cleaning products.

"Getting a jump on the spring cleaning?" I ask.

Rick looks up and smiles. "What do you think?"

"Looks nice."

"I'm just starting the floor. It's going to be beautiful."

The sound of water sloshing in a pail makes me turn. Across the lawn, Marlene approaches from the direction of the garden hose spigot, leaning sideways with the weight of a brimming bucket. Behind her, I'm surprised to find Eli carrying a second bucket, barefoot, his jeans rolled halfway to his knees.

"You enlisted some help," I say. "Hi, Marlene. Hello, Eli."

As he passes, my younger son gives me a bashful smile. Not a knowing smile or an ironic smile, but a bashful smile. Something's gotten into the boy. I'm just happy to see that he's back.

"I thought we'd be done before you got back, Beth, but this is taking a lot longer than I expected. There's a lot of dirt in here."

"I think it looks great."

"Eli's gonna help Marlene with the windows. That'll make a big difference."

"Wow. I'm impressed." Lowering my voice: "Don't make it *too* nice, though. I don't want you to get any ideas. You're not moving back out here."

He straightens himself up and leans the mop in the corner. Behind him, Jed stops scrubbing. Marlene and Eli stand over their respective buckets, frozen in place. At my elbow, Holly watches, arms folded.

"Beth," he says, loud enough for everyone to hear. "I'm not moving back here, don't worry. That's why I carried all my things out. I'm out of here and never coming back. And this—" He holds his arms wide, striding to the center of the shed. "This is for you."

"For me?"

"The shed. It's yours."

"Honey, you don't have to—"

"I really do," he says. "It should've been yours all along. And now it is."

"What am I going to do with it?"

"Whatever you want," he says. "You can knock it down for all I care. Or put up those window boxes you were always talking about."

"That's so sweet," Holly says. "You can't knock it down, though. It's too pretty."

She crosses the threshold for the first time, her heels tapping on the damp wood. The others resume their tasks, relieved the moment has passed. Eli catches my eye, grinning.

"Rick, I don't know what to say."

He puts those outstretched arms around me and pulls me close. We sway a little on the shiny floor, occupying the same space, breathing each other's air. It feels all right. No, it feels good. Or like Rick said about the mural, it's very good.

Apology accepted. For real, this time.

"Why don't I pitch in and help?"

Gregory calls later that evening.

"I'm pretty sure this is too soon," he says. "But it's what Sam wants. She thinks it's important if she's gonna move forward."

"She thinks *what's* important?"

"To apologize," he says. "And to say thank you."

"She doesn't need to thank me—"

"It's actually Rick she wants to thank."

Ouch.

"There's something else," he says. "She wants us to take her back *there*. To talk to the nun."

Bad idea, I'm thinking. Really bad. But then I remember the beach, the sound of the storm clouds rumbling through my body.

This is you, I think. *Part of your plan*.

And then it dawns on me, I'm not thinking these words. I'm praying them.

"That sounds great," I tell him. "Tomorrow's fine, if that works for you."

"I'll call you from the road," he says, a note of surprise in his voice. He must have expected me to put up resistance.

*

"This is it?" Rick asks, doubt in his voice.

Last night, after the call from Gregory, I told him all about Mission Up. It was his decision to come along, which is why the four of us are now sitting across the street from Mother Zacchaeus's inner-city lair. I'm at the wheel, with Rick beside me and my brother straight behind me. In the rearview mirror, Sam's eyes stare back at me. Clear eyes, I should add. You wouldn't think, seeing her now, she was the same girl I first met under the coil of sheets, her face a mess of black makeup.

"Maybe I should go first," I say. "Let Mother Zacchaeus know we're coming. She doesn't handle surprises very well."

"Are you sure?"

Gregory leans forward, clears his throat. "That might be the best idea."

They arrived on our doorstep around noon, having driven up from the community college in Virginia. The thought of being the object of Sam's pilgrimage had kept Rick up for hours last night. He squirmed all through the morning too. But once he saw her, once he saw the transformation just a few weeks off the needle had made, his nerves disappeared.

I was proud of him.

While Sam and Rick spoke in the living room, I led Gregory back to the kitchen and brewed some tea. He filled me in on the girl's progress over the past couple of weeks, how he had gotten her into a counseling program, which she seemed to be taking seriously.

"There's a long road ahead, but she's off to a good start."

"And what about her mother?" I asked.

He turned shy. "What about her?"

"Hmm . . . based on your reaction, I assume you're now more than friends?"

"With everything that's happened, we've gotten close. That's understandable. I really like this woman, Beth. I think she might be . . ."

"What? The one?"

"You're laughing, but yeah."

"I'm not laughing," I said. "I'm just happy for you."

Through the doorway, I could hear Rick speaking. Although the words were indistinct, I recognized the tone of paternal advice.

"Remember Christmas Eve, back when I was a freshman? The time we went looking for that meetinghouse?"

Gregory thought a moment, then nodded. "When you had that crappy Bug. Not much has changed, has it?"

"You were really good to me, you know. I was thinking about it the other day. With everything you must have been dealing with, I remember you telling me everything was going to be okay. Reassuring me."

"Hey, I was right, wasn't I? You never found that place, and everything still worked out. You have a couple of great kids, a mentally ill husband, this house, an even worse Volkswagen than you had then—and with an embarrassing piece of religious art on the bumper, to boot."

"You're right. I'm truly blessed."

I took the steaming tea mug from his hands, then clasped them in mine.

"Seriously," I said. "Thank you."

He pulled away, abashed. "It was nothing."

Down the block from Mission Up, a couple of kids in puffy vests bounce a basketball off the front stoop of a narrow house. I watch them a moment, waiting for cars that pass. The windows of the house are boarded up. They bounce the ball off of them too.

At the pink door, I glance back to the car, then take a deep breath. Reminding myself to keep an eye out for Mother Zacchaeus's right hook, I knock.

This time there are no locks to turn, no bar to move. The door shudders open and Mother Zacchaeus appears. She wears an apron over her black priest's shirt, hiding most of the pins on her chest.

"Well, well, well," she says. "Look who it is. You come to take another one of my girls away?"

"I've brought one back."

She squints at the car. "Well, well, well. Yes, you have."

"She wants to talk to you. I think she wants to apologize, and to thank you for saving her life."

"Come again?"

"For saving her life."

"She don't need to do nothing like that. You tell her for me."

"I'll go get her," I say, motioning toward the car.

Rick opens the passenger door, then Gregory gets out and circles around, the two of them flanking Sam protectively as she crosses. It's a sweet gesture, but maybe a little over the top. They glance around suspiciously, like bodyguards on the presidential detail.

Mother Zacchaeus backs into the vestibule and I follow her in. A couple of girls in spangled jeans and hooded sweatshirts are coming down the stairs; some kids in the lounge are running, their laughter nearly drowning out the sound of the television. As always, Mission Up is a hive of activity. As always, every surface looks encrusted and contagious.

"That pink box of yours," I say. "I talked to a friend of mine about trying to fill it."

She perks up. "And?"

"He did some kind of background check."

"Uh-huh. And didn't like what he found? I see."

"I'm sorry," I say.

"No need to be."

"It was kind of hard explaining to him what this place is all about."

"This place?" She shakes her head. "You not trying if you find this hard. People gotta need, somebody gotta do something. Simple as that. They don't gotta be perfect, they just gotta be breathing. Nobody down here expects you to be perfect."

"Can I ask you something, though? You're not really a nun, right?"

"Me, a nun? Where you get that idea?"

"The outfit," I say. "Calling yourself Mother Zacchaeus."

"This outfit, this my armor. My name, it makes perfect sense. When a person change, they name gotta change as well. Don't you know the Bible none, you good Christian lady? What happened to that man Saul when the Lord gotta hold of him? New man, new name."

"But your real name is Rosetta Harvey."

"Lady, I don't know what my real name gonna be. But what it is for now is Zacchaeus. It means white, pure, like the heart of Jesus himself. I don't answer to nothing else."

"Well, my name's not Lady," I say. "It's Beth."

She holds out her small, thick hand. "Good to meet you, then, Beth."

On the threshold, Sam waits anxiously, her hands clasped at her waist. She looks quite delicate with the daylight shining in around her. I could easily imagine this girl in Deedee's painting, a square halo atop her head. And I could picture Zacchaeus there too, perhaps her more than anyone. *"She may not be a nun,"* I can hear Deedee's deep voice saying, *"but that doesn't mean she's not a saint."* Aren't we all, though, in Deedee's world?

Aren't we all?

Mother Zacchaeus leads Sam through the lounge, where several people recognize her. They coo in amazement at how greatly she's changed. While they're occupied, I turn to Gregory. "Why don't you show Rick around the place?"

The two men disappear up the stairs while I linger at the entrance to the lounge, my back to the entryway and the unused check-in counter, watching Mission Up's inmates make a big to-do over the prodigal's return. Eventually, Sam manages to draw Mother Zacchaeus into the next room. I'm sure she has a speech all prepared, and while the nun (I can't think of her otherwise) won't enjoy the process, she'll find the grace inside her at least to endure it.

"You back," Aziza says, circling around me to get to the couch. She plops down heavily, then reaches into her V-neck shirt to produce a pack of cigarettes.

"Ain't no smoking in here!" one of the kids shouts.

"Go on with you," she says, patting his head. But she puts the pack away. "Didn't think you would be, after last time. Back, I mean. The way Big Z hauled off and slapped you. You got some guts, girl. If you can stand up to that woman, you can stand up to whatever. Still, she told me you wasn't done with this place."

"She did?"

Aziza nods. "She say she could see it in you. You was coming back."

"I wasn't planning on it. Not then."

"Well," she says, drawing the word out. "If you brought your kid down here, I guess she figured you was making yourself at home."

"Speaking of him, I didn't appreciate the way you were coming on to him."

"Coming on to him?" She smirks. "Now that I thought you *would* appreciate. You were trying to scare him, right?"

The problem with this place, I think, is that they see you coming a mile away. And they've got your number too. They've had it all along.

"Maybe," I say.

When Mother Zacchaeus and Sam emerge, I see something I never expected. The nun's arm hangs from the girl's shoulder, and

I am almost positive there's a damp shine to Mother Zacchaeus's eyes. They walk through the lounge and out, drawing me along. The men come downstairs, pausing midway when they see the aproned nun in their path, afraid of being caught. But she doesn't seem to notice. She's still pondering whatever Sam had to say.

As the others file out, I linger. Mother Zacchaeus leans on the doorpost, her legs crossed, grinning after them. At least, I think it's a grin. Her lips can't hold the unfamiliar posture long enough for me to make sure.

"I want you to know something. I'll be back."

She nods, not looking at all surprised.

"I don't know how to help you," I say. "But I'm going to find a way."

"That won't be difficult," she replies. "The one thing we never run out of here is need. We got a bottomless pot of that, and you welcome to as much of it as you want."

The urge to say something stupid is strong. I can almost hear myself forming the inane words. Channeling Bogart at the end of *Casablanca*: This is the beginning of a beautiful friendship. But I suppress it as best I can, not wanting to spoil things. She must sense my internal conflict.

"Get on," she says, patting my shoulder.

I walk down the steps onto the sidewalk. I look around, seeing the neighborhood for the very first time. Apart from the boys bouncing the basketball, the immediate block is empty. In my mind's eye, I populate it with Deedee's medieval souls. As far away as this is from Lutherville, you're never so far that you've outpaced them.

chapter 20

All Saints

"You brought me all the way up here to say no?"

Even if I couldn't hear the disbelief in his voice, the expression alone would tell me Jim Shaw is angry. He sits on the edge of the sofa, Kathie by his side, wringing his fingers together with so much force it wouldn't surprise me if they started popping off.

"I brought you up here," Rick says, "to show you *why* I'm saying no."

It's a strange thing, seeing Jim at a social loss. Usually he's so quick to patch over the cracks, to smooth the rough spots. But Rick has blindsided him, and it shows.

"Fine," he says. "Show me."

"In the morning, Jim. Come to church with us, then afterward I'm gonna take you somewhere. I want you to see this for yourself."

But Jim is already shaking his head. "I'll be honest with you, sport. I'm not going back there. Nothing against you, but when we left The Community, we had our reasons. I wouldn't have given you an opportunity to leave the place if I didn't think there were problems."

"I'm not asking you to go back there."

"'Come to church,' you said."

"That's right. But The Community is not the only church in town."

"It's the only one you work for."

"Not anymore," Rick says.

The room falls silent.

Ordinarily I would have jumped in by now, trying to defuse the situation. But the news Rick broke to Jim just now, he didn't share with me until right before the Shaws arrived. I'm still trying to fathom what's going on. When he told me he was leaving The Community, chucking the Men's Pastor job, I assumed that meant yes to Virginia, yes to leaving our home, our neighbors, our friends—the old ones and the new ones.

Then he'd turned around and declined the megaphone in Richmond too.

I didn't see *that* coming.

Except that I did. Ever since I told him about Mission Up, ever since he saw Deedee's painting and I repeated to him the words she'd said about not being distracted by your own reflection but looking through the glass, this rupture has been coming. A new giddiness has entered our relationship.

"Are we really going to do this?" he'll ask.

"I think we are."

Maybe it was like this in the days after I told him about my pregnancy. Without skipping a beat, he'd started making plans for our future. One of the things about Rick I admire is how quickly he can reorient. When that reorientation involves an "everything fast," I hate it, but now I love his spontaneity again.

Next to Jim, Kathie's pressing a finger into her temple, moving her head from side to side. She opens her mouth, as if to adjust for changing air pressure. The ringing in her ears must be getting to her. I've been watching for this since they arrived. Now more than ever, I feel for Kathie. Longing for the clarity that comes through silence.

"You wanna take a walk?" I ask.

She blinks. "Okay. Yeah. That would be nice."

The men both rise. Rick is anxious. "If you leave, what am I supposed to do when people come to the door?"

I'm not sure if it's the trick-or-treaters he's worried about or being left alone in the house with Jim.

"It's simple," I say. "They'll do all the talking. You just hand them the candy."

As if on cue, the doorbell rings. A toddler in a tutu, a ten-year-old princess, and a couple of teenage vampires stand in a huddle under the porch light. They hold out plastic jack-o-lanterns, a shopping bag, and a very optimistic pillowcase. Into each of them, I dole out candy from the bowl stashed near the entrance. Out on the sidewalk, the toddler's mom waves hello. She's pushing a plump little devil in a stroller.

"See? That wasn't so hard."

I hand the bowl to Rick and lead Kathie out into the night.

She wears a lovely pair of knee-high leather boots that make a sharp *tap-tap-tap* on the pavement. I ask about the tinnitus, which she says is getting worse. Despite the doctors, she has stopped believing the problem is stress-induced. There's something wrong with her, objectively wrong, only they haven't managed to diagnose it.

"Cognitive therapy is a crock, Beth. Don't let anybody ever talk you into it."

"I'm sure it helps some people."

"It makes me want to stick needles in my ears. I wouldn't mind losing my hearing, honestly, if only this ringing would stop."

"You don't mean that."

"I don't know. I can't think straight. Don't listen to me."

A couple of high school vamps walk past, their legs sheathed in fishnet. Kathie turns to watch them. I shake my head.

"We didn't do it that way when I was in school."

"Didn't you?" she asks. "I was a wild child, remember? Lots to regret."

The way she says it doesn't sound like she regrets too much.

We run into a tiny ghost wearing an old-school sheet with eyeholes. True to form, the holes are slightly misaligned, which forces him to wobble as he walks. Too young to be out on his own, I think, but this is Lutherville. There are people here who still leave their doors unlocked. I can only imagine what Deedee must think, seeing all the Halloween ghouls standing in for her desert fathers.

"I have to say, for a woman whose husband has just quit his job and then turned down the opportunity of a lifetime, you seem amazingly calm."

"You'll see why. We're on the same page, me and Rick. Things are a lot like they used to be. I have plenty of good reasons to worry, you're right. But I'm a lot less worried than I was a month ago."

We circle the block before heading back. To my surprise, as we pass the Smythes' house, Margaret and Deedee are out on the front porch, handing precious Zagnuts out to the children of Lutherville. We line up behind a couple of Harry Potters, a Dr. Who, and some zombies, waiting our turn to say hello. Margaret insists on our taking some candy.

"I've never had one of these before," Kathie says.

Margaret gives her a sly grin and gestures with her cast. "You be careful, then. They'll ruin you for anything else."

"Will we see you in the morning?" Deedee asks.

"We'll be there."

As we walk across the yard, Kathie asks what I meant.

"One of the things Rick wants to show you is a mural in the church up the hill."

"The Catholic church?"

I nod. "Then there's something else. Down in the city."

*

When it's time for bed, Rick and I walk the Shaws into the backyard, where we have a little surprise for them. I have converted the shed into a guesthouse. There's an antique bureau on loan from the Smythes, a lovely four-poster bed, and heavy drapes over the windows. In the hearth, a golden fire gives the room a warm glow.

"It's so . . . romantic," Kathie says.

It is certainly that. Rick and I exchange a look.

"In the morning, we'll all have breakfast, then start over to the church."

*

I've rarely been to a Catholic service. It's the opposite of the formless meetinghouse ritual of my youth, but also unlike the stage show at The Community. Apart from the costumes, there are no production values to speak of. The priest's voice, in contrast to the majesty of his getup, has a droning, high-pitched quality that never varies. There's a lot of kneeling and standing, and by the time I get the hang of it, the whole thing is over except for communion.

Rick squeezes my hand. "You trust me, right?"

"I guess I have to."

"Seriously. You do trust me."

"Yes. I do."

Kathie sits beside me, heavy-lidded but for once apparently not in pain. Beside her, Jim continues to fidget as he's done all morning, not a big fan of being kept in suspense. Even Roy, who isn't much of a churchgoer, sits on the pew in front of us, not bothering to attempt the liturgical movements, contenting himself to gaze absently at Deedee's mural, which is now revealed.

After the final prayer, we join the press of parishioners moving toward the nave for a closer look at the newly painted wall.

"This is what you want me to see?" Jim asks.

"It's one thing, yes."

Every time I look at the mural, I see something new. A familiar structure I hadn't noticed before. A huddle of saints underneath one of the basketball hoops at the park. Since the first time, I've come back almost every day. The individual saints no longer resemble each other. I feel like I can tell most of them apart. Someone made a count and reported back to Deedee that there were two hundred and thirteen figures in all. "Better count again," was her reply. I suspect they missed the halo in her mother's bedroom window.

Standing next to Jim, I can feel his resistance. Still frustrated by Rick's decision, he doesn't want to submit to whatever plan is in store. The whole experience has left him irritated, from the dodged calls to the terse bids for more time to the cryptic request that he travel up to Baltimore for his answer. As the crowd thins and he gets closer to the wall, however, I can sense a change.

"It's very unusual," he says. "I've never seen anything quite like it."

"She's a famous painter."

"Your next-door neighbor? I am impressed." Then he casts his gaze higher and notices St. Rick. "What in the world?"

Last night, while Kathie and I walked, Rick took the opportunity to explain his retreat to the shed. I'm not sure how much detail he went into, but it doesn't take Jim long to make the connection between the hermit-like Fast and Deedee's painting.

"Are you beginning to understand?" I ask.

"No, Beth," he says, trying to laugh. "I think it's a little over my head."

"You know what I think? Rick thought he'd find the answers by getting away from everything. He felt so strongly he had to shut the world out . . . including us. When he saw this, he realized that the answers weren't in the shed. They were out in the world. They always had been. We just didn't see them."

"We?"

I nod. "We started off on separate paths, but we seem to have arrived at the same place. Literally."

What I don't tell him is this: Rick and I spent our own night together in the shed. We talked and talked the way we hadn't done since before we were married. At nightfall, we had separate ideas we both wanted to share, two different stories of our autumn apart. By morning, there was just the one story, and just the one ending too.

"You can't do it alone," he said. "We can't do anything alone. Not anymore. We have to be together on this, on everything."

And he means it.

Deedee and Roy join us for lunch after church. One of the surprises of the last couple of days of October: Deedee's interest in Mission Up. I forget she doesn't fit the cloistered, fearful suburbanite mold I try to shove everybody into. Though she's never been to the place, she has already started talking about it with her circle of friends. Roy has already felt the pressure: "I don't know what I'm donating to, but Deedee tells me I have to do it, and I'm to see you about the details."

After lunch, there's a negotiation over which cars to take. Jim offers the Maserati and Roy the Rolls, but after a lot of persuasion, they agree we can all pack into the Volkswagen and Deedee's old Saab. Marlene and Jed turn up, and she offers to take Eli with them. We set off with me behind the wheel and Rick beside me, the Shaws in the backseat. In Deedee's car, Roy looks nervous to be a passenger. I imagine he's accustomed to doing the driving.

Once we're on the highway heading into town, the general vicinity of our destination dawns on Jim, who concedes the logic of going as low profile as possible, not taking the fancy, eye-catching cars.

"I don't think my insurance covers driving in West Baltimore. With any luck, we'll get in and out before anybody knows we're coming."

Rick turns around in the passenger seat. "Oh, they'll know. We're going to make quite an entrance. There's a whole mob of people waiting for us."

I put the blinker on to make a left. I've made the journey

often enough now that the route is familiar. As I begin my turn, a red SUV streaks head-on through the intersection, forcing me to slam on the brakes or be flattened.

"Is everybody—"

My words are cut off by the screech of brakes over my shoulder, followed by a jarring *thump* as the car rolls into us. The VW bucks forward, metal grinding.

"—okay?"

Nobody's hurt. We get out to inspect the damage. A young man in a little Japanese pickup hops out and starts sputtering apologies: "My bad, my bad."

Deedee, stopped behind the pickup, cranes her neck out to see what's happened. As we gather around the back bumper, Marlene pulls alongside with Jed beside her and Eli in back.

"Go on ahead," Rick tells them.

The little pickup appears undamaged apart from a scrape on the chrome. The VW has not been so lucky. The bumper has a notch in it that looks like somebody chopped it with a giant, blunted axe blade. The left taillight's busted too. On the ground there's a shower of yellow and red plastic bits, some fine slivers of metal, and a bent Jesus fish.

I stoop down and retrieve the fish. The shiny surface has lost its sheen. The collision's impact had an effect similar to scrubbing the plastic with a wire brush.

The pickup driver offers Rick his insurance information, still murmuring apologies. To my surprise, Rick declines. "It doesn't look too bad. Nobody's hurt. The guy responsible is the one who ran the light. Let's just call it even, all right?"

"Are you sure?"

After much reassurance, we all get back in the VW.

"Maybe you should drive," I tell Rick. "That was nice, letting him off the hook."

"Today of all days, I'm in the mood to be forgiving."

"If he'd rear-ended my Maserati, I don't think I could be so calm," Jim says.

Rick laughs. "I hear you. Anyway, that guy did us a favor. I've wanted to get rid of that fish ever since Beth stuck it on the car."

"Don't be down on the Jesus fish," I say. "We've been through a lot together."

In my lap, I nestle the broken Jesus fish, carefully probing the damage with my fingertip. All beat up, I think I like it a whole lot more.

*

Chas Worthing knows how to turn a drum circle into a street party. A row of grills stands along the sidewalk outside Mission Up, manned by Chas, Barber, and even Vernon, who turns out to have at least one shirt in his closet not devoted to the legalization of cannabis (even if it does read BAN WALL STREET in angry black letters on a white background). Most of the familiar faces from the Rent-a-Mob have shown up, along with friends roped in for the occasion. True to his word, Chas has even managed to get a WBAL news van out here. Get Mother Z on camera and hopefully she'll receive some more support for the community. She was game. I think she's got a lot of showmanship inside that body.

"You're a pushover," I say, giving him a big hug.

He laughs, unaccustomed to the contact. "Hey, I get it. Like I told Marlene, I'm not above helping out other people's causes."

One day Chas will see there are no such things as causes.

Only people. But that's not going to come overnight. Believe me, I know.

I say hello to Barber, who's already handing out hot dogs to some neighborhood kids, then sidle up to Vernon.

"You're here," I say.

"Are you kidding? I wouldn't miss this. There's actually something to *do* here. That's what excites me. And besides, if things get out of hand, turn a little ugly, we both know I can handle myself."

"Yes, we do."

Marlene passes behind us. I reach for her hand before she can get away. "Thanks for everything."

"It's cool," she says. "I told you they'd love to be part of it."

"And you were right."

I give her a hug before turning her loose. If I'm not careful, hugging people is going to become the theme of the day. And so many people! I have to walk up the steps for a better view of the crowd. In addition to the Rent-a-Mob, there are the women and kids of Mission Up, along with plenty of others from the neighborhood. The news cameraman jerks this way and that, uncertain what exactly to film. I feel the same way. The amazing thing is, most of these people weren't even a part of my life a month ago. Now they're all here together, mingling, getting to know each other.

Holly arrives, dragging a reluctant Eric behind her. She's dressed to work in paint-flecked jeans and a pullover sweater. Eric carries swinging cans of paint in each hand. She finds Deedee and in two minutes flat, they've got the cans open and they're discussing color. From a distance, I see a dipstick covered in hot pink.

"Have you seen Marlene?"

I turn to find Jed, his arms filled with a huge bag of hot dog buns. "She went that way," I say, then watch my son ducking into the mission in search of the girl he loves.

At the foot of the stairs, Jim and Kathie are taking it all in. Rick leans close, explaining everything. I walk over to check on them.

"Beth felt something coming here, and I feel it too," he says. "We're not going to spend the rest of our lives chasing after fulfillment. We're going to spend them serving."

"Sure," Jim says, "but how are you planning to pay the bills?"

"I'm not going to take the job in Richmond. But we can go to work for you right here. Beth and me. I've talked to the folks at The Community, and they're open to this as well."

I make my exit, not wanting to dwell too much on the financial uncertainties. I don't know what's going to happen, I really don't. But I'll take this uncertainty any day over the cloud I lived under before October. We'll get by, I'm certain of that. When I told Rick I trusted him, I wasn't lying. But it's not him I'm depending on. Not by a long shot.

Seeing Jim and Kathie here, the couple who, without realizing it, set our family crisis in motion, brings everything full circle for me. We are all together now, either in body or in spirit, all of us players in a drama we had no idea was being performed.

Each with a role to fulfill in this jigsaw of happenstance.

Mother Zacchaeus made this place out of nothing; she gave shelter to Sam, whom Gregory brought me here to fetch.

Eli, whose flippant remark drove me into the arms of the Rent-a-Mob, and whose experimentation made me return to Mission Up. Marlene and Jed, whose budding attraction healed my relationship with Chas and his group.

Even Holly, who finally got me to the beach where everything seemed to click.

Rick, my husband, more like himself than ever before, who taught Deedee the answer without knowing it, so she could teach it to the rest of us through the medium of her art.

And what was I in all of this?

I started out hoping to reconnect with my lost sense of purpose. My life once had a course that, in their own way, each of these people had helped to derail.

Or so I thought.

Now I find that what life was making of me, what God was making of me, was not an arrow to trace a path through the sky, but the hub of a wheel. I am the intersection, I am the connection between them all, and the purpose I've been given isn't mine alone. It is for all of us to share. What I needed wasn't something I could take. What I needed was something I could give.

"Look what you did," Mother Zacchaeus says, after telling the reporter all about Mission Up. The woman is a star.

"It wasn't me."

She smiles. "Good answer."

Do we hug? I'm not sure if she'll allow it. There's only one way to know for certain. I reach for her, and she submits to the embrace.

"All right," she says. "All right."

"I know it must seem like a lot, like we're trying to take over—"

"You got that medal I give you?" she asks, cutting me off.

I pat my pockets in vain. "Not on me."

"Come here, then."

She plucks another pin from her chest, then comes at me. I'm sure this time she's going to sink it deep. But no, she pulls on my shirt, sticks the pin through, and reaches under to fit the back with surprising grace. Not so surprising, though: I imagine she's been doling out such rewards for quite some time. I peer down at my new decoration, which bears a red cross within a white flower.

"It's lovely."

"You done all right," she says. "I knew you would."

"How?"

"I know these things, Beth. Jesus help me, sometimes I wish I didn't!"

Behind us, Rick has roped Eric Ringwald into the circle, and now Eric is explaining to Jim that, yes, he's going to see to organizing the nonprofit. His wife, Holly, he says, will be on the board. Hearing her name, I turn to find her. She and Deedee are just inside the mission. While the crowd outside grows and some local trumpeters join in with the drums, my two friends are on their knees side by side with a pair of paint scrapers, making quite a mess.

"Elizabeth, the more I looked at this thing, the more I felt I had to do something about it."

So I spend ten minutes watching my famous neighbor, the only person I know with a Wikipedia entry, teaming up with my soul sister to lay a fresh coat of hot-pink paint on the front door. It's a beautiful sight, indeed.

"Have you seen Eli?" I ask.

Holly shakes her head. "Maybe out on the street?"

I head to the street, interrogating Jed and Marlene, who can only shrug. I ask Rick, who's too caught up in conversation, then scour the lines in front of the hot dog grills. When I've nearly given up, when my heart has just started to contract, I hear the sound of basketballs bouncing on boards. Down the street, among a group of neighborhood kids, Eli throws the ball, lets it bounce, then jogs over for the rebound, only to have it snatched from under him by a boy half his size. He wheels around, jumps, and misses as the kid sails the ball over his head.

"You even let that one come down here again."

Aziza, right beside me, exhales a cloud of menthol into the air.

"He can't play basketball too good, though, can he?"

"He's holding back," I say.

She harrumphs.

"Okay," I admit. "He sucks at basketball. He's better at lacrosse."

"White boy sport."

"Yup."

We cock our heads at one another and laugh.

Maybe he senses that he's being talked about. In the middle of a throw, Eli ditches the ball and turns. He sees me, gives me a nod. Coming from him, it's as potent as a loud "halloooo" and a grin from ear to ear.

"What's those glasses he's wearing? Those are girls' glasses."

The white plastic frames look terrible on him, I have to admit.

"Those are mine," I tell her, feeling so proud.

They're all here, the people I love and the people I want to love. There are no robes, no halos, not that the eye can see, but there are souls, plenty of those. We are all packed in together, filling a small block in a small part of a big city in a big world, overlooked by the blue throbbing fullness of a sky that was always there.

And all the raised voices and the music and the spring of balls bouncing rise together like so much incense, an offering of noise, the sound of people living.

Nothing here is empty.

No space is void.

No place unoccupied or unclaimed.

Reading Group Guide

1. Have you ever felt your world turn upside-down like Beth does—the "sky beneath her feet"? How did you respond? What did you learn from the experience?
2. As a pastor's wife, Beth's life and choices are often dictated by others' expectations. How does she handle those expectations? In what ways do they affect her own faith and relationship with God? Is living under such close scrutiny unique to families of clergy or does everyone experience this?
3. When Rick decides to retreat to the shed in the backyard, what do you think he could have done differently so Beth wouldn't feel abandoned? What could *she* have done differently?
4. *The Sky Beneath My Feet* is rife with symbols, e.g., the Jesus Fish and the portrait of St. Rick. What are some others? What do they represent within the story? Do you have similar symbols in your life?
5. How have Beth's views of the Quaker faith changed since she was a teenager? How does her faith change over the course of the novel?
6. Beth is emotionally close to her brother, Gregory, despite—or maybe because of—his messy past. When he asks for her help with Sam, she agrees. How would you react in a situation like this? Would you be afraid of Mother Zacchaeus or of being around the people at Mission Up?
7. Eli's experimentation with marijuana seems to be a growing occurrence among teens these days. How do you teach your children to avoid drugs? When they ask why it's wrong, what will you tell them?
8. Beth experiences a very profound moment under the hut at the beach. How is her life changed by that moment? Have you ever had such an experience?
9. When you are offended or done wrong by a loved one, how do you handle the situation? Does forgiveness come easy for you or do you find it to be a challenge?
10. What has Beth's journey taught you about your own life?

Acknowledgments

My deepest thanks to J. Mark Bertrand, without whom this novel would never have come to be what it is. And to my agent, Chip MacGregor, a man who sees possibilities I never knew existed, thank you. Ami, thank you once again.

About the Author

The Christy Award-winning author of *Christianity Today*'s Novel of the Year *Quaker Summer*, Lisa Samson has been hailed by *Publishers Weekly* as one of the "most powerful voices in Christian fiction." She lives in Kentucky with her husband and three kids.